Your Christmas Love

LAYLA HAGEN

Dear Reader,

If you want to receive news about my upcoming books and sales, you can sign up for my newsletter HERE: http://laylahagen.com/mailing-list-sign-up/

Chapter One

Sienna

"I've got the list with gifts ready," I said into the phone, surveying the spreadsheet I'd labeled *Christmas presents*.

"Wow. You're way ahead of me, girl. I'm still working on it," Pippa said. "But that doesn't mean we can't start shopping already."

"I agree."

Buying gifts was my second favorite part of the holiday season. My absolute favorite was hanging up Christmas ornaments. My office was proof of that.

"See you at six thirty?"

"Perfect."

Some might think that starting to shop so early for presents was overdoing it, but there were a lot of people in the Bennett clan, and buying the perfect present for each took time and dedication. Pippa Callahan-Bennett was my favorite aunt, and my partner in crime when it came to shopping.

"Your boss is arriving today?" she asked.

"Yep."

"Good luck."

"Thanks. I'll need all the luck I can get."

I sighed after hanging up. My boss had been working out of the Seattle office until now, but he was officially moving to San Francisco today. We'd only communicated through phone calls and emails until now.

Everyone was in a frenzy this morning, waiting for him to show up.

"Think the boss from hell will be late?" my colleague Mara asked, poking her head in my office.

"Don't call him that," I said on a smile.

"Why? Everyone else is."

"True. But I don't think he'll be late. Not his style."

He was impatient and demanding, but he was also brilliant. Winston Statham was a genius. He took over the chain of department stores from his parents at only thirty years old. He was just five years my senior. I'd learned more in the months I worked with him than in two years at my previous job.

I'd joined Statham Stores one year ago as a branding junior. My superior had to unexpectedly go on maternity leave early, and Winston decided I was equipped to take over her duties until she returned.

Since then, I'd been working with him to revamp our online store.

My dynamic with Winston was... interesting to say the least. When we weren't sparring over details, we were productive, building on each other's ideas. Would working face-to-face impact our dynamic?

I'd find out sooner rather than later.

I looked around my office, smiling. I'd already hung Christmas ornaments everywhere. Sure, it was still early in the year, but I'd barely held back until Halloween. After, I unleashed myself on the office.

I jumped when I heard a familiar voice by the elevators and hurried out to the corridor. My palms were sweaty. My mouth was dry. I was determined to make a good impression. I spotted Winston immediately, because everyone was gathered around him.

Currently, I was looking at the back of him: charcoal black hair, impressive height and build. He was speaking with several of my coworkers. When he turned around, my breath caught. I'd never even seen a picture of him.

Thank heavens he'd never wanted to do any video conference calls, because those mesmerizing green eyes would have messed up my focus. Everything about him just spelled sexy and manly. He stood out in the crowd, and not just because his suit was tailored and molded around his fit body to perfection.

Everyone was introducing themselves. I waited until he was right in front of me to say, "Sienna Hensley."

"Nice to finally meet you in person." His eyes widened in surprise. I couldn't ignore the way my stomach flipped during the few seconds we made eye contact.

After he greeted everyone who'd gathered in the lobby, we all went into the meeting room. Winston had asked me to prepare it so he could address the team upon his arrival.

There were too many of us for all to sit, so I stood by the door. I just couldn't get over how damn attractive he was. Those eyes, the way he walked… even the way he ran his fingers through his black hair was sexy.

"Good morning, everyone. Thank you for gathering here. As you know, I've been working out of the Seattle office until now, but San Francisco is home. Besides, this is our flagship store. It's the place to be. Let's make this Christmas season our best one yet. I'm confident we can reach a new record in sales on Black Friday and during this quarter in general if we put our minds to it."

He looked around the room as if expecting everyone to nod in agreement, but was only met with skeptical expressions.

Way to make an entrance, Winston.

Only last Friday, half of my colleagues were betting that he wanted us to gather so he could get to know the team better, that in person he wasn't really the boss from hell he seemed from his emails.

Winston's parents had retired before I joined Statham Stores, but my colleagues said that they were warm and friendly. Winston's leadership style was different. He went on to talk about more specific sales goals and ways to reach them.

Well, that speech didn't help anyone warm up to him.

"Okay, everyone. Let's get to work," he finished. Everyone practically darted out of the room. I was about to join them when Winston's voice stopped me in my tracks.

"Ms. Hensley, let's go to my office. I want to talk to you alone."

He pinned me with his gaze, watching me intently. I was a little breathless.

"Sure."

"Is all the documentation for the Christmas program ready?"

"Yes."

"Good. Bring it with you. I want us to review it together."

"Can we do it in about an hour? The sales team has a surprise for you. They're waiting for you down in the store."

The Statham Department Store in San Francisco was so huge that there was plenty of space for our offices on the upper level.

He cocked a brow. "I don't have that on my schedule."

"Well, no. It's a surprise."

"I don't have time right now."

"I'll let them know and then be right with you."

"Okay. And for the record, don't let anyone plan any more surprises. There's no time for that."

Ouch. Everyone had been so anxious for his arrival. It was practically a company-wide event. So many employees had stayed with Statham Stores for decades because they were loyal to the family, because they loved and respected his parents, and him by extension. They wanted to meet him.

How could someone so good-looking be so grouchy? I had to suck in a breath and steel myself when Winston walked past me. *Damn, damn, damn.* The closer he came, the more handsome he seemed, even though his expression was serious. Did the boss even know how to smile?

I was making it my mission to find out.

Chapter Two

Winston

The second I entered my office, I realized that I should have structured my opening speech differently. I should have spent more time preparing it, but if there was one thing I didn't have, it was time. I'd never been under so much pressure, and if the numbers didn't improve, I'd have to close this store.

I refused to even consider that possibility. I would come through for my parents, who trusted me, but also for every single employee working in this store. Their livelihoods depended on it. Statham Stores owned twelve department stores around the United States and eight in Europe, but I refused to close even one—especially this one. I had so many great memories of this place.

I practically grew up on these floors, watching Mom and Dad run it. They'd shared this very office space. Back then, there were two desks in opposite corners. Now they'd been replaced with a long one for me.

Someone knocked at the door.

"It's Sienna."

"Come in."

I took a deep breath. It didn't help much. She was so beautiful, I just couldn't look away from her. Her light brown hair reached the middle of her back. Warm brown eyes complemented her bronze skin tone perfectly.

"I have the Christmas program here. The sales team would still like to meet you, whenever you have time, and personally, I think it's a good idea."

I didn't have time for pleasantries, but I'd already made that clear. If she insisted, it meant she disagreed. I'd call her out on it, but one of the reasons I chose to promote her instead of hiring a replacement for the branding VP was precisely because she never held back.

Sure, that led to some verbal sparring, but also very creative and productive solutions for the website redesign. Modernizing Statham Stores wasn't an easy task, but Sienna hadn't shied away from any challenge.

We sat side by side at the long desk. She'd brought the printed version of the Christmas program. It covered everything from pricing strategy to Christmas-themed events. At this point, I'd be screwed if she quit. She was indispensable for what I had in mind to save the store.

I refused to be attracted to her. And yet, I could barely keep myself from moving closer to her.

"Did our usual band for Christmas Eve confirm?"

"Yes, but we're also holding auditions for a second band. It's good to bring in some new blood."

"I agree."

I loved that she took initiative. Damn, this wasn't helping curb that attraction; quite the contrary.

"I've put Post-its on pages seven and twelve. I think we need to change a few details. I think we should move the Meet Santa session to Saturday rather than Sunday. Parents get too anxious if the line is too long, because they have to go to work the next day."

"That's a great idea. Go ahead and change it."

"Perfect."

The woman wasn't only smart, she also had more empathy than anyone I'd ever worked with. She easily put herself in others' shoes. It was perhaps because she wasn't always thinking about profit maximization but customer satisfaction that her suggestions were so spot-on.

"Ms. Hensley, I also called you in here because I have a new project in mind."

"I'm listening."

"This store… it needs a rebranding. We've kept the original structure and branding for far too long. There's a fine line between respecting the history of this place and losing revenue. The new merchandising systems we've implemented in the other stores are more productive, but given that this is our flagship store, we need to go about it differently. Deeper. On a structural level."

"I've got you. Okay. I definitely think there's room for improvement. We could focus on that in the New Year."

"I want us to have a concept ready in eight weeks."

"Christmas is in seven weeks."

"I'm well versed in the art of counting, Ms. Hensley," I said dryly.

Her eyes became fiery. "Then you'll probably also know that I've booked two weeks of vacation starting the twenty-second."

"I don't remember approving that."

"It's still with HR." Her voice was less certain. "I promised my brother I'd visit him in London. I don't want to disappoint him."

We had that in common. I didn't like to let the people I love down either.

"The concept needs to be ready before the thirty-first of the year, Ms. Hensley. I'm sure we can come to an agreement. We can incorporate it in our current workload."

On top of our current workload was what I actually meant, and she knew it. Finishing the concept would mean late evenings at the office, possibly even working weekends… all before Christmas. I practically saw that fire in her eyes intensify.

She opened her mouth, then pressed her lips together as if deciding she shouldn't voice her thoughts. That was a first, but perhaps I'd finally pushed her too far.

"Yes, I'm sure we'll find a solution." Her tone was colder than before. Judging by my reaction to her, maybe it wasn't such a bad thing. One of us needed to keep a cool head. And that someone wouldn't be me.

Chapter Three

Sienna

At six o'clock I left the Statham building, hurrying to meet Pippa. I'd just rounded the corner to where I'd parked when a guy I hoped I wouldn't see again unhitched himself from the building wall, watching me. My ex, Trevor.

"What are you doing here?" I asked.

"You've been ignoring my calls and messages."

"That didn't clue you in that I never want to speak to you again?"

"Don't be difficult," Trevor said at the same time I heard Winston's voice to my right.

"Is everything okay?" He was holding a takeout bag, looking between me and Trevor.

I nodded, pulling myself to my full height. Just what I needed. To be humiliated in front of my boss.

"I want to talk to you alone," Trevor said.

"There's nothing to talk about." I crossed my arms over my chest. I really wished Winston would leave. I didn't want him to see this.

"That's not true."

"You wanted distance, remember? I broke up

with you. End of story. There's nothing to talk about. I don't want to see you again. I moved on."

I still had a scar the size of a football in my heart from the whole experience, but no one needed to know that. He'd called me suffocating and demanding.

"Thought maybe you didn't see my messages."

"I did. Not interested."

What did he think? That I'd be available for a booty call?

"You hear her," Winston said. His voice was calm… *too* calm.

"Stay out of this," Trevor said.

"You show up here again, and I'll get a restraining order."

That caught Trevor's attention. I blinked. Had Winston really said that?

"Who do you think you are?" spat Trevor.

"Someone who doesn't tolerate men like you."

"Trevor, go away. Don't call me, don't show up at my workplace."

"We have unfinished business," Trevor insisted.

"You wanted out. With me, out is out. There's no unfinished business here."

Trevor took a step forward. I didn't move, but Winston did, taking a half of a step in front of me, shielding me with his big, strong body.

"Leave!" His voice still sounded lethally calm,

even though a vein was pulsing in his temple.

Trevor looked between the two of us for a few seconds before backing off and turning on his heels.

"I'll walk you to your car," Winston said.

"Thanks. I didn't park far away."

He walked behind me. I could feel the heat of his body with every single step. When I reached the car, I opened my door slowly, turning to him. Damn. I'd miscalculated the distance. Winston was so close that his warm exhales breezed against my cheek.

"Has he shown up here before?" he asked.

"No."

"I want you to tell me if he does again. Or if he bothers you at all."

"Why? You're really going to get a restraining order?"

"That, or I'll kick his ass."

I cocked a brow. Somehow, with those crisp suits, I couldn't see it.

"You doubt I can?" he asked in a challenging tone.

"Can't really see you getting your hands dirty, no." I was only half teasing.

But as Winston's mouth curled up into a seductive smile and he rested his hand on the roof of the car, just next to my arm, I realized I'd pegged him all wrong.

"I can get very dirty if the situation requires it."

Oh yeah, very, very wrong. I'd thought he was

cold and distant. Tonight, I'd seen this other side of him. He was passionate, possibly hot-headed too, he just kept it all under a tight leash. But right now, it was simmering at the surface. Holy hell. It was right there, in the glint in his eyes and the unmistakable double entendre in his words.

"I doubt Trevor will show up again. He's not used to working for anything, just likes… easy prey. I'm guessing he thought I'd fall at his feet. Thanks for tonight."

"No problem."

"You're heading back to the office?" I asked, pointing to his take-out bag.

"Yeah. Just bought something to eat."

"Doing overtime already, boss?" I grinned, even though he cocked a brow.

"Told you I'm on a tight schedule."

"Yes, of course. I'll leave you to it." I was still grinning when I got in my car. I might have just fallen a little for Winston and his gruff ways. He'd stood up for me. The man was getting a huge-ass Christmas present, whether he wanted it or not.

Damn. I didn't want to be attracted to my boss, no matter how good-looking he was. Or how smart. His brain was fascinating to me. Yes, that was a weird thing to say, probably, but for me, smart was sexy. I *liked* working for him while we were elbow-deep in presentations and brainstorming sessions.

I was still reeling from tonight's events, and so, so happy that I was meeting Pippa. She was one of my favorite people in the world. My sisters, Chloe and Victoria, were supposed to join us on our shopping trip this evening, but Chloe's school had called a parent-teacher conference at the last minute, and they were both stuck there. They were joining us later for dinner.

I had a huge family. Victoria was twelve years older than me, Chloe thirteen years younger. We also had a brother, Lucas. He was seventeen and currently doing an exchange year in London. I missed him like crazy.

We'd lost our parents when I was seventeen, and Victoria had become our guardian. The huge age difference between all of us was because my parents had adopted Lucas and Chloe. After Victoria married Christopher Bennett, the term huge family took on a whole new meaning.

I was meeting Pippa—Christopher's sister—at Union Square, and then we'd scour the boutiques in the area together. On the way there, I reviewed the list of gifts I'd made on my phone.

There were a dozen kids to buy gifts for, and even more adults. There were nine Bennett siblings, and their parents, Richard and Jenna. All the siblings had married, and most had kids. Some of the spouses also had extended family.

Buying Christmas gifts was honestly a project in and of itself. Pippa was spearheading the effort. We had a spreadsheet with shopping days, and she'd divided all the adults into six teams. I loved buying gifts, especially for the kids. It was a lot of work because I had to keep up with the latest entertainment trends for children between three and seventeen. Last year I made the mistake of buying DVDs of a movie I'd liked as a kid. I was still scarred by the looks of disappointment on their little faces.

I was determined not to repeat the mistake.

There was a light mist in the air tonight. Just barely visible, but enough to make me wrap my jacket tighter around me. I loved San Francisco, even though it was a bit colder than other parts of California at this time of the year. But living here had its perks, and sometimes I visited touristy spots for no reason other than to soak in the energy of the city. Pier 39 was among my favorites. On lazy, sunny days, I loved watching the sea lions there.

When I arrived at Union Square, Pippa was already there, eating a donut. She had another one for me.

"You've read my mind," I said.

"Carbs and sugar. We need both for the shopping session."

"Hear, hear," I mumbled through mouthfuls of the sweet treat.

We were both silent until we finished eating, watching the palm trees adorned with twinkling lights in the square.

Pippa usually wore stilettos and either a dress or a pencil skirt and a shirt. Today, she was dressed in shopping attire: sneakers, jeans, and a brown jacket over her white sweater. Her blond hair was pulled back in an elegant ponytail.

She was overall the most fashionable person I

knew. She was warm and feminine, and I just loved her.

She was also a successful matchmaker. So successful, in fact, that I hoped Pippa would turn her focus on me any day now. Any day now. I was happy with my life, but I wouldn't mind having a man to go home to. Someone who gave good foot rubs and excellent bear hugs. Someone who could make my panties catch fire with a single look (Winston did that in spades, but I quickly dismissed that thought). Most of all, I wanted someone to take care of and love.

"How is work?" Pippa asked as we headed to the first shop on our itinerary.

"The boss is even grouchier in person."

I kept the part where he proved he had a knightly side to myself, because I didn't want anyone knowing about my ex showing up at work.

"You know you're always welcome at Bennett Enterprises, right? We'd love to have you there. Any department you want."

Bennett Enterprises was the most successful jewelry company in America. The oldest Bennett siblings had founded it years ago: Sebastian, Logan, and Pippa—she was the head designer. Five of the Bennett siblings worked in the company, including Christopher, Victoria's husband. It was a family affair, and I couldn't wait to be part of it.

"Thanks, Pippa. I promise I'll take you up on it one day. I just want to gather some experience so I can be of use to you guys when I finally make the jump."

"You don't have to prove anything to anyone."

Yes, I did… to myself. I wanted to know that I could count on myself, that I could stand on my own two feet. Losing my parents as a teenager shaped me—I'd had that security blanket ripped from around me. Victoria had done her very best, but I'd been old enough to fully understand our financial worries. I wanted to make sure I had a solid career—one I'd earned, not simply been given because my sister had married into the Bennett family.

And I meant what I told Pippa—I did want to gather more experience before joining them. Ava, Sebastian's wife, was leading the marketing department, and she was a genius. She'd cut her teeth in a marketing consultancy, working with various companies for years.

By the time I finally joined Bennett Enterprises, I was determined to be a marketing and branding ninja.

"So how is he in person?"

"Grouchy."

"You already said that. I'm gonna need some more details, please."

I was conflicted, unsure of what to say.

"Wait a second." Pippa slashed the air with her finger, bringing it closer to me in small circles. "He's hot, isn't he?"

And, that, ladies and gentlemen, was the secret power of Pippa Bennett-Callahan. She could honest to goodness read thoughts.

I had made the mistake of not fessing up right away exactly twice, but I knew better than to try again. It simply didn't work.

"Yes, yes he is."

"Well, well, well. And *you* have the hots for him."

"No… I absolutely do not want to have the hots for my grouchy boss." I sighed, closing my eyes. "I've dated enough assholes, Pippa. I need to change my type."

True, after tonight, I wasn't sure he was an asshole. Sure, he was grouchy, but an ass wouldn't have done what he did. It didn't matter, though. I still couldn't go there, and he wasn't even interested in me.

"As a matter of fact, can you use your matchmaking skills on me? Please?"

"I think you're the only one who's ever asked me that."

"That's because I'm not too proud to admit I need all the help I can get in the dating department."

"I'll see what I can do."

I shimmied my hips, clapping my hands. "Awesome. I'll have a boyfriend by Christmas."

Pippa's eyes widened. "I think you have a little too much faith in me."

"Nope. I've just had enough proof of your success. I am not picky. I just want someone nice and funny who knows how to laugh."

Pippa grinned, rubbing her hands. She flashed

YOUR CHRISTMAS LOVE

me her trademark *I'm plotting* smile. I could sense my luck already changing.

"Let's review the list before we hit the stores," I suggested.

"Let's. I can already feel the energy from the sugar kicking in."

I winked. "I think that's just the adrenaline."

"That too."

We put our heads together over my phone. It would have been more efficient to split up and go through my list, but spending time together was way more fun. We discussed the pros and cons of every gift as if we were debating the next presidential election, then ended up buying twice as many things as we'd intended to.

We met Victoria and Chloe at our favorite Mexican restaurant, Eduardo's Tacos, just one block away from Union Square.

Victoria whistled, looking at our hands.

"I was expecting you girls to have twice as many bags."

"Victoria!" Pippa exclaimed in mock offense. "This was just the second round. We've already schlepped the first one to the car."

Victoria laughed. "My bad. You two really shouldn't go shopping without supervision."

Pippa flashed a grin. I tried not to look too guilty.

"What did you get me?" Chloe asked, batting her eyelashes.

"You're not going to find out until Christmas

23

morning," I warned, fully knowing I had failed to surprise my baby sister for the past four years. I didn't even know how she found out every time. I fiercely guarded my lists.

Chloe sighed but didn't insist, which only confirmed my suspicion that she already had a plan to find out anyway.

"Hope you didn't buy me a kid gift though," she said.

"You'll see." She was twelve and had declared that she wanted to be included in the teenager group.

"What kind of tacos are you girls in the mood for?" Victoria asked.

"How about one of everything?" I said. The aromas of freshly baked tortilla and chili, and the displays with guacamole, chicken, chips, and salads were making my mouth water.

Victoria rubbed her belly. "I like how you're thinking."

"I'll go order at the cashier," Chloe offered.

"How was the parent-teacher conference?" I asked once Chloe was out of earshot and Pippa, Victoria, and I headed to a table for four at the back. She was a great kid and never got into trouble, and yet I couldn't help worrying about her.

After our parents passed away, I'd desperately wanted to shield the little ones from hurting. Lucas was a few years older than Chloe, and there had been no sugarcoating the loss for him. But it had been a blessing that Chloe had been so young. In many ways, Christopher and Victoria were the only parental figures she knew.

"The usual. She hates math, reads fantasy books under the desk. I pretend I'll be stricter; the teacher pretends she believes me. What's new with the two of you?"

I glanced sideways at Pippa, who gave me a small smile. Aha! She'd keep my secret, thank goodness.

No need to get Victoria involved in the matchmaking game as well. Unfortunately, my sister completely lacked any skill in that department, but she persisted, which had resulted in several cringe-worthy dates.

But I had a lot of faith in Pippa. She could somehow sense when two people had that spark together.

I was in such an excellent mood that I'd nearly forgotten I'd be chained to my office building for the next few weeks.

After downing the last taco, I made the mistake of checking my email. Winston had sent me a calendar invitation. He'd blocked the meeting room next to his office from six to eight p.m. every evening until Christmas.

That wasn't my favorite meeting room. It was small, and it was the only one I hadn't decorated for Christmas yet.

As the VP of branding, part of my job was spearheading the department store's Christmas program, and that included decorating every floor and window display.

I'd loved, loved, loved going with Mom and Dad to Statham Department store as a kid during the Christmas countdown weeks, and now I was part of creating that magic. How amazing was that?

Since we'd bought new decorations this year, I'd used the old ones to decorate the offices. Why let them go to waste? Everyone loved them.

I'd skipped the small meeting room because no one used it, but I'd take care of it first thing tomorrow morning.

I always felt like a kid around this time of the year. It was perhaps why I loved decorating everything. I always felt much closer to my parents. I surrounded myself with a Christmas *feeling* for as long as possible.

I cringed as I looked at the calendar entries for the next few weeks. At least he'd left Thanksgiving free.

I couldn't deny that I was inexplicably drawn to him. All that masculinity and knee-weakening sex appeal. And I'd felt so protected with him by my side tonight.

Maybe working so closely with him wasn't smart. I could easily say no. It was against company rules to do more than two hours overtime a week. But I liked the work. I'd learned so much until now, and we'd only been communicating via email and phone. A few weeks in which I worked one-on-one with him for two hours every day? That was fuel for my nerdy soul (and for my lady bits, but I wasn't ready to admit that even to myself).

Chapter Four

Winston

I loved being back in San Francisco. I'd been gone for too long, but this city was home. Hell, this store was home. The first few years out of college, I worked in banking before joining Statham Stores. I should have accepted my father's offer to take over the company three years ago, but I'd felt too young. I wanted more experience.

Dad handed the reins to his years-long general manager, who meant well but wasn't equipped to lead this business. When he'd retired last year, the financial status of this unit had been in shambles. It still was.

I was determined to turn things around, to save this store. It was the pinnacle of my parents' work.

I couldn't even imagine the look of disappointment on Mom's face if we lost it. She knew every employee by first name. Knew their life story too. If I didn't save this, I wasn't letting down just the loyal employees who'd been with us for years. I was letting my parents down too.

Saving the store had my full focus. Despite loving it, I'd been dreading to come into the office…

until I met Sienna face-to-face. That permanent smile that lit her up was branded in my mind. She was fascinating.

Two hours after the incident in front of the store, I was still riled up. That asshole had some nerve, showing up here. I was so lost in thought that I didn't realize my phone was ringing right away.

I chuckled at the screen when I saw Mom was calling.

"Hi, Mom!"

"Winston, hi. I want to cook dinner tonight for all of us. Can you make it?"

I ran a hand through my hair. "Can we do it on the weekend? It's crazy at the office at the moment."

"That's nonsense. We can have a late dinner."

"Weekdays are really busy," I insisted.

"You moved back, and I see you just as much as I did when you were gone."

I'd been back for two days.

"Mom, don't guilt me into coming over for dinner."

"Why not? It's a mother's prerogative to use guilt against her children. Late nights, sleepless nights; I have a whole lot of arguments."

"I bet you do."

"Did I mention morning sickness? I had my head in the toilet for months when I was pregnant."

"Mom." I chuckled but didn't give in. I couldn't. There was too much at stake. I hadn't told them just how precarious the situation was. There wasn't anything they could do about it. They'd just worry.

"It's the countdown to Christmas, Mother. We're under pressure to fulfill all orders."

There, that wasn't a lie. It just wasn't the whole truth. That wasn't the only reason I was under pressure.

"At least you know Christmas is coming. Wasn't sure you did. Don't forget to relax."

"I won't."

After hanging up, I googled a delivery service. Mother loved flowers and chocolate. I placed the order before going back to work. Two hours later, she called again.

"I just got your gifts," she exclaimed. "This is not a replacement for you not coming to dinner, young man."

"No, it's not."

"Also doesn't mean I'll pester you less."

I grinned. "Wouldn't dream of it." Checking my schedule, I made a spur of the moment decision. "I'll drop by the house this week in the evening, but not for dinner. Just a glass of wine."

I could practically feel my mother's joy.

"I knew I'd guilt you into it eventually."

Chapter Five

Sienna

The next day, I arrived before anyone else at the office, so I could take care of the meeting room. It wasn't that hanging decorations was frowned upon… but the way I did it might raise a few brows. I didn't just hang them. I made an experience out of it.

Case in point, I put a Christmas playlist on my phone, not bothering with earbuds because my floor was empty anyway. I tapped my foot along to the rhythm, mouthing every line to every song: "Jingle Bells," "Frosty the Snowman," and even some commercial Christmas songs that I loved: Mariah Carey's "All I want For Christmas," Bill Nighy's "Christmas is All Around Me," and my all-time favorite, "Santa Baby," the Kylie Minogue version. Eh, that one was more sensual than Christmassy, but hey, grown-ups needed to have fun on Christmas too.

I kept that one for last and put it on repeat as I hung the last of the twinkling lights along the windowsill. There, the room looked so much better now. I could see myself spending two hours a day in this little box.

"What's going on here?"

I froze mid hip shimmy, drawing in a deep breath.

Shit, shit, shit. Winston was here. It was still only seven thirty. No one arrived before eight.

Slowly, I turned around, wishing I could turn off the music by sheer force of will, because Kylie was just singing a particularly suggestive lyric.

My face was red, I was sure of it. It felt on fire. Damn it. My goal was to impress him so he'd hand me more responsibility. Dancing unrestrainedly around the office was not going to help. How was he going to take me seriously from now on?

I'd been expecting him to be looking around the room with disapproval, but his gaze was fixed on me, and those green eyes seemed darker than I remembered them from yesterday. He looked down my body slowly and then back up. His eyes were smoldering. Oh my God. Was he checking me out?

I broke out in a sweat at the mere thought.

"Ms. Hensley, what is all this?"

"Christmas decorations."

"I see that. What are they doing *in here?*"

"Thought this place could use some Christmas spirit. This was the only meeting room without decorations."

"Did it occur to you that maybe that's why I chose it? The entire floor is overflowing with twinkling lights and whatnot."

Wait a second… was he picking on my decorations? He was losing all the points he'd earned yesterday evening.

"It's not against company rules to decorate the workplace. I checked."

"No, but blasting music isn't appropriate."

"You don't like Christmas carols?" I countered. I had no clue why I was so riled up all of a sudden.

He narrowed his eyes. "This is not a Christmas carol."

I was surprised that he listened to enough music to know the difference. In my mind, Winston was always working, wearing one of his crisp suits and shirt, and holy hell, the man was rolling up his sleeves. His forearms were impressive. Muscular and toned. A sudden desire slammed into me to know what else he was hiding under that shirt. Those pants.

I cleared my throat, hoping that would dispel the sinful images. I failed, of course. But I needed to get my bearings and apologize, be professional.

"I'm sorry about blasting music. You're right, this is… inappropriate. I just didn't think anyone would be here. I know everyone's schedule. Except yours, of course." Why hadn't I thought about that? "But I am *not* sorry about the decorations. Everyone here is on edge to make the targets. We're all working our asses off. We need a little bit of cheering up."

I'd expected him to retaliate in his usual gruff manner, tell me to take it all down.

"Fine. The decorations stay. You're right. It's motivating for everyone else." His tone was surprisingly soft. For everyone else, but not him?

There was a story behind that. Something didn't compute.

I was determined to make him come around.

"But I don't want to hear that song again," he added. The bossy tone was back.

I couldn't help a grin and brought my hand to my temple in a mock salute.

"Yes, boss."

"Sassy, are you, Ms. Hensley?"

"You haven't seen sassy yet, Mr. Statham."

Fire danced in those deep green eyes again, as if the heat had been there all along and I'd lit the match with my words. I licked my lips, quickly looking away. I had no idea what was going on here, what to do with this sudden… tension. I'd never met someone so masculine, so dominant.

When I chanced a look at him, I startled. He was still watching me intently. Could he tell that my entire body felt ablaze just because he was *looking* at me?

"The song, Ms. Hensley. It's still playing." There was amusement interwoven with bossiness in his tone.

"Right, yes."

I felt his gaze on me every step of the way to the table where I'd set my phone. When I finally paused the damn song, I heard him chuckle.

He stepped away from the doorway, making just enough room that I could pass by him. I nearly brushed my shoulder against his chest on my way out.

I couldn't ignore these energetic vibes rolling off him. I couldn't ignore *him*, period. His presence was too overwhelming. Those suggestive lyrics were at fault for this… flirty tension we had going on.

I hoped.

Otherwise, spending two hours alone every evening with this sinful man might just be my undoing.

***

The rest of the day felt like a sprint. Winston was sending me about ten emails per hour. Judging by the occasional grunt and whispered curse from my colleagues, he was spamming them too.

At eleven o'clock, he called a meeting with the branding and marketing team. I was anxious about it for reasons I couldn't explain.

When I stepped inside the large meeting room, I sat as far away from the front as possible. One by one, my colleagues filtered in, sitting around the oval table. Winston himself arrived last. I sucked in a breath when he stepped inside, looking away. Somehow, I could tell he was looking at me. When I chanced a glance at the front, I bit my lip. I'd been right. Winston's gaze *was* trained on me.

Once everyone arrived, Winston started speaking. He talked extensively about the webpage. To my surprise, he didn't mention the rebranding.

"Thanks for coming, everyone, despite the short notice," he finished. "I've communicated with many of you extensively via email and phone calls until now, but I look forward to meeting everyone in person. This is my family's legacy, and I intend to do right by it. I assure you, the well-being of this company and everyone who works in it is front and center for me. My door is always open."

He looked around the table once. Did he have any idea how intimidating he was? He had this dominant allure that seemed almost dangerous, as if there was a real chance that if you walked into his office, you wouldn't walk out the same person.

He followed that intro with a round of Q and A where everyone could open up about the most pressing issues.

He was brilliant; there was no other word to describe him. He had a quick solution for almost every issue, and I knew that even though everyone was still intimidated by him, they also respected him.

I relaxed and was beginning to think that the tension from this morning had really just been because of my unfortunate choice of music, but then Winston started moving around the table with slow, deliberate steps. When I felt him behind me, I sucked in a breath. He wasn't close enough that I could feel his body heat, but I still felt his presence. All that power and energy were inescapable.

When he dismissed the meeting, he waited for everyone to leave. I felt him watch my every move as I gathered my notepad. Was he thinking about this morning, or could he tell the effect he had on me?

I only took a deep breath when I was out of

the meeting room.

My reprieve was brief, though. Ten minutes later, Winston called me into his office. When he looked up at me over his laptop, I broke out in a sweat. My lips were dry.

"Ms. Hensley. That keynote for this evening is still missing."

"I sent it before the general meeting."

"I don't have it." His tone was impatient. Oh, this infuriating man.

"Have you checked your spam folder? The attachment was large. Sometimes our servers flag that as spam."

He clicked on his laptop twice. "It's in spam."

When he glanced up at me, I squirmed, feeling trapped in my spot. My skin simmered. I felt as if the distance between us had vanished.

I was *not* attracted to this man. He was moody and… my boss. I couldn't be attracted to him. And yet, I was.

"Thank you," he said.

"You're welcome." With a small nod, I hurried out of his office.

At lunch, everyone on our floor crammed into the kitchen, eating pizza and talking about the boss.

They were grilling me because I'd had more contact with Winston than anyone else, but honestly, I couldn't tell them more than they already knew. The man was an enigma for me too. A sinfully hot enigma, but still.

When I returned, I passed Winston's desk and heard him on the phone. He'd been talking to the same supplier since before I left for lunch. Had he eaten at all? It seemed unlikely.

Well, I couldn't let him starve. The last thing we needed was for him to go into hangry mode.

Delivery would take a while, so I hurried to the food hall on the ground floor and had fun trying to guess what he'd like to eat. I ended up buying him a chicken sandwich. You couldn't go wrong with that, right?

He'd finished the phone call when I returned to his office. I knocked briefly at the door, even though it was open.

"I bought you a sandwich."

He looked at me in surprise before rising from behind his desk, crossing the room to me. I tried to steel myself against all that sexiness and masculinity, but it was as pointless as it had been this morning in the boardroom.

Every step dripped with confidence, a hint of dominance, as if the world was his oyster. His for the taking.

"Thank you," he said, taking the sandwich from me. The tips of our fingers touched. I felt as if he'd stroked my entire body. His gaze became even more intense.

"Figured you didn't have time to grab lunch. It's chicken."

"And poison?" He gave me a half smile that made my heart beat faster. I couldn't even imagine how I'd react if he'd flashed me a full-on smile.

He knew he wasn't quite forgiven for his impatience before I cleared up the spam misunderstanding. Good.

"Can't have that. I still need you to approve my vacation days, remember?"

"Did you have lunch?"

"Yes. Everyone else did. We order and eat together in the kitchen."

He nodded, taking a step back. I was about to head out when he said, "Ms. Hensley, come in. And close the door please."

I did as he said, feeling trapped. Especially when he motioned to the armchairs around the small round table in the corner.

"Sit down with me."

Why did his voice have to be so rich and deep?

"How is the mood out there?" he asked after we sat down.

Was he genuinely concerned about what people thought about him? I couldn't get a read on him.

"How do you mean?"

"Let's put it this way. If I left my sandwich unattended, is there a chance someone would slip poison in it?"

I grinned. "I wouldn't try my luck if I were you."

"Noted. What would you suggest I do to improve my odds?"

"Why are you asking me?"

"Because someone who dances to Kylie's "Santa Baby" first thing in the morning at the office will give it to me straight."

He looked at me as he said it. I maintained eye contact, even though my body temperature rose so quickly that I felt the need to splash cold water on my face right away.

"No one really knows you, Winston. You arrived less than two days ago, and everyone's had at least two emails from you with shouty capitals. Your parents were everyone's friends, and I think most people expected you to be the same. Everyone has different leadership styles, of course, but many of the long-term employees have stayed with Statham Stores because they're loyal to your family. Because they love your parents."

Something flashed in those dark green eyes. I had no idea why, but it made me want to reach out and pull him closer.

"Thank you for your honesty."

"I wanted to ask you something. You didn't mention the store's rebrand in the meeting. Was that on purpose?"

"Yes. Please keep it to yourself for now."

I stood, because his tone was final. He stood as well. I pointed to the unopened sandwich.

"Eat your sandwich. We wouldn't want you to get hangry. Not the way to improve your odds."

"Yes, ma'am."

This time, he didn't just give me a half smile,

but a full one. I'd fulfilled my mission!

Only now I wasn't just feeling that the distance between us was smaller, but that it was nonexistent. Those alpha vibes were simply too much. Well, well. Winston Statham was waving a white flag. A tiny one, but still, we were making progress.

I left his office because I didn't think it was smart to be alone with him for longer than necessary. Then I remembered that I was meeting him at six o'clock *alone*.

Things weren't going to get any easier today, were they?

Chapter Six

Sienna

At six o'clock, as everyone left, I gathered my laptop and notepad and headed to the meeting room.

I instantly lit up when I entered the room. I'd done so well with all the decorations, I couldn't be in here and not smile. Mission accomplished.

I hurried to turn on all the twinkling lights. Fingers crossed that Winston wouldn't object. On second thought, even if he did object, I'd find some way of convincing him that this was productive for work morale. After all, I'd convinced him this morning.

Okay. New resolution. I would *not* think about this morning. I was still mortified and hoped that Winston had already forgotten the incident. On the other hand, I was fairly certain that my semisexy shimmy around the room had been what had convinced Winston to let me keep the decorations in the first place.

And speaking of Winston, where he? I was five minutes early, but it wasn't like him to be late.

As if on cue, the door to the meeting room

opened and he stepped inside, carrying two take-out bags. A delicious and familiar aroma filled the air.

"What's that?" I asked.

"Dinner." My stomach growled at the smell. "I'm keeping you hostage here. The least I can do is feed you dinner."

I was suspicious. He'd waved the white flag this afternoon, but I'd assumed it would be a fleeting thing.

Was this our newfound chemistry? I could get used to this.

"Thank you," I said.

When he placed the bags on the table, his arm very nearly touched mine. He smiled at me, taking my breath away.

Oh, yes. I was already getting used to this.

"What did you buy?"

"Chicken masala."

"That's my favorite." I perked up. This evening was looking better and better. He hadn't even commented on the explosion of lights around us. We were definitely making progress.

"I know."

I stopped in the act of unwrapping the lid of my bowl. That caught me off guard.

"How?"

"Asked Mara where you usually buy lunch, then asked the cook what your favorite is."

I lowered my eyes to the bag. Okay, so this wasn't just waving a white flag. It was thoughtful.

"Great choice. It's the best masala in the city

as far as I'm concerned. I don't know why he's not more well-known. But I've talked to my family about maybe bringing him in as a visiting chef at the Blue Moon."

"Blue Moon? The one owned by Blake and Alice Bennett? You're related to the Bennett family?"

"Yes. My older sister married Christopher Bennett," I said as we sat next to each other, digging into our dinner.

"So what are you doing here putting up with me? Half the family works at Bennett Enterprises, and the other half own successful businesses."

"I know. They keep tempting me into joining them, especially Pippa. The designer. I'll work at Bennett Enterprises someday too, but I want to have as much experience as possible so I can be an asset when I join them."

He scrutinized me, as if he was seeing me in a different light. Having all that focus on me, all that simmering heat, was overpowering my senses. I lowered my eyes to my bowl, drawing in a deep breath.

I felt at his mercy—his gaze was inescapable.

We ate in silence, and I was proud that we'd managed to put the awkwardness from this morning behind us.

Almost unwittingly, I looked at the corner where I'd been shimmying while I'd hung twinkling lights. I realized one second too late that had been a mistake, because Winston followed my gaze. When he snapped his attention back to me, I knew he was thinking about that morning again.

I squirmed in my seat, suddenly feeling hot. Winston's gaze fell to my lips. I inhaled sharply, pushing the empty container to one side, opening my laptop.

I glanced stubbornly at the screen, even though it was still loading. I chanced a quick glance upward. Winston was watching me with a half smile. My senses were on high alert, on the brink of being overpowered by him—*again*.

"Should we begin?" I asked.

"Whenever you're ready."

His own laptop was open next to him. I hadn't prepared a presentation, per se, just Power Point slides with keywords to help our brainstorming.

"What spurred the decision for the rebrand?" I asked, hoping for more info than yesterday.

"It's good to renew a company's image from time to time," he said vaguely.

I wasn't buying it, but fair enough. He didn't need to explain himself to me, even though it would have helped to know why he wanted to scrap the current one.

"The Christmas branding stays," he said. "It's part of the store's DNA, and customers would feel cheated if we dropped it. But we need something more, a draw all year round to put us ahead of Macy's and other similar chains."

"How about something seasonal?" I suggested. "Each season could have a different theme."

He nodded slowly. "I thought about that too. We'd build up to the new season in the last month of the current one, instead of running sales. That's one thing we need to change—sales shoppers. It's a drain on profits. That in turn affects liquidity."

I pressed my lips together.

"What?"

I'd never been afraid to speak my mind, even if I was wrong. How else was I going to learn? And Winston had always been fair to me in that regard. He might be bossy and demanding but had never put me down for saying the wrong thing.

"Sales shoppers can become regular customers eventually. For years, I could only afford to buy marked-down items, but as soon as my financial situation improved, I bought full-priced items too. It's a matter of building brand loyalty. If you didn't have those sales, I would've just gone over to Macy's."

He tapped his pen on the table, frowning. "We have data on that. Sales shoppers use our fidelity card most. Let's track how many became regular customers over the years and go from there."

"I'll run the stats tomorrow."

"Great. I like the seasonal plan."

"Well, winter is going to be split in two, right? We can only play the Christmas theme until the end of the year, at most. Then we can play on Valentine's Day, although it's not my favorite holiday."

I was the type of person who thought while

speaking out loud. Sometimes I came upon a solution *while* talking.

"Why not?"

"It feels like a retail gimmick, honestly. And the single people feel left out."

"I agree. Let's take a look at January historically. See what other holiday we can find. Maybe we can make a celebration out of it. And then in February, we can already drum up the new season."

"Perfect."

We made a slide for each season, just jotting down ideas and keywords as they came to us.

"How wild can I go?" I asked. Ideas were running amok in my mind.

"Nothing is off limits, Sienna." His voice was a low rumble, and it sounded dangerously close.

I'd been so focused on the presentation, hunched over the laptop, that I hadn't noticed he'd drawn his chair nearer. He was right next to me. He smelled like pepper and the ocean, and the scent was overpowering. *He* was overpowering.

I couldn't move away. His nearness might have been knee-weakening, but I craved more of it.

"You sure you can handle it?" I asked playfully.

A spark popped in his eyes. "Try me."

"What if we made a huge *bid winter goodbye* event running from mid-January to mid-February? We could remodel part of the food court in a festival-type setting. Even add a playground for kids where parents can drop them off while they shop. Add a slide maybe. Come to think of it, we could have that playground all year round."

"I like the dynamic element," he said appreciatively. "But we need something we can implement right away. Including the slide and everything else would take structural changes to the building."

"Got it."

We went on discussing the pros and cons of the ideas for the winter schedule for what felt like hours. Finally, the well of ideas dried up. Hell, my mouth was dry from talking so much.

"Let's call it a night," he said.

I leaned back, stretching my arms. Finally, Winston pushed his own chair away, massaging his temple. I immediately missed his nearness.

I packed my things quickly, then turned off the Christmas lights. I was even more hyperaware of Winston's presence than before. He could have left, but he was still in the room. I was about to bring a chair so I could reach the string of lights I'd put on a shelf when Winston said, "I'll do that."

He must have been closer than I'd thought, because I felt the heat of his body behind me almost immediately. He was so close that if I leaned back a few inches, my head would touch his chest. I stood completely still while he extended a hand, reaching the switch with ease, turning it off.

"There."

I waited a few seconds before turning, but

he'd only taken a step or so back. He was far too close for my peace of mind, and he knew it. That amused glint in his eyes was a dead giveaway. I cleared my throat, smiling, attempting to diffuse this... energy that seemed to grow more intense each time we were alone.

"See, want to tell me this didn't help? Put us in a Christmas mood?"

He cocked a brow.

I rolled my eyes. "Fine. Put *me* in a Christmas mood, and makes me feel as if I'm home with my family. That fuels my creativity."

"Noted." Unexpectedly, he added, "Do your parents also live in San Francisco?"

"They passed away when I was a teenager."

"I'm sorry for your loss."

"Thanks."

"How many siblings do you have?"

"An older one, Victoria. Two younger ones— Lucas is seventeen and Chloe twelve."

I rarely spoke about my parents, least of all to people I wasn't close to. But he'd fed me my favorite food, and I was surrounded by twinkling lights and all manners of Christmassy things. How could I not let my guard down?

"My mom was a nurse. For a long time, I wanted to be one too. But I don't like the sight of blood and sick people. I just couldn't do it. One summer in high school, Christopher arranged for me to intern at a hospital, and I just couldn't go through with it. I felt as if I was letting her down. But

Christopher was really supportive and said I should intern for the rest of the summer at Bennett Enterprises. I was in the marketing department and loved every second of it. You know the saying 'Don't try to be an apple if you're a banana, because you'll always be a second-rate apple'?"

"Love that saying. And you're brilliant at this, Sienna. You've definitely found your place."

"Thanks. Anyway, Mom used to bring us all here for the Christmas program. It's one of my favorite memories."

His eyes softened. That only loosened my tongue more.

"So when I saw an opening in the marketing department, I jumped at the opportunity. I'm a Christmas enthusiast."

"You mean a Christmas dork."

"Hey! Don't say that," I teased. I'd meant it rhetorically, but Winston shifted closer again. It was intoxicating, taking my breath away.

"Or what?"

That challenging tone, the whiff of pepper and ocean were too damn appealing to me. I could almost feel the warmth of his skin, even though he wasn't touching me. This energy between us had turned sensual again. Everything was like that with Winston. It was his superpower.

"Anyway, being in charge of the decorations fits me like a glove," I said.

"I can see that."

The Statham Department store was a fixture

in San Francisco's Christmas season. Every single trip here during my childhood had been pure magic. I'd loved every detail: the huge red bows hanging from the tall ceilings, the live carol singers, the shopping assistants dressed as elves on each floor, Meet Santa Day.

When no one had wanted to be in charge of setting up this year's decorations, I'd volunteered with a big grin. It had soon become clear why no one had wanted the job. I had to start my day earlier than everyone else, and on occasion stay later. The decorations were only put up when the shop was closed to customers. Since most of the Christmas temporary staff were students, I had the unpleasant surprise of them just not showing up for work and having to hastily replace them, but all in all, *I loved the job*.

"Mom, my older sister, and I had this tradition where we watched a Christmas movie every evening in December. I do that now as well. But this year, I'm locked in here with you instead of watching my movies,"

"It's still November," he pointed out.

"I amended the tradition. Started it earlier to prolong the holiday season. So you'd better make it up to me," I teased.

He took the bait, leaning in closer. For some reason, it made me feel like *he* was baiting *me*.

"I can do that. Dinner is on me again tomorrow."

"You'll have to up your game if you want to

make up for making me skip my Christmas movie."

"I plan to up my game, all right."

"How?"

"You'll see."

"More details, please?" I felt compelled to ask because I wasn't sure we were on the same page.

"You're used to making all the rules, aren't you, Sienna? Won't work with me. I make the rules."

"Don't be surprised if I don't stick to them." Was he only talking about work?

"You'll follow them. You'll see." His voice had changed. It sounded lower, rougher.

In a fraction of a second, the atmosphere between us changed. I swallowed hard, fiddling with my thumbs.

"Same time tomorrow?" He wasn't taking his eyes off me, and the constant attention was too much. He definitely wasn't just talking about work. *OhGod, OhGod.*

The attraction wasn't one-sided. The realization wreaked havoc on me. My pulse was out of control. Heavens, I would have been better off not knowing.

"Sure."

Chapter Seven

Winston

Usually, I looked forward to Christmas, but this year, every bit of decoration had just been a reminder of what was at stake.

Except, looking around the offices every time I went out of mine, I didn't feel stressed; quite the opposite. Sienna had been right; this *was* relaxing.

I couldn't get the sight of her dancing out of my mind. Every time I'd seen her since, I remembered the sway of her hips, the passionate way she'd sung the lyrics. I'd very nearly walked over to her, pinned her against a wall, and claimed her mouth.

I'd worked with her for months but hadn't gotten to know her on a personal level. The desire to do so now slammed into me.

She was smart. I knew that. I'd asked myself more than once why she put up with me. Last night, I'd gotten my answer. I respected that she didn't want anything on a silver platter. She wanted to earn her place.

A vein pulsed in my temple when I thought about that guy on the first night. I didn't know the whole story, but just seeing Sienna's vulnerable expression had been enough to make me want to punch that idiot, ensure she never had to see him again, or deal with him in any way.

In the evening, I went into the meeting room first. I'd bought burgers for dinner, another of Sienna's favorites. She arrived a few seconds later, and her eyes widened when she saw me. Then she lit up completely at the sight of the burgers. Damn, she looked even cuter radiating happiness like this.

"I love burgers," she exclaimed.

"I know. I did my homework." I tilted closer as we opened the take-out bags side by side. Her skin flushed, and her fingers faltered for a second. I loved her reaction. This tension between us was undeniable, but it felt so damn good that I just didn't want to stop. I barely kept myself from reaching out and touching her smooth skin.

"What's with the huge boxes next to your desk?" I asked.

"I had some stuff delivered. I'm having some work done to my house, but I didn't want to have them sent there. They're too big to fit into a delivery box, and it's a pain to collect them from the post office. Tried to bribe the delivery guy into bringing them to my car, but he wouldn't hear of it."

"I'll help you bring them to your car."

"That's okay, I can handle—"

"I'll bring them to your car," I said in a definitive, no-argument-accepted tone.

She tilted her head. "Is this part of your plan

to convince me you're nice?"

"I'm not *nice*, Sienna. But I think you know that."

I held her gaze. She didn't reply.

"What's in the boxes anyway?"

"Some materials for renovations. I'm working on that every evening. Progress is slower than anticipated, obviously, since I'm here so late. I need to have everything ready in a week, when some new furniture arrives. This weekend I'm painting my walls."

"I'm handy with construction. I can help you this weekend."

"Wow. Thanks. You want to paint my walls? Why?"

"I feel guilty for keeping you here so late."

Her face opened up into a huge smile. "Well, then, bring it on, boss. What can I do to also get you to sand my floors?"

"Sassy again?"

She shrugged one shoulder. Her smile didn't dim. I loved the positivity and playfulness she carried with her all the time. I wanted more of it—all of it.

I wanted *her*.

"I am officially upgrading you from boss from hell to dictatorial and grouchy."

"You what?"

She grinned. "You said you liked my honesty."

"I do." I just wasn't sure that *dictator* was an improvement.

"I have to warn you. I like doing housework while watching Christmas movies in the background."

"You're joking."

"No. It keeps me distracted."

"I'll keep you distracted." I shifted in my chair until there were just a few inches between us. This time, I couldn't resist touching her. Just a light scrape of my fingers on her wrist. The fine hair on her arms stood on end. When I looked up at her, she bit her lower lip before opening a new document on her laptop.

"How?"

"You'll see." I winked at her before turning to the screen. We still had a few hours of work ahead of us. She'd run the stats on the reward cards, and we laid out the pros and cons of cutting off sales.

Branding required a lot of number analysis, and Sienna was excellent at it. We created half a dozen graphics, but I wanted to mull it over for a few days before deciding on a course of action.

"I feel like my brain is fried," she said after two hours.

"Let's stop here," I said. "I need to get going anyway."

"You have plans?"

"Promised my parents I'd stop by for a drink. If I don't, my mother is liable to show up at the office. Do you know a good place to buy chocolates? I've been away from San Francisco for a while, and my old go-to store closed. I don't want to go empty-handed. Ordered some online a few days ago, but if you have a recommendation, I'll go with that."

"Sure." Her tone was softer. I was sure I'd just earned a few points. Between yawns, she gave me the address of a shop.

"I've kept you here for too long."

"We've got some very long evenings ahead of us if you want to roll it out starting in the new year."

"Once we finalize the concept, I'm going to bring the VP of operations into this. But yes, it will be a lot of work. Hence why I won't take time off for Christmas."

She pouted. I knew it was on the tip of her tongue to ask me about her time off.

"Sienna. I approved your vacation time on my first day. HR is still processing it."

"Really? Thank you, thank you, thank you. I think my brother would have disowned me otherwise. Come to think of it, my whole family probably would have."

"What are your plans? Spending the whole vacation in London?"

"Just one week. And then part of the family is going to Aspen. It'll be amazing. I'm going to be the skiing instructor for the kids."

She spoke every word with warmth. Her exuberance was addicting.

That was perhaps why I looked for every opportunity to be near her. Sure, I felt guilty about keeping her here, but that wasn't the only reason I'd volunteered to paint her walls.

"Sounds like a full schedule."

"It is."

"Be sure to send me pictures. It'll keep me entertained while I slave away here."

"Is that a ruse to actually send me work while I'm away?"

I was longing to touch her again, so I put my hands in my pockets. Easier to resist the impulse this way.

"No need for ruses with me. When I want something, I ask for it, Sienna."

***

I arrived at my parents' house half an hour later than I said I would.

Predictably, Mom was already suspicious.

"I was afraid you'd call us with an excuse, saying you won't make it after all."

I pulled out the box of chocolates.

"I see. Brought this to soften me up."

I winked at her before shaking hands with Dad. Clapping my shoulder, he said, "You did well with those chocolates."

"Had the best teacher."

I learned my tricks from him.

My parents lived in a two-bedroom house in Pacific Heights. I'd grown up in a larger house, but after I left for college, they downsized, insisting that all the empty rooms just served as a reminder that I was gone.

Predictably, Mom had dinner laid out. Dad and I exchanged a look, smiling. He patted his belly. "Second dinner for me."

"For me too. I had something to eat at the office."

Mom gave me a stern look.

"Why is the Christmas countdown stressing you so much?" Dad asked.

"Your dad and I always made it a point to come home for dinner," Mom said.

"I know, but it's my first year as the company's president. The team in San Francisco barely knows me."

"What's that supposed to mean? I talked everyone's ear off about you right until my last day at the office," Mom said.

"They know *of* me. But not me. Establishing a relationship of trust goes a long way."

"What you need is a general manager you can delegate everything to, like we did with Gerald," Dad said.

I didn't reply. Gerald was still a sore point where I was concerned. And I did plan to hire a general manager as soon as I got the store back on its feet.

I immediately thought about Sienna. At twenty-five, she was perhaps a few years too young for that position, but then again, I was too young to be president too. But the company needed a young, energetic management team. I could see Sienna building such a group.

I'd seen her sitting with the others at lunch. She had a knack for people. But she'd made it clear this job was temporary for her. Bennett Enterprises was the endgame, and I respected that.

I smiled to myself. Here I was, thinking about her again. I had no idea what it was about this woman that made it impossible not to think about her, want to be near her.

"When can you drop by for a real dinner?" Mom asked.

I pointed to the potato salad and grilled chicken. "Does it get more real than this?"

"You know what I mean."

I laughed. Dad shook his head. "You're not getting out of this, son."

"The weekend, Mom. I'll let you know tomorrow if Saturday or Sunday is better."

She placed both hands on her hips. "Do I have to use my guilting tactics to get you to commit right now?"

I held up my hands. "No, no. Absolutely not."

"Next time, bring two chocolate boxes," Dad said under his breath. I grinned in response. I loved that some things never changed.

Chapter Eight

Sienna

On Thursday evening, Christopher and Blake surprised me by dropping by to help me with renovations. I was surprised they'd brought Sebastian too.

"What are you doing here?" I asked him.

"Christopher told me you're running behind on your renovation plans. I'm at your service," Sebastian said.

Oh my God, I wanted to hug the living daylights out of him. All three of them, actually. Renovating my house before Christmas had not turned out to be one of the best ideas. Delivery of materials was unreliable, workers were overbooked. I planned to cover the furniture in the living room with plastic, so Winston and I could paint on Saturday.

But honestly, I'd never anticipated that just moving the furniture around could take so long.

"Thank you so much!"

Blake winked. "Hey, what's the benefit of a bazillion Bennetts if not to help each other?"

That was honestly the family motto. I did feel a little guilty though, because Christmastime was a stressful period for everyone. Christopher and Sebastian had their hands full at Bennett Enterprises—demand for jewelry went up at this time of the year. Blake's restaurants were booked with Christmas parties and whatnot.

We got to work immediately. Everything was so much easier and quicker when you didn't have to do it by yourself. Besides, it was always a *hoot* to have them here.

"Just saying, if Daniel and I had had the identical twin card to play, things in the Bennett clan could have been completely different," Blake said. I smiled to myself. Christopher had an identical twin, Max. They'd been dubbed the serious brothers, even though they'd always been pranksters.

"Doubt it," Christopher said.

The two sets of twins were forever in a competition with each other.

"Hey!" Sebastian said. "How about you focus on work? Sienna and I are twice as quick."

We finished in under one hour.

"When are you painting?" Sebastian said.

"Saturday."

"We can drop by and help you," Blake said.

"No, no. I won't hear of it. I know you're all busy at Jenna's house."

Christopher cocked a brow. "But you won't be able to finish by yourself in one day."

The tips of my ears were red. Shit, could they tell? For some reason I wanted to keep my day with the boss to myself. I was an easy prey for the Bennett men to sniff out that I wasn't going to paint alone.

"I'll make do," I reassured them as I bid them goodbye.

***

On Friday, I was on pins and needles. Especially when a certain grumpy but sexy-as-hell boss reminded me that I'd see him on the weekend too.

"Let's grab breakfast first on Saturday morning," he suggested after I gave him my address. We were in the food court on the ground floor, discussing my idea of adding a permanent entertainment center. Even though he didn't plan to add it right away, we wanted to get a cost estimation.

"There's a great deli in your area."

"No time. I'll have some sandwiches ready."

"Sienna—"

I shook my head, pointing a finger at him. "You don't get to make the rules."

"I'm your boss."

"Not in my home, you're not."

"We're still at work."

"Making plans for the weekend… at my house."

Winston's eyes flashed. I could tell he wasn't used to anyone saying no to him. He was about ten feet away from me, but even from a distance, I couldn't ignore all that masculinity rolling off him. I tried, but it was becoming increasingly harder.

Thank goodness the ground floor was already bustling with activity as early shoppers ate breakfast before hitting the shelves.

He cocked a brow. "You're feisty."

I grinned. "I know. Besides, I've upgraded you from dictatorial *and* grouchy to just grouchy. Don't lose all that progress over a breakfast. There's a lot of work to do. If we eat breakfast out of the house, we'll start too late."

His eyes bulged. "You've upgraded me... I see. How come?"

"I have my reasons."

Plus, I think that deep down you might be a dreamy, romantic guy. Because who else would bring his mom chocolate?

Nope. I absolutely did not want to look deep down. I wanted to keep things on the surface. Piercing green eyes, sinful lips. That surface was far too hot to be of any help. I lowered my gaze to the notepad I was holding, focusing on it as if my life depended on memorizing the words I'd scribbled there.

"I've got a good enough idea for what we want to ask for a cost estimation, but I'll stick around to take some measurements. You can go back to your office," I said.

He jutted his hands in his pockets, tilting his head slightly.

"Why, afraid that I'll get my way if I stay here any longer?"

I smiled, shrugging one shoulder.

"No. Can't boss me around in my free time, Winston."

That amusement grew even more pronounced. "We'll see about that." A knowing smile played on his lips. I instantly felt as if he'd come closer, as if there was a wall separating us from the bustle of the food hall. Goose bumps broke out on my skin as he passed me on the way to the elevators. Once he was gone, I took a deep breath.

Yup, Winston was the reason for my jumpiness today, no doubt about that. When I'd accepted his help, I hadn't banked on this energy between us growing so intense. Canceling our weekend plans now was out of the question. I needed to have the walls ready as soon as possible. There was no getting around that. My fellow Bennetts and Hensleys had gone above and beyond, helping me with the renovation. I hadn't wanted to hire a team because I would've had to take time off to supervise them.

I'd only planned small changes in the beginning, and then I started adding so many things that it became a renovation project.

I'd scheduled everything down to the minute. If it weren't for Winston's extra project, I would have been on time with everything.

No, I couldn't back out of our weekend plans. Besides, the arrangement did have some perks... chiefly, the fact that I'd see Winston do some physical work. I could already imagine him wearing a thin shirt—I was keeping my fingers crossed for a sleeveless one—all sweaty and flexing his muscles in my living room.

There was a real risk I'd never look at him the same after that, but oh hell, that sight was definitely worth the risk.

In the afternoon, Mara approached my desk. She kept looking over her shoulder.

"Mara, hi! What can I do for you?"

"Are we still on for trying to make the boss participate in the Secret Santa game at the Christmas party?" she asked.

"Shhh… don't say that out loud."

"Winston's cooped up in his office with his door closed."

"Ears of a bat, that one." I dropped my voice to a whisper. "Haven't brought it up yet, but I have a good feeling about it."

I felt as if Winston and I were making progress. But he'd only just *accepted* the decorations. If I brought up Secret Santa now, I could lose all the progress we'd made.

Baby steps.

Holding the Christmas party the week after Thanksgiving had been my idea. The store usually had the employee party closer to Christmas, but I'd attended it last year, and everyone had been too stressed to enjoy it. The final bonus announcements were the next day, and every discussion had centered around that. Besides, I'd found the party to be a little stiff.

This year, I was organizing it. Secret Santa had also been my idea. We'd done that at the company I worked for previously, and it had been an excellent way of bringing people closer.

I wanted to convince Winston to participate as well. Having the boss join in a common activity would go a long way in everyone warming up to him.

"You do?" Mara lifted her eyebrows.

"Yeah. He's not the ogre everyone thinks he is."

Her eyebrows went even higher. "Aha. If you say so. Anyway, any chance you can tell me who's buying my present? Then I can drop them hints."

I waggled my finger at her. "Mara! That's cheating."

Everyone knew who they were buying gifts *for*, but not who was buying *them* gifts.

She grinned. "I know. But I'd rather cheat than end up with a crappy present."

"Absolutely not."

I'd organized the drawing, so I could technically look up who'd been paired with whom, but I definitely *wasn't* a fan of cheating.

Besides, if I convinced Winston to participate, I'd have to run the pairing program again.

"One little hint?"

"No chance."

Mara sighed. "You're mean."

"No, I just believe in following the rules." I laughed as Mara left, wondering about Winston and *his* rules. I tried to tell myself that he wasn't attracted to me, that I was just imagining things. It was safest if I told myself that.

I'd done my best to stay out of the boss's way after this morning, but when six o'clock came around, I had no choice but head to the meeting room. Winston was already inside, and he was every bit as irresistible as he had been this morning.

"No more breakfast talk," I warned.

He pointed to his open laptop and our dinner. "We're not on your territory yet, Sienna."

Fire sparked in his eyes. The professional environment around us had been a buffer. But tomorrow at my house? All that would be gone.

Chapter Nine

Sienna

On Saturday, I groaned when my alarm clock rang at six. I usually slept in on weekends, but now, duty called.

I was still half-asleep when I started sanding the walls, dressed in overalls and with my hair pulled into an old-lady bun at the back of my head. I had a Christmas movie running in the background. I'd watched this particular one so often that I knew the dialogue by heart. Even though I'd covered the TV with a sheet of plastic, it didn't take away from the experience.

I got so lost in the movie and the activity that I completely lost track of time. I winced when the doorbell rang. It was nine. Winston was here. *Shit. Shit. Shit.* I'd planned to shower and change before he arrived, but I couldn't just let him wait on the front stoop.

Drawing in a deep breath, I opened the door. Winston's eyes bulged as he took stock of my appearance.

Damn. This might be the weekend, but I didn't want to appear unprofessional. There nothing I could do but soldier on, though. I led him inside.

"Decided to make headway?" he asked.

I yawned. "Yeah. I usually sleep in on Saturday, but…" Yet another yawn swallowed the rest of the sentence. "I made sandwiches."

Grabbing the plate, I held it up to him.

"No poison, I promise."

"Why? Already approved your vacation days."

"Yes, but you still have to paint my walls."

It was only after drinking another cup of coffee and eating two sandwiches that I was awake enough to take stock of *his* appearance. *Oh, la, la.* He rocked work jeans and a sweater perfectly.

He stared at the TV. "You weren't kidding about playing Christmas movies in the background."

"No, but for you, I'll shut it off. Can't torment you this early in the morning."

"That's an unexpected act of mercy."

"I'm much nicer when I'm half asleep."

"I'll keep that in mind."

I felt ridiculous in my overalls with my messy hair. But I'd feel even more ridiculous if I went to shower and change now. I was going to keep working anyway. I did head to the bathroom to brush my hair and pull it up in a high ponytail though. I almost put on makeup.

That would be ridiculous.

I splashed some water on my face, happy I was finally waking up. When I returned to the living room, Winston was already sanding the walls. He'd gotten rid of his sweater. He wore a white shirt that was so thin he could just as well be naked.

I allowed myself a few moments in which I did nothing but check him out. A girl needed to take some time for herself and indulge. Nothing wrong with that.

"I can feel you looking at me," he said lazily, glancing at me over his shoulder. Aha... nothing wrong until I got caught in the act.

"I was just assessing your skills," I said as nonchalantly as possible.

"And? Did I pass the test?"

"With flying colors."

"So why don't you get to work too?"

"Maybe my devious plan was to get you here and let you do all the work. Boss you around for a change."

"That's not how it works, Sienna."

He was doing that thing again where he was turning my knees weak even from a distance. Those alpha vibes were traveling at the speed of light.

With shaky legs, I got to work. He was just doing me a favor. Because I was doing him a favor. We were basically scratching each other's backs. And then my thoughts derailed completely... I could imagine my fingers scratching that perfectly toned back, and those abs. Yum.

Damn. I needed to concentrate on my task. I had trouble reconciling the bossy suit from the office with the man in front of me.

I was starting to believe that Winston really might not be the hellish boss I'd pegged him for, just under a lot of stress. Sometimes that could stretch one's tolerance and patience.

The more time we spent on the rebranding campaign, the more I believed that this wasn't just change for the sake of change. He was under a lot of pressure; I just couldn't imagine from whom. He was the boss. His parents were calm, gentle people from what everyone told me, so I couldn't imagine the pressure coming from his family's side.

Not having a movie run in the background meant silence stretched between us. I'd never done well with silence, so I started talking.

"It's good I've already done the upper floor. We should finish this in the evening."

"Why do you live by yourself in a house this big? Does it have two bedrooms?"

"Three large ones and a smaller one. I lived here with my siblings for a while, before Victoria and Christopher got together, and then we moved into his penthouse. But I've always loved this house, so when it was time for me to get my own place, I came here. We moved here after losing my parents. It had been shabby back then too, but we'd made it a home. Victoria is a decorator, so she knows how to turn any space around."

"How come there is such a huge age gap between you and your siblings?"

"They had Victoria when they were young, and I was a late surprise. After me, they adopted Chloe and Lucas. My parents had always wanted a big family. We did so many things together as a group. Decorating for Halloween and Christmas was always a huge deal."

"I'm surprised you haven't hung any Christmas things here."

I placed my free hand on my hip. "Do not mock my love for Christmas."

"Wouldn't dream of it." His lips were curled into a smile. Oh, this insufferable man.

"I just wanted to finish the renovations first, so the decorations don't get all dirty."

"You and my mom would get on well," he said.

"How come?"

"I can't explain. She's just as exuberant about everything as you are."

"Everyone's always praising your parents. I feel like I've missed out on a lot by not meeting them."

"They're great people. Hard workers. They have respect and understanding for everyone."

"Don't they miss the stores?"

He barked out a laugh. "They love the stores, but they like their retirement even more. They didn't take vacations very often before. Now they're making up for that."

"Sounds like they're enjoying themselves."

"They are."

"Did your mom like the chocolate?"

"Loved it. I'll buy two boxes tomorrow for dinner."

"Why? What did you do?"

"Who said I did anything?"

"Aha. So you're just buying her sweets for no reason at all?"

"Is that illegal?"

"No, just unexpected."

"Why? Doesn't fit with the dictator you've painted me to be? I'm sorry… grouchy, right? Unless you've upgraded me again?"

My heart was beating out of my chest. There was more to him than the brilliant man I was learning a lot from. I was curious to know more, and he didn't seem opposed to opening up. "I'll reconsider… depending on how today goes."

"So, I'm on probation right now?"

"You could say that."

"Let me get this straight. I offer to paint your walls, and I'm still on probation?"

"You could have an ulterior motive."

His eyes flashed. Oh my God, he *did* have one. I was about to ask what it was, then decided not to. Sometimes ignorance was bliss.

Except now that was all I could think about. Tearing my gaze away, I focused on the portion of the wall I was currently sanding, and then the next one. Before long, I got lost in the rhythmic task. I was still talking Winston's ear off.

"Can't believe you're willingly spending your Saturday doing this."

"Sounds like it should earn me points." I jumped, because his voice sounded much nearer than I'd expected. Somehow, I was right next to him again. How had I ended up here? It was as if I was gravitating to him without even realizing it.

I smiled to myself. "It is."

"Anyway, it's a reward for me."

"How?" I asked, perplexed.

"As you said… ulterior motive."

This push and pull were messing with my mind, and my senses. Winston was looking at me as if I was wearing some sexy lingerie, not dirty overalls. My breath caught. My pulse jackhammered in my ears. I wanted to look away—move away—but I couldn't.

I had no idea how to navigate this. The tension was all-consuming. I wasn't just aware of *him*; I was more aware of myself.

"I knew it," I said in a teasing tone. "You're here to make me work."

He curled his lips in a half smile. Clearly, work was the last thing on his mind. But I clung to this excuse and started talking about the rebranding campaign. It was neutral ground and kept me distracted from the *ulterior motive.*

Six hours later, my back started to hurt, but I persisted. We'd used coarse sandpaper, then a thin one before applying a coat of paint. We had half a wall left, and we still had to apply a second coat.

I wanted to be done today so I could make it to the Bennett gathering tomorrow.

I must have given my discomfort away somehow, because Winston suddenly asked, "What's wrong?"

"Nothing. My back is a bit sore."

He pointed to the couch. "Let's take a break. Sit. Rest."

"Back to bossy, are we?"

"You haven't seen bossy yet, Sienna. Sit."

When I turned around, a bout of dizziness hit me. The room swam in front of my eyes. My vision faded at the corners, and then I couldn't see at all anymore. I could feel myself losing my balance and expected to hit the floor any second. Instead, a strong arm curled around my waist. Warm fingers splayed on my neck.

"Sienna?"

I blinked a few times, until my vision returned.

"What happened?"

"Whoa. Just some dizziness. I'm fine now."

He still hadn't let go of me, but I didn't mind. Honestly, I still felt a little unsteady. But the more my senses returned, the more aware I became of *him*.

The soft palm, yet callused fingers. The nearness of his lips. The concern in his eyes.

"Sienna, are you sure you're okay?"

I nodded, but that just triggered another round of dizziness. I closed my eyes again.

"Fuck, you're not. Come on, let's get you to sit."

He walked me backward to the plastic-covered couch, pushed me down on it. I fell like a stone and nearly made him tumble too. He propped his palms on the headrest, stopping his fall. I was trapped between those muscle-laced arms.

He grinned. I grinned back. Holy shit, he was close. His mouth was hovering just above mine. I barely resisted pulling him closer.

"I didn't eat anything since this morning. I think my blood sugar just dropped."

"I'll get you some water."

Before I could even open my mouth to tell him it wasn't necessary, he was in the kitchen already. I liked having this sexy man in my house, fussing around me.

So, when he returned with a glass of water and a piece of chocolate from my stash, I just whistled appreciatively.

"You've just earned that upgrade."

I rose to my feet. Winston frowned, stepping right in front of me.

"What are you doing?"

"We still have a wall to finish."

"You should sit still for a few more minutes."

"Winston, I don't need you to babysit me."

"I disagree."

"I'm fine, really. The chocolate did the trick. I'm good as new."

I was too close, and yet, I didn't seem to have the wits or strength to step back, even though I knew I should put some distance. I needed some reprieve from the constant tension that had surrounded us today, pulling me toward him like a magnet. But my feet just wouldn't move, and Winston stayed put as well.

"Sienna—"

"Winston—"

I didn't realize what he intended to do until I felt his hand at the back of my head and his mouth on mine. I couldn't think beyond how much I wanted this—him. Fisting his shirt, I pulled him even closer, felt him smile against my mouth before his tongue coaxed mine.

He kissed me until I trembled with anticipation and need. He tugged at the straps on my shoulders, as if he wanted to yank them away. His mouth was hot and urgent, exploring me.

The hand at the back of my head kept me exactly at the angle he wanted. The deeper he kissed me, the more I wanted. As if knowing how much I yearned for his touch, he brought a hand around my waist, bringing me flush against him. My breasts pressed against his chest. Energy speared me, zapping every cell. My nipples turned hard.

My body thrummed with need. I was greedy for more of him. I wanted his fingers on my bare skin, his mouth… everywhere. I felt like I was about to lose my mind—my decency for sure.

When he pulled my lower lip gently between his, drawing little circles with his fingers at the back of my neck, I clenched my thighs, trying to ignore the ache between them. He'd turned me on with nothing more than a kiss! And when he pulled back gently, I groaned in protest, almost pulling him back to me before reality tugged at the corners of my mind.

Winston was my boss! What had I been thinking? Well, I hadn't. But in my defense, the man kissed so well, I was proud I could even remember my own name.

His eyes were full of lust. His grip on my waist was so strong that if it weren't for the thick fabric of the overalls, I might have finger marks on my skin. Winston did *not* look as if he had any intention of letting me go.

Honestly, I didn't want him to. I liked the feeling of having his arms around me, his body pressing against mine.

I didn't know if it was because he'd shown up here to help even though he didn't have to, or because we'd shared personal tidbits about each other, but this was not just about attraction. I felt vulnerable. It scared me, yet I wanted to hang on to everything he made me feel.

"You taste so good," he murmured. His lips were hovering at the corner of my mouth, his hot breath tickling me. I slowly let go of his shirt but drew my hand downward in a small spiral, past his navel. I had no idea what I was doing. I just wanted to touch him, explore him.

He gripped my wrist, stopping the descent.

"Stop doing that or I'll kiss you again, and this time, I won't stop at a kiss."

His voice was rough, almost strangled. I pulled back a notch, looking straight in his eyes. They were darker than I'd ever seen them and so intense that my breath faltered.

I cleared my throat, and he dropped his arm. I was so nervous that I was tongue-tied. I didn't know what to say, or what this meant.

"So, thanks for today," I said awkwardly.

He flashed a wicked smile. "My pleasure entirely."

My skin prickled. Holy shit. I took another step back, just in case.

"I can finish what's left to do."

"You want me to leave?" His tone was playful, but there was still something wolfish in his expression.

I blushed. "No, but we've worked for hours."

"You don't think I'll leave you alone, do you?"

"You won't?"

"No."

I hadn't expected this. "Why not?"

"I want to make sure you're okay. I'll keep an eye on you. And cook us dinner in the meantime."

I stared at him. "Are you serious?"

"Yes, ma'am. I have a proposition for you. I'll finish the last wall. We need to wait two hours before applying the second coat of paint anyway. I'll cook you an early dinner in the meantime."

I was silent for a few seconds, processing this unexpected turn of events, then decided to just go with it. So far, this day had surpassed even my wildest imaginings. I was looking forward to what more it could bring.

I had giant butterflies in my stomach. *He wanted to take care of me.*

That was... I couldn't even process it. I was too overwhelmed by warm and fuzzy feelings, and my fingers itched with the need to grab his shirt and pull him closer.

"Well, okay then."

"Sit and relax while I finish that wall."

"Okay. On second thought, I'll take a shower. I'm all dirty."

He frowned again. "What if you get dizzy again from the hot water?"

"You want to babysit me in the shower too?"

"Are you inviting me to watch?"

I blushed, licking my lips. Winston held my gaze. Lust replaced the amusement in his eyes.

"Winston..."

He smiled. "Don't turn the water temperature too high."

"Wow. You want to check the temperature too?"

I crossed my arms over my chest. I wasn't mad at him; quite the contrary. I detected real concern in his voice, and I just wanted to hug him for it. But I had a hunch that I was better off pretending like I wasn't onboard with this, or who knew what kind of ideas this stubborn man might get?

"Don't say that twice, or I'll take you up on it."

I'd been right. If I didn't draw a line in the

sand, he was liable to get naughty ideas.

"I was joking."

"I wasn't." His voice, his entire body language was dripping sensuality. Licking my lips, I drew in a deep breath.

"I won't be long, but in case you finish the wall, wait for me to start on dinner."

"You don't trust me around here alone?"

I pointed a finger to the spot where he'd nearly set my panties on fire with that sinful kiss.

"I think it's safe to say I don't know your true intentions, mister."

"I can lay them all out for you. Better yet, I can show them to you." He stalked closer to me, and I was instantly too caught up in him to step back and keep a safe distance. "I'll kiss you until you beg me for more, Sienna."

"Don't."

"Why not?"

My heart was pounding furiously. Somewhere in the recesses of my mind, I had a whole list of reasons.

But I just shook my head, smiling lightly. "I'll go shower now. And if you insist on starting dinner, I won't say no. I just wanted to help."

"Go shower. I'll take care of everything else."

I couldn't hide my smile, and when he winked at me, I grinned like a schoolgirl. This day was just full of surprises.

I was glad for the excuse of taking a shower, because I needed some time to think. Of course, thinking was impossible knowing that this sexy man was just a few feet away, cooking me dinner.

Those fuzzy feelings were still wrapped around me like a warm blanket. I just couldn't shake this sense of joy, and why would I?

I liked being happy, and Winston decidedly knew how to make me smile. Scratch that. I was still grinning.

Who would have thought that the man I'd dubbed as grouchy was a skilled charmer?

To be fair, I had a lot of emails to prove my initial assumption, so I wasn't feeling *too* guilty.

I dressed in jeans and one of my good tank tops. I wasn't trying to impress. Okay, maybe I was. But the man had just seen me in stupid overalls the whole day. Before leaving the bathroom, I also splashed a little makeup on. Just some mascara and blush. It wasn't obvious, just made me look fresh. I wanted to redeem my image of consummate professional somehow.

But I was afraid I'd completely messed that up when I'd let him kiss me. Hell, I hadn't just *let* him. I'd practically jumped his bones.

I squared my shoulders. There was no point chastising myself over what happened.

I just had to do better from now on.

The minute I left the bathroom, I realized that I had no idea what doing better meant.

Winston had finished painting and was cooking in the small kitchen. He'd taken out a carton of eggs, vegetables, rice, and some condiments I hadn't used in… forever. I hoped they hadn't expired.

"What's that?" I asked.

"Fried rice with veggies."

"Looks yummy."

He made a come-here motion with a finger. My legs moved toward him of their own accord. Winston didn't take his eyes off me. Before, he'd watched me as if I'd been wearing sexy lingerie. Now, he watched me as if I was naked.

At any rate, I *felt* naked.

As soon as I stepped next to him, all my doubts and questions faded. It was impossible to be near him and not be completely consumed by him.

He took a spoonful of rice, holding it in front of my mouth.

"Tell me if you want me to add anything else."

"I trust you," I said.

He cocked a brow. "You just made a big show of not trusting me."

"I trust you when it comes to food." I amended with a huge smile on my face.

"Taste it." He sounded bossy, and I hoped it wasn't too obvious just how much I liked it. This was different than at the office. Playful. And the kiss had changed things between us, I just wasn't sure how.

"This is delicious. Wow. So that's why everyone uses condiments. I just kind of forget about them. Except vanilla, rum, and cinnamon when I bake. I'll make a salad—"

"No, you won't. I'm cooking everything."

Before I could add anything more, he placed his hands on my shoulders, walking me to the chairs, making me sit down. Feeling his fingers on the bare skin of my shoulders, his thumbs pressing gently at the sides of my neck, made me simmer all over. The skin on my arms turned to goose bumps.

"I see. So this is what you meant when you said I hadn't seen bossy yet. Just so you know, I'm reconsidering that upgrade."

"I'm more than happy to prove my case. I know how to go about it."

He lowered his gaze to my mouth. I was past simmering right now. A full-on inferno billowed inside me. Oh yeah, another kiss would convince me. I wasn't even sure of what anymore, but it didn't seem important.

How could I be so smitten already? This man affected me unlike anyone before.

"I like the sight," I commented.

He half turned, cocking a brow. "Do you now?"

"Enjoyed it all day. At least now I don't have to pretend I work while doing it. I am memorizing all that display of muscle… to have something to replay in my mind when I'm alone."

His gaze darkened. I was flirting, but it felt so good. Maybe the tension between us had escalated because we'd both been reining ourselves in.

"Keep that up, Sienna, and there will be no dinner."

"No can do, mister. I'm super hungry. Is this how you're planning to take care of me? By starving me?"

"How about I just kiss you until you forget about everything else?"

I narrowed my eyes. "That doesn't count as taking care of me. Get back to work."

His smile was deliciously happy as he returned his attention to the pan. The rice was preboiled, so it took no time at all for dinner to be ready.

When we both sat at the kitchen table, I became aware of how tiny it was. I could barely move in my seat and not touch Winston: either his hand or his legs under the table.

Okay, so my previous assessment was incorrect. Here we were, openly flirting, and yet the tension was escalating.

I laughed, pushing a strand of hair behind my ear. I wanted to know more about him.

"So, what made you decide to finally take over the stores?" I asked.

He chewed carefully, eyeing me intently.

"The store's previous general manager didn't do a great job. When he retired, I took a look at our numbers. He took additional financing from banks to solve short-term liquidity problems. He put the store in San Francisco as collateral and screwed up everything."

"Wow. I didn't know that."

"No one does except the CFO and her right hand. So I didn't want to trust someone else with the stores during such a delicate time. This company feels like home to me. I practically grew up on Statham's floors or in my parents' office. I want to preserve it."

I was speechless. He was a remarkable man. I hadn't thought it possible that I'd find him even more endearing, but he'd just proven me wrong.

"Why don't you take on investors? Or a partner?"

"No. Banks are one thing, but a partner or an investor would want decision-making power, possibly equity. The stores are a family business. I don't want strangers in the mix."

"Okay."

"Please don't talk about this with anyone. I'm handling it, and I don't want to cause panic."

"My lips are sealed."

I was in his confidence. The news he'd shared was definitely not an occasion to smile, but I was smiling nonetheless.

"Winston, you're brilliant. You'll get the store through this, I'm sure of it. Every company that's been active this long has its ups and down and moments of crisis."

"Thanks for putting it in perspective."

He looked troubled. I had to get his mind off the store. But how to do it? I could flirt, of course, but instinct told me I should stay on neutral ground. Who knew where that flirting might escalate? When it came to Winston, I couldn't foresee even one step ahead.

Praise was my weapon of choice today.

"I did a course in crisis management in college, and we did about thirty case studies of big companies going through tough moments. And they didn't have someone as brilliant as you at their helm."

That brought a smile to his lips. "You're extra nice with me, Ms. Hensley. Any particular reason?"

"Just saying it like it is."

"I didn't know you held me in such high regard."

"Now you do. And…no more talking shop." I continued with the praise, though. It was working. "Your veggie rice is delicious. Whenever I cook this, it tastes like nothing."

"It's all in the seasoning," he said with a wink.

"Shucks. I guess I should have paid more attention to your recipe instead of ogling you."

He trapped my legs between his under the table. "I guess you should have. Or I can just drop by again and we can cook together."

Damn… the way he said *cook* had the same effect on me as if he'd said *shower* together.

"Why would you do that?" I asked.

"You know why."

I lowered my gaze to my plate, feeling warm all over. After we finished eating, we cleaned the table together.

"Anyway, we still have to apply the second coat of paint."

"I like a man who keeps his word. I'd

forgotten all about it."

Winston wiggled his eyebrows, leaning in until I thought he might kiss me again. I was ready this time.

Instead, he simply spoke against my lips. "I've earned that upgrade, haven't I?"

I laughed. "Still considering. Better be careful. Not in the bag yet, so don't mess things up."

"Wouldn't dream of it. I have great plans for us, Sienna."

Heat simmered on the surface of my skin, as if he was touching me. I didn't have to ask to know that those plans were definitely of the dangerous variety.

Chapter Ten

Sienna

I couldn't sleep after Winston left, despite all those hours of physical work and the dinner. The man consumed my every thought… and then my dreams. Next morning, I was surprisingly full of energy.

The drive to Jenna and Richard Bennett's house took me by Lombard Street. I ran into a traffic jam on the crooked portion of it. Honestly, though, I didn't mind. From the top, I had a gorgeous view of the most crooked street in the world and of the city. Some complained that San Francisco had the most boring weather: not warm enough in the winter months to enjoy the sun, and not cold enough for snow. I disagreed. While I loved snow in the holiday season, the climate here had an undeniable perk: the greenery was always lush and brilliant.

I drummed my fingers on the wheel, cranking up the music while driving.

Gatherings at Jenna and Richard's house rated in the top five things I loved. The entire family there, meaning things were loud, and on occasion, crazy (such as when Christopher and Max teamed with Pippa's daughters to pull a double identical-twins prank).

My brother, Lucas, fit right in with the prankster group (although his humor fell more on the sinister spectrum). Everyone else was content sitting on the sidelines and allowing themselves to be surprised. I missed Lucas like crazy.

Around Thanksgiving and Christmas, we met up more often. The kids had various school events that required prepping costumes and such, and everything went much faster if we worked on them together. I grinned when I arrived. The house had a bright red roof and cream-colored walls. Jenna and Richard had already hung figurines and lights everywhere. It looked as if an army of tiny Santa Clauses was climbing the walls. The enormous yard was empty because it was too chilly to be outdoors.

The inside of the house smelled like vanilla, caramel, and a whiff of roasted peanuts. Yum. I joined the large group in the living room.

Today, we were working on elaborate costumes for the nativity play that everyone under ten seemed to be participating in. Logan Bennett's wife, Nadine, was a successful evening gown designer, and her staff had done the brunt of the work. Now we were just personalizing every costume.

I was sitting between her and Ava. She was trying to sell me on moving to Bennett Enterprises just as much as Pippa. When I eventually moved, I'd be working directly with her. But I wasn't ready to change workplaces just yet. Later, I moved next to

Chloe, and we immediately started discussing the latest trends in belts.

"I'm confused by all the conflicting advice in magazines," Chloe concluded.

"You know what? I'll just ask one of the advisors on the women's floor to give me the rundown, and I'll tell you."

"You're the best." Chloe was positively beaming. I couldn't help myself and gave her a half hug and a huge smooch on her cheek. She pulled back.

Right. I really had to stop doing that. She was twelve. I remembered those years. I hadn't liked our mom's constant doting and had tried to escape it every time. Until we lost our parents, and then I'd treasured those memories. I would have given anything for one more hug from Mom. But Chloe had been so young that she didn't remember our parents very much.

During a break from costume adjustment, I showed Victoria a video of the decoration pieces in the store that I wasn't sure about.

"This bow could be smaller. And this would look excellent with a golden chest beneath. If you don't have anything on hand, I can find you one," Victoria said.

"Thanks, sis. Wow, you're right. A chest would absolutely work. I'm sure I'll find one."

"Let me know if you need me to search for one," Victoria assured me. My sister was a great interior designer. In my opinion, she was actually the best. I'd wanted to get Victoria on board as an official consultant this year, but she was always overbooked around Christmas.

"How are things with your boss?" Victoria asked. I'd told her all about Winston... well, almost everything. We hadn't had a chance to catch up, so she didn't know about the kiss. I planned to rectify that immediately. Besides, maybe talking about it would help me not replay it in my mind so often.

"So... a few things happened." Under my breath, I described the kiss in exquisite detail.

Victoria's expression grew from curious to incredulous. "Holy shit. This is... wow. Unexpected."

"Crazy?" I suggested, smiling when I saw Pippa approach us. Her grin left me no doubt that she'd heard at least part of the conversation.

"What's crazy?" she asked. Pointing a finger at me, she added, "You look like someone who can't believe things escalated so quickly. My money's on things with the boss from hell having gotten... hot and heavy?"

I laughed, blowing out a breath.

Victoria smiled. "Can't hide from Pippa."

"Details?" Pippa beckoned.

"You mean to tell me you didn't eavesdrop on our entire conversation?"

She shrugged one shoulder, batting her eyelashes. "No, just the ending. I want to know the full story. How else can I give you advice?"

Here I went again, recounting every detail.

Unfortunately, talking about it wasn't helping me think about it less. If anything, I was breaking in a sweat while remembering his hot and determined lips on mine, the way he'd simply *claimed* me. His kiss was branded not just in my memory but on my mouth too. And the way he'd made me feel had just been out of this world. I'd wanted to stay there in the cocoon of his arms for the rest of the evening. He'd cooked for me. He'd taken care of me. I was melting *again* remembering all that masculine charm, that determination, and his unexpected protective side.

How was I supposed to forget about all that until Monday?

Pippa tilted her head, flashing a smile that told me I was in trouble. "Just saying, but you sound as if you want a repeat."

"I do, don't I?"

Victoria nodded sagely. I shook my head, then pressed my lips together as Christopher approached us.

"The girl council is in action, I see." He laced an arm around Victoria's shoulders, the other around Pippa's. The girls both had their poker faces on, but that didn't fool Christopher.

"You're keeping secrets," he declared. Victoria sighed, giving me an apologetic look. Big mistake. Christopher had just been trying to get a feel for the situation, and she'd confirmed his suspicions.

"Spill it," he demanded.

"The point of a secret, brother dearest, is that no one is supposed to know about it," Pippa said sweetly.

"If it concerns my wife, I want to know."

"It doesn't," I piped up. "It concerns me."

I had no idea why I thought that might appease Christopher.

"Also my concern."

I laughed, which only made him frown more. The Bennett men were a mixture of brother and father figure for me, especially Christopher. His protective ways had annoyed me as a teenager, but as an adult, I appreciated them.

"This time, it's girl business," I assured him.

He cocked a brow. I surreptitiously motioned the girls to put the *distraction plan* into motion.

"Babe, before I forget, we have to pick up my new catalogs tonight," Victoria said.

"I thought we had time until next week."

"Yes, but I don't want to leave it until the last moment."

"And there's a real risk the crowd will be insane around Thanksgiving. Can you also pick up mine? If you bring them to the office, I'll take them from there," Pippa added.

It worked. Ha! I smiled to myself. Operation Girls-Against-Bennett-Brothers still worked like a charm every time. It was a simple strategy, really. Bring into conversation mundane tasks, which gave everything a trivial air.

Our odds for success were always better when Pippa joined us.

"Sure. We'll get them." Christopher focused

on me again, and for a brief second I thought our tactic hadn't worked.

"How's work?" he asked.

"Just fine."

"Your boss is back, right?"

"Yup." I was working hard on my poker face.

"Then why so jumpy? Is your ex causing you any trouble?"

"Nah. Forget about him, Christopher. I already did." I flashed him a brilliant smile. I hoped I was convincing. The last thing I wanted was for Christopher to waste any time thinking about Trevor.

"Let me know if he gives you any trouble."

"Sure."

Over my dead body, but Christopher didn't have to know that. He'd get all up in arms, and there was no reason for it. I really wished I'd listened to him when he'd said he didn't have a good feeling about him. In my defense, he'd said that about most of my boyfriends, which was why I dismissed his concerns most of the time.

I was afraid Christopher might smell our distraction tactic if we weren't careful, but Blake saved me. He joined our little group, throwing me a furtive look before assessing his brother.

"Don't suffocate the poor girl," Blake warned Christopher.

I patted his shoulder. "Finally, a Bennett man taking my side."

Christopher chuckled. "Not always."

"Hey, I have my moments of weakness,"

Blake replied solemnly. "But most of the time, I'm firmly in Sienna's squad."

"Except that one time you scared off my date," I reminded him. "Don't think I forgave you for that."

Blake clutched at his heart theatrically. "Five years later I'm still not forgiven?"

"I've got a long memory, Blake." I was grinning at him. I couldn't be mad at Blake if I tried. He had that unique charm that just won me over instantly. He didn't take himself seriously, or most things around him.

"Seems I still have a lot to make up for." He waggled his eyebrows. "But I'm up for the task."

"Don't say that twice, or I'll find something to torture you with."

"Can't wait. How did it go with the walls?"

"All finished."

Blake whistled. "Never thought you'd make so much progress on your own."

I felt the tips of my ears turn beet red and avoided Pippa and Victoria's eyes, hoping Blake wouldn't catch on to our knowing looks.

Something must have tipped him off that I wasn't being one hundred percent truthful, because he asked, "Everything okay?"

"Sure."

"Is anyone giving you any headaches?"

Christopher fist-bumped the air. I dropped my chin to my chest. "Blake. You just lost all your coolness points."

"Impossible."

"I already told Christopher that everything's fine."

"But—"

Blake was interrupted by Sebastian, who clapped his hands once.

"Hey, chatty group over there, how about going back to work?"

I smiled sheepishly, glad for the excuse, and scurried back to my place next to Chloe.

Two hours later, we'd finished all the costumes and the set piece. I smiled as we all headed to lunch. Spending time with the Bennetts was the perfect way to recharge. No matter how tired I was coming in, I was always filled with a giddy energy and a renewed sense of optimism.

After lunch, we all headed to the Embarcadero in time to catch the lighting ceremony. It was one of the most famous events in town. The four office towers along the Embarcadero were lit up with 17,000 twinkling lights amid a display of fireworks. We came each year, and I was still just as mesmerized by it all as usual. It was so clever to use the architecture to showcase the Christmas spirit. My thoughts flew to Winston, to the way he'd frowned at the twinkling lights I'd hung in the meeting room that day. What would he say to this?

I snapped a picture of my view and almost messaged him, then stopped. Would I be overstepping boundaries? Would he even want to hear from me?

I hovered with my thumbs over the keyboard for a few seconds before deciding to wait for him to make the first move.

Afterward, we walked to Pier 39, which boasted one of my favorite Christmas trees in the city. The smell of sea salt mingled with eggnog and cinnamon from the several booths around us. Even though I was already full, I couldn't help indulging in a cookie.

As we strolled around, Pippa pulled me to one side. I knew that smile she had on. It spelled trouble.

"So... want an update on my matchmaking work?" she whispered.

"Um... yeah." I had completely forgotten about that. To my surprise, I wasn't looking forward to the update.

The prospect of going out with a stranger just wasn't exciting. In fact, I didn't want to go out with anyone she found at all.

Pippa pointed a finger at me. "Aha."

"What?"

"I knew it. You're not excited about it anymore."

"No." I wasn't sure where she was going with it. Maybe she was just checking if she should back down and not waste her time.

She smiled triumphantly. Silly me. Pippa never talked just to talk.

"You know what that means, right? You've got it bad for your boss, whether you want it or not."

Oh, Pippa, Pippa, Pippa.

When you weren't sure about something, she was right there to spell it out for you.

As I left for my house, I was still thinking about Winston. Could things at the office still go on the same as before? I had no idea.

I took my phone out to check my emails, only to discover I had a text from Winston. He'd been thinking about me! I giggled, covering my mouth with my hand even though I was alone.

Winston: How was your Sunday?

Sienna: Perfect!! I've had family time and SO MANY cookies. I'm in heaven.

Winston: Happy to know.

Sienna: Yours?

Winston: Much less interesting than my Saturday.

I was smiling from ear to ear already.

Sienna: I see. And what made your Saturday so interesting?

Winston: A certain amazing, smartass Christmas dork.

Sienna: !!!!!

He was right, but come on. He didn't think he could get away with being mean, did he?

Winston: I spent all day today thinking about her.

And just like that, I was a puddle of fuzzy feelings again.

Sienna: You didn't have enough

yesterday?

Winston: Not by a long shot. Lucky I'm seeing her tomorrow.

I had a grin the size of the moon. Yeah... things definitely wouldn't be the same between us at the office.

Chapter Eleven

Sienna

I'd been right. Things at the office were not the same. Whenever I saw Winston, his focus was unapologetically on me. After a particularly long meeting, I thought about ordering a fan, having it shipped with Amazon Prime. By the looks of it, I'd have plenty of use for it.

On the plus side, his mood had improved somewhat, and it did not go unnoticed. My colleagues were a little more relaxed around him. Emphasis on a little.

Winston went one step forward, then two steps back. He praised everyone in the meeting, then immediately sent a mass email where he emphasized some deadlines using strong wording.

Knowing what was on the line, I had more understanding for him. I couldn't even imagine what it would feel like to have that weight on your shoulders. Still… the strong wording just added to the overall stress level in the office, and I thought it was my duty to let him know it was counterproductive.

I poked my head in his office.

"Grouchy boss, you're scaring everyone again.

Just thought you should know. It's not good for work morale."

He leaned back in his chair, looking every bit the powerful man he was. His frown lines disappeared, a naughty light popping up in his eyes.

"What's your strategy to change that?"

"*I'm* supposed to do that?"

"You have a good track record of lifting my mood."

I tried not to look too pleased, but I was ready to do a happy dance.

"And I need a strategy? Hadn't thought about anything that elaborate."

"I'm a demanding man." He grinned. I felt as if my bra and panties were suddenly on fire.

"And don't I know it?" My tone was a little too sassy, but he kept grinning. Mission accomplished. "I'll think about it."

"I can give you a few suggestions."

I narrowed my eyes, certain he was baiting me again. "I'm good. My phone's ringing. Have to get back to it."

"You afraid to be in here with me too long?"

I shook my head. He laughed, clearly not buying it. I wasn't afraid, per se… I was just not ready to trust myself around him.

I felt him watch me as I left the room. My breath was a little shaky. Honestly, so were my legs.

Things were definitely getting too intense around here.

In the afternoon, I received a surprise phone call. I was just about to go on a short coffee break when the phone rang.

"Sienna Hensley," I said.

"Hi, Sienna. You're the interim branding VP, right?"

"Yes. Who am I talking to?"

"Winston's mother."

"Wow. I've heard so much about you. It's so great to meet you. Even through the phone."

I was rambling. But the woman was practically a legend. I pressed my lips together, determined to sound professional, not like a fangirl at a concert.

"I've been told that you're closest to my son out of the entire team."

"Yes. You could say that."

I had no clue what else to add. How did she even know this?

"So, here is the thing. My son's back, but I almost never see him. He keeps saying he needs to work until late in the evening."

"That's right, ma'am."

"Don't call me that. Makes me feel like I'm a hundred years old."

I smiled. "Mrs. Statham."

"So, what's with all these late-night work sessions?"

"We're preparing some big changes. Can't work them into our regular schedule."

"So you're working with him?"

"Yes, ma'am. Sorry. Mrs. Statham," I

amended with a laugh.

"Right. What's with all the changes? And for how long are you two going to keep that draconian schedule?"

I opened my mouth to answer before thinking better of it. Wait a second. *Wait a second*. Was she trying to fish out information from me? Oh my God, she totally was.

I'd been around the Bennett clan long enough to recognize the tactic. I'd cut my teeth on Jenna, Pippa, and Christopher. Victoria was completely harmless (and usually so obvious that I could easily dodge her questions) by comparison.

"I don't know all the details. Why don't I ask Winston and get back to you?"

"No need for that," she said quickly. I smiled to myself. "How is it working with my son, Sienna?"

I frowned at the change of subject, unsure what to brace myself for.

"He's brilliant, and I love working with him."

"That's lovely to hear. We're always wondering how things are at the office, you know. It's weird, after forty-six years of going in there daily, now suddenly not being there at all. We're so happy Winston decided to carry on the legacy."

I relaxed in my chair. She just wanted to know how things were in general. No nefarious goal behind it.

"He's doing a fabulous job."

"My son knows all the tricks. Perhaps if you told me what the big change is, I could help? My husband and I have had some great ideas in our time, you know."

I blinked, sitting up straighter again. Holy hell, I'd been close to falling right into her trap. I should have seen this tactic coming. Pippa was a master at it.

Step one: get the poor unsuspecting soul you're planning to question to relax—usually by talking about something else.

Step two: once they've lowered their defense, jump in for the kill.

"I assure you, Winston's got the hang of things," I said.

"Well, then. Have a great day, Sienna." Something in her voice told me she wasn't giving up. "It was nice talking to you."

"You too."

Stathams were forces to be reckoned with. That was true as much for the mother as it was for the son.

I shook my head, smiling as I hung up. I was fully awake now, no need for a coffee break.

But I thought I should let Winston know what his mom was up to. So when I saw him in the hallway, I waved at him, motioning for him to come to my office.

I dropped my voice to a whisper once he was inside.

"Funny thing, your mom called."

"My... mother?"

"Yup."

"Why?" he checked his phone. "I have no

missed call from her."

"Well, no... I think she was hoping for extra information from another... source."

"Should I be afraid?"

"Yes. She's onto you."

"How did she even have your number?"

"I'm guessing she's a resourceful woman. She knew who I was and that I worked closest with you."

"What did she ask?"

"Mainly about your schedule. She was very interested in our late-night project."

Winston sighed. "What did you tell her?"

"That we're preparing something big. That was a mistake. She became even more suspicious, but I was very evasive after that."

"I haven't told them about the financial issues."

I'd suspected that, but hearing him confirm it stirred something in me. He was protecting everyone else, but who was protecting him?

"Well, she won't find out from me."

His eyes turned soft. "Thanks. By the way, I've seen the memo about the Christmas party. It's earlier than usual." It was next week.

I'd waited too long to bring this up to him. No time like the present.

"Yes. I thought everyone will be more relaxed at the beginning of the month."

"I agree."

"We're also playing Secret Santa this year. I think everyone would love it if you participated."

"Secret Santa."

"Yes. It's a game where everyone's name—"

"I know how it works, Sienna."

I perked up.

"Just making sure. So, can I add you to the list?"

"On one condition."

"What?"

"You'll find out on the evening of the party."

"You want me to agree to something without knowing what?"

He didn't answer, merely pinned me with his gaze. *Oh my God.* He absolutely did expect that.

The tips of my ears felt hot. "Your mom was right."

"About what?"

"You knowing all the tricks."

"She said that?"

"Yes. Though I don't think she meant this kind of trick. But if you keep at them, I might conspire with her."

"For what?"

"Don't know yet, but I'm sure this isn't the last I'll hear from her."

Winston had been standing close to the door, but now he walked toward me.

"Are you blackmailing me, Ms. Hensley?"

***

Winston

"Of course not. I'm just... setting forward very good terms, *Winston*."

Sienna got up from her desk, walking in front of it. I was close enough to smell her perfume. It was fresh, but also so sensual that I wanted nothing more than to bend her over the table and get her naked.

I took one step forward, instinctively bringing a hand to her waist.

"And you think I'll agree to them... why?" I teased her.

She winked. "Because they're very agreeable."

I rubbed my thumb an inch or so up and down, watching her react to my touch with a delicious blush.

"My office. My way, Sienna."

She narrowed her eyes but said nothing.

"I'll participate in the game."

"Perfect. And by the way... how do you feel about having a plant in your office? Like a philodendron?"

"Why?"

"I looked up plants that are supposed to help one relax and have clarity of mind—they basically increase the oxygen supply."

She'd looked that up... especially for me. I wanted to kiss this woman and just not let go. Did she know how much that meant to me?

"You just... looked that up?" I asked.

"If you don't like that idea, tell me what would help you relax, and I'll make it happen."

That need to kiss her gripped me completely.

I wanted to feel closer to her in every way possible.

I smiled, moving my hand up to cup her cheek.

"Are you sure about that?"

"Yes."

She must have realized that what I had in mind wouldn't exactly be HR approved, because she averted her gaze, taking in a deep breath. I should have stayed put, but I just couldn't.

"You in my office. That would help. You want more details?"

"Winston, I'm serious."

"So am I."

I moved my thumb over her lips, felt her shiver. When I dropped my hand to her neck, she licked her lips. I leaned closer, bringing my mouth to the corner of hers, placing a small kiss there. Sienna moaned softly, and I knew I couldn't kiss this woman here, in the office, because I wouldn't be satisfied with a simple kiss. I wanted to lock us in the room and throw the key away. Keep her there, claim every inch of her.

"I'd kiss every inch of your body, Sienna."

Her cheeks turned red.

"Winston, don't!"

"You don't want me to kiss you?"

Sienna sighed, dropping her head in her hands. "I'm just… I don't know."

Damn, she was cute. I was close to throwing her over my shoulder and leaving, just get out of the building with her, but clearly things were moving too fast for her. She probably had no idea what to make of this. Hell, *I* didn't know what this was. But I was going to find out.

"I see. I'll give you some space to figure it out, then."

"Okay."

Blushing, she nodded, biting her lip. I stepped back, allowing some distance between us. Ever since I'd told her about the store's precarious situation, I felt lighter, as if the simple fact that I told her had liberated some of that pressure.

Her perspective on life in general was refreshing. She could focus on the big picture without allowing working for her goals to take over her life. Since finding out about the store's finances, I made space for little else in my life. I'd been working tirelessly to get us out of this mess at the expense of everything else, including my parents, and that wasn't okay. I could learn a thing or two from Sienna. Something told me that everything was better next to her.

"I'll get back to work," I said.

"Great idea."

"Afraid to be too close to me?"

She grinned. "Don't want to give you a chance to change your mind."

"We can't run that risk, can we?"

Chapter Twelve

Winston

That evening, I went out to meet some friends I hadn't seen since college. The day after that, I took my parents out to afternoon tea at the Fairmont hotel in Nob Hill.

"This is a pleasant surprise," Mom commented.

"Mom, it's tradition for us to go out for holiday high tea," I said as we sat at a round table. We'd come to Laurel Court, the hotel's restaurant, for years. I took in the circular room with Ionic columns and murals. The plush leather seats and light blue carpet were just as I remembered them. The restaurant was full, but the tables were spaced out enough that the atmosphere was intimate.

"Well, yes, but lately, you're so lost in your own head. Didn't expect you to take us out this week." I'd chosen this week because Dad had informed me that Mom had been working tirelessly on Thanksgiving preparations and needed a break. She refused to give in to him, but she wouldn't tell me no.

"My phone call helped, right?" she asked after the waitress brought us an assortment of scones and pastries.

"Mom…"

"What? Sienna wasn't very talkative, but I still think it helped."

I looked at Dad. "Feel free to jump in at any time."

He held his hands up. "Trust me, I tried."

Mom elbowed him. "And I hope that was the last time you did. If I want to hover around my son, I damn well will. I only have one."

I shook my head, laughing. I thought about what Sienna said about every old company going through cycles and different crisis. She made sense, of course. I remembered tense periods from my childhood, when my parents were working until late.

I almost asked them about those crisis periods, then decided not to. They'd catch on, and besides, the whole point of taking them to dinner was to stop thinking about the stores and just enjoy life.

"See, son, this is how things are after forty years of marriage."

"Whose side are you on?" Mom asked in an accusatory tone.

"Yours, of course."

I chuckled. Man, I'd almost forgotten my parents' dynamic.

Few of my married friends were as lucky as my parents. Most were semihappy, but some swore they were the luckiest bastards alive.

I agreed with them. Luck played a huge role in

finding the person you're supposed to be with.

I'd had several relationships that fizzled out. I'd never envisioned myself with someone for the long term. I'd been in a relationship for about a year when I first realized the stores would implode if I didn't take drastic measures. I barely had time to breathe after that, and things between us fell apart a month later, when Diane said she just couldn't live with the constant pressure *I* was under.

It's easy to make a relationship work when everything runs smoothly, but when things get rocky, that's when you know if you have what it takes for the long term.

"Mom, I'll make you a deal."

"I'm listening."

"You stop pestering my employees, and I'll tell you what you want."

"Pester? That's dramatic, don't you think?"

"You called five employees—I checked—until one of them gave you Sienna's number."

She sighed. "Well, I had to do what I had to do. But it brought you here. Am I forgiven?"

I laughed, shaking my head. How could I say no?

"Let's ask for another round of scones," I suggested.

Dad nodded. "And it's time for champagne."

As a kid, they'd first brought me here because I was crazy about the gingerbread house in the lobby. Then we started attending high tea. When I turned twenty-one, we changed the traditional tea for champagne. I managed to push some worries to the back of my mind that evening, even though Thanksgiving was in two days, and Black Friday just after that. It was the biggest shopping day, and it had to exceed expectations for the board to be satisfied. But the holiday atmosphere at the Fairmont was relaxing me. Sienna was already rubbing off on me.

***

Next morning, I arrived late at the store. I walked through the main entrance as usual. I liked to feel the store's pulse, to check for details.

We'd officially kicked off our Christmas shopping weeks. That meant that all the shop attendants were wearing Santa caps. In addition, one person on every floor wore a full-on elf costume. They handed out sweets to kids and informed adults of the special Christmas sales. To some it might seem like trying too hard, but we ran surveys, and our customers had stated they like the additional Christmas spirit the elves brought.

I nearly did a double take when I reached the second floor. The "elf" there looked very familiar. Sienna. She noticed me too and quickly looked away. She was blushing.

And what was she wearing? Her costume was a different shade of green than anyone else's. Seemed to be made of another type of fabric too—a stretchier one. It showcased every dip and curve. I wanted to throw her over my shoulder and not allow anyone else to see her wearing that.

"Ms. Hensley."

"Good morning, *Mr. Statham*." She emphasized my name with a wink.

"You can't be doing a second job. I'll talk to HR about a raise."

"The student in charge of this floor bailed. I requested someone else at the agency, but she can't be here for another two hours. I'm filling in until then."

"Have someone else fill in. I need you upstairs."

I held her gaze. She drew in a deep breath.

"No, you have a phone conference starting in ten minutes. It'll last about three hours. You won't even know I'm gone."

I didn't back down. "It's not your responsibility to fill in this role."

"Well, no, but I like it. Pity I don't have an actual costume. I had to improvise with leggings and a sports shirt."

That explained the stretchy fabric.

"You look so damn sexy dressed up like this." My voice was practically a growl.

Her eyes widened. She looked around. "No, I'm not. I haven't even gotten one hot look until you came. It's your own fault for thinking about inappropriate things."

"Sienna—"

"Winston."

I had to stop; I just didn't know how. I knew

I was being unreasonable. I didn't even have a claim on her.

"I'm just proving my commitment to the company." She pulled at the top of the cap, then twirled once. I had to jet my hand into my pocket to keep from reaching out. I didn't think I could touch her and not pull her into a kiss. She was a little flushed when she stopped twirling. Her smile was so wide, it lit up her entire face. Scratch that. It lit *me* up.

"I should be rewarded, not scolded," she went on.

I stepped closer. I didn't trust myself to touch her, but I wanted to claim every bit of her that was out in the open... like her personal space.

"Come into my office when you're done, Ms. Hensley, and I'll reward you."

My attention span was nonexistent during the phone call. Every time I attempted to focus on the conversation, all I could see was Sienna in those clothes, acting as if it was the greatest honor to wear them. She hadn't been acting though. She'd had pure joy written all over her face, and I wanted to know the story behind that. I wanted to know everything she wanted to tell me and lure out her secrets. What else did she love? What else made her happy?

"Winston, are you listening?" the business partner at the other end of the line asked.

"Sure."

I finally managed to focus on the conversation, even though part of my mind was still on Sienna.

She knocked at the door of my office an hour later.

"Come in."

She stopped just in front of my desk. She was carrying a plant.

"This was just delivered. You never told me yes or no, so I bought it. If it annoys you, throw it away. If you like it… you can add it to the list of things you need to reward me for."

Even though she was wearing regular clothes, the sight of her wearing those stretchy pants was branded in my brain.

"Thanks, Sienna. I really appreciate it. This is very considerate of you."

She blushed. I held her gaze until she looked away, tugging with her hands at the hem of her shirt. I relished the fact that I affected her just as much as she affected me.

I rose from behind my desk, rounding it, feeling a visceral need to be closer to her.

"Took longer than I thought," she said. "The replacement took her sweet time. We really need to come up with a better alternative than students. They're cheap, but you can't count on them."

She spoke very quickly, still looking away.

"I mean, I know it's not fun for many to stand for hours on end, but it's a job."

"It's fun for you. Why?"

"I don't know. I guess I just like how playful

it all is. And it's useful in gauging customers' experiences, watching them react to certain items and prices. Also, I had an idea... Just putting it out there, but what if we'd rotate management employees in that role? Not for an entire shift, but maybe just a few hours? And then we could exchange impressions about our customers' experiences."

I smiled at her. "That's brilliant, but not many would be as excited as you are about it."

She grinned. "Probably not. But I still think it's worth thinking about it."

"Tell me what your observations are."

"Well, for example, mothers tend to complain that we've separated kids' clothes by ages on opposite sides of the floor. If they come shopping with all their kids, they have to run around a lot more. I also spoke to the cashiers, and they say that they get a lot of complaints about books being on a separate level from the candles and presents corner."

"Can you write all that down somewhere?"

"Already ahead of you, boss. So, what did you need me for?"

"What?"

"You said you wanted me to come straight here after I was done."

I tipped forward, grinning. "I was just looking for any excuse to be alone with you. Your sexy little costume was messing with me."

Her mouth popped open. I very nearly closed the distance and kissed her.

"Doesn't happen often," I said.

"So, I'm special?"

"Damn right, you are."

She pushed a strand of hair behind her ears. There was some commotion on the corridor, and I stepped back to what would pass as professional distance. She glanced at the plant she'd placed on my desk.

"Thank you for the plant, Sienna."

"Of course. Just thought you'd like it. I ordered some for the other departments a while ago."

"So I'm not special at all?" I pushed. Her eyes lit up with fire.

"We've moved on from simply upgrading you from grouchy boss to special treatment?"

"You're saying I'm not deserving of it?" I teased. She laughed.

"Well, you're about fifty percent less grouchy than before. I'll give you that. Points earned."

"You're not easy to negotiate with."

"My family keeps saying that too." Flashing a smile, she added, "So I just saw a new entry in your calendar. You're leaving for a meeting?"

"Yes. Take the day off."

She snapped her gaze to me, finally. I'd been *very* close to touching her cheek, turning it so she'd look at me.

I was looking for any excuse to touch her. Any at all. Only if I did, if I gave in to that impulse, there was no saying how much further I'd push both of us.

"What? Why?"

"You said you're expecting a reward. Here it is."

"But I'm not tired. I mean, I can do my job."

"You're never going to just agree with me right off the bat, are you?"

"I think you know the answer to that. So, about the meeting?"

"It's an old college friend of mine who specializes in brand consulting. I want his input on the slides we have so far."

"Okay. Let me know what he says. You didn't put in the end time for it."

"That's because I'm not sure how long it'll last."

"Does that mean we won't work tonight?"

"No. That's why I said you could take the day off."

I'd been expecting her to seem relieved, but she merely gave a small "Oh."

"You look disappointed."

She shrugged, but her eyes were bright and fiery.

"I like our evening sessions."

"And you still insist I'm not special?"

She pointed a finger at me. "I won't answer that. Who knows what other ideas you'll get?"

"Indeed. Who knows?"

I caught her hand, keeping it to my chest. She licked her lips. Her eyes widened. I almost pulled her closer, but then I'd kiss her until she admitted I was special, that she did think about me just as often as I thought about her, and we weren't that far along.

Yet.

***

The meeting was across town, in my friend's consultancy. Thomas and I went way back to our college days, and I trusted his feedback. I wanted his advice. I wasn't leaving anything to chance.

While opening the presentation, I realized I should have taken Sienna with me. She was eager and smart, and she'd worked on the presentation just as much as I had. It was an opportunity for her to gauge Thomas's reaction in real time.

I texted her right away.

Winston: Want to come over to the meeting? You worked on this too.

I wasn't sure where she stood after today's encounter, but Sienna answered in less than a minute.

Sienna: YES! DO I GET TO PRESENT TOO?

I chuckled. I could imagine her dancing around the office again. No, damn. I had to get that image out of my mind.

Winston: Sure.
Sienna: I'm on my way
Sienna: !!!

Only Sienna could send an extra message with exclamation marks. Chuckling, I informed Thomas that my VP of branding would arrive soon. I began explaining in broad strokes what this was about but waited for Sienna to dive into the presentation.

I kept telling myself that I'd asked her here because it was a great opportunity for her, and not because I wanted to see her, be near her. I'd almost convinced myself, and yet, when she entered the room, I automatically smiled.

"Hi, Mr. Dunhill. I'm Sienna. Nice to meet you."

"Likewise. Call me Thomas."

"Okay, Thomas."

"Shall we begin?"

"Yes."

"Winston tells me you're walking us through the first half of the presentation."

She nodded excitedly, walking to the wall where the presentation was projected. She talked with eloquence and authority. She was magnificent. I'd been right in asking her here.

After she finished the slides, I presented too before we all sat at the table.

"You have a solid, fresh approach. I'm surprised at how well you've integrated the new ideas into the traditional aspects people associate with Statham. You've run the profitability numbers to see when you'd break even?"

I nodded. "Yes. It's looking good."

"And we're not done with that yet. We've got a financial expert doing some liquidity modeling, just to make sure we're on the right track," Sienna said.

"Sienna did a lot of the heavy lifting," I said.

He turned to her.

"I'm impressed. Winston, you didn't tell me you had such a brilliant branding expert. Any way I can persuade you to leave Winston for me?"

No way, no how. I accepted that Bennett Enterprises was her endgame, but I wouldn't lose her to anyone else.

"I can match any offer you make," I informed him, hoping he took my dismissal for what it was: a warning to stop.

He didn't.

"I don't know, Winston. I'm sure I can add a few perks to steal her away."

He was watching Sienna with curiosity, which was when it became clear he wasn't interested in her just on a professional level. A vein pulsed in my temple.

"I'm happy at my workplace," Sienna said. "Do you want to look over some of our backup ideas? We haven't fully finalized those, but between Winston and I, we can cover most details."

"Sure."

For a second time today, my focus was split between Sienna and the subject we were discussing. I respected Thomas as a business brain, but he was a jackass in his personal life. In college he'd proudly told everyone about the notches on his bedpost. He hadn't changed, and I wouldn't allow Sienna to fall in his trap.

By the time we'd debated the pros and cons of each tactic and idea, it was very late.

"I can't stay any longer, but I think we've

covered everything," Thomas said. "Sienna, I have tickets to a horse race next weekend. Would you like to join me? I think you'd like it."

He was looking pointedly at her.

"Sienna and I have an appointment all day on that Saturday," I said sternly. I had no intention of giving him the slightest opportunity to make a move on her.

Sienna's eyebrows shot up. Thomas shook his head. "He's making you work overtime? Just putting it out there, but that's rarely the case in my consultancy."

"Stop trying to steal my branding expert, Thomas." I tried to sound casual and teasing, but by the way Thomas jerked his head back, I'd failed. Sienna pressed her lips together.

"Thank you for your time," I told him as he walked us out.

"Sure. Let me know how it goes."

Once we were alone outside, Sienna turned to me, crossing her arms over her chest.

"So what are those big weekend plans I don't know anything about?"

"Sienna…"

"Don't Sienna me. I don't understand what's happening."

"I went to college with Thomas. I know him. He wasn't just inviting you over because he thought you'd like the race."

"I caught on to that, Sherlock. He was asking me out." She blinked. "Wait a second. You were jealous."

"I was."

"Oh my God, I can't believe this." She covered her mouth with a hand, but I still caught her giggle.

"You find this funny."

"Yes."

"Sienna, I think about you all the time. All. The. Time. This morning, I could barely concentrate on my call."

She giggled. Again. I stepped closer, swallowing hard. I almost kissed her, just to see how she'd react.

"About those plans. I'm going to Burlington to talk to the board next weekend. If they think the rebranding is going to save the store, they could persuade the bank to vote for an extension of the credit line. I wanted to ask you to join me."

"Wow. I… I didn't expect that."

"You're smart. I think it would be a great opportunity for you to meet them."

"Of course it would. But are you sure? It's an important presentation."

"And you're more than up to being the one to present. Honestly. It might be even better if they hear certain things from you rather than me. Your enthusiasm is genuine."

"Why Burlington?"

"That's where the board meetings always are. It's tradition to go to Vermont. Do you already have plans?"

"On Sunday, but I could shift them around."

"No need. We can come back Saturday with the last plane. I'll tell the travel agency to take care of the plane tickets and hotel."

She bit her lip, running a hand through her hair.

"Come on, Sienna. It's not like you to turn down an opportunity."

"You're getting better and better at those tricks."

"No trick. I just know what you want. What fuels you, what motivates you."

"Fine, I'll come to Vermont. But just so you know, you're playing dirty."

"Nah, it's just smart negotiating. Just like you did with me to convince me to join the Santa game at the party."

"Hey, that's different. It's good for the team to see you as being one of them."

"You think that's why I said yes?"

Her eyes widened, and she gave me a nervous laugh. I knew exactly what she was nervous about. I also knew one thing for sure: things between us would change during the Christmas party. I'd see to it.

Chapter Thirteen

Sienna

The rest of the week was so busy that I barely had time to breathe. Everyone was in a rush to get everything ready for Black Friday. Winston had put our evening meetings on hold because there was so much going on. On Thursday evening, I was so tired that I could barely keep my eyes open.

Thanksgiving at Jenna and Richard's house was just as fun and loud as usual. The whole house smelled like sweet potatoes and pumpkin pie. The turkey was roasted to perfection. I especially loved the signature blend of cranberry and orange stuffing. Usually, delicious food and being surrounded by my favorite people was a recipe for relaxing, but tonight I was on edge. Everyone at the table had tomorrow free, but I didn't, since it was the biggest day of the year for everyone working in retail. Winston had instead given us the Friday after that free...well, my colleagues had the day off. Winston and I were flying to Burlington.

I returned home early from dinner but was so pumped about the next day, running numbers in my head, that I could barely sleep. When I woke up, I felt a little groggy. The day was as wild as Black

Friday could be, and we hit record sales, not just at the San Francisco store but all Statham branches.

As the next week rolled in, the Christmas office party and my trip with Winston were consuming my thoughts. On the morning of the party, I arrived at the store with pep in my step. I'd come before everyone else, once again, mostly because I wanted to get a head start on my tasks. I knew that once the afternoon rolled in, my focus would drop. I'd probably walk around giddy until the party. I'd bought a present for Wanda from accounting. I knew Wanda pretty well, but I'd slyly interrogated her after I found out she was the one I was buying a gift for. Grinning, I plugged in earbuds, listening to my favorite remix of "It's Beginning to Look a Lot Like Christmas" and filling the spreadsheet I'd promised Winston would be ready by the end of the week. It was Thursday today, but I wanted to send it to him early. He was giving me a huge opportunity by inviting me to present alongside him, and I wanted to prove that I was worthy of that chance.

I liked to exceed expectations, not only those of others but my own. Which meant drastic measures were necessary. I took a small hourglass out of the top drawer of my desk. It only had enough sand for twenty minutes, so I turned it upside down periodically, allowing myself a five-minute break every hour so I wouldn't get a stiff back.

I was so focused on the spreadsheet that I

didn't realize I wasn't alone until Winston said, "Good morning."

I startled in my chair, looking up to find him standing right in front of my desk. My heart rate immediately accelerated, as it usually did around him.

"Winston, you scared me. I thought I was the only one here."

He smiled. Good Lord. Why did he have to look so damn sinful and sexy?

"I have something for you."

"Oh?"

He placed a small gift bag in front of me.

"What is this?"

"It's Secret Santa day, right?"

"Yes. Wow. You drew my name?"

"No."

I frowned. "I don't understand. Oh, no. You misunderstood the rules. You have to buy a present for the person whose name you picked. And you can't let them know it's from you."

I regretfully looked at the bag. I already thought about it as *my* present. But Winston *had* bought it for me, so… technically it was mine, right?

I mean… it probably wouldn't be a good fit for just anyone.

"It's yours, Sienna. I've bought a present for the person I've been paired with, but this… this is for you."

I looked up at him, my heart beating at lightning speed now.

"What is it?" I asked.

"Open it." His voice was low, commanding. Heat coiled through me. Licking my lips, I grabbed the bag, setting it in front of me. My breath caught. I focused on the bag again. It was easier that way, even though the energy between us wasn't lessening in intensity. If anything, it increased.

I felt Winston round the table, coming nearer to me. The skin on the back of my neck prickled as I pulled at the bow that kept the handles together.

Inside it was a gorgeous hairpin with a butterfly on it.

"Winston, this is stunning." My voice wasn't quite right.

"I saw this and imagined how it would look on you. I wanted you to have it. I knew you'd love it. You always wear these things in your hair."

The fact that he'd paid so much attention got to me in an unexpected way.

"And I'd love to see it on you. Let me put it on."

My breath caught. I made the mistake of tilting my head, looking up at him. The ferocity in his green eyes made it impossible to do anything but cave to whatever he demanded.

I nodded slowly, handing him the pin and staying as still as possible.

I felt so exposed, so open. I held my breath when his fingers brushed my temple, replacing the hairpin I was wearing with the one he'd bought for me. He dragged his fingers from my temple down my cheek. I hoped he wouldn't go even lower, that...

ahhh, turned out to be just wishful thinking. He only skimmed his fingers down my neck, but I was barely hanging in there.

"There. It looks great on you."

"Thanks, Winston."

He took a small step back but was still close enough to make my body hum.

"Ready for tonight?" I asked. "It would be cool if you could stay a while."

Winston's smile grew more pronounced.

"Of course I will. Have to cash in on that open promise you made."

"I never promised!"

"Yes, you did. Got me to join, didn't you?"

"If you were so sure I'd accepted, you wouldn't bring it up."

"Just thought I'd remind you. Say yes, and I'll stay however long you want me to."

"You're negotiating?"

He tilted his head. "Anything to get what I want."

"And what's that?"

"A 'yes' from you, Sienna."

My palms grew sweaty. Just when I thought I had a grip on things, Winston changed the rules of the game. I couldn't say no, could I? If it kept him here, it was good for everyone's morale. Who was I kidding? I wanted to say yes to whatever this man demanded of me, pure and simple.

I nodded, and his eyes turned almost feral. That hum in my body intensified by the factor of a million.

For the rest of the day, I had a ball of anticipation and euphoria lodged in my stomach. Every time I touched the hairpin, I couldn't help smiling to myself, just as I couldn't help the butterflies in my stomach or the electrifying heat jolting through me.

Later that afternoon, one of my colleagues, Jane, approached my desk.

"Hi, Jane. How can I help you?"

"I want to ask your advice on something."

"Sure."

"So, in the gift exchange, I got Winston."

"Okay."

"I bought him socks. You think that's okay?"

Okay? That was *terrible*.

I wanted to reassure Jane in some way, but I'd never had a good poker face.

"He won't like it, will he? I just had zero time for shopping."

"You know what? I'll head down into the shop and pick something up. We'll just add that to your gift."

"You're a lifesaver, Sienna. Thank you, thank you, thank you."

After she left, I checked the rest of my to-do list before promptly deciding I wasn't going to get anything else done today anyway. We only had two hours left until the party started, and everyone was already in a Christmas mood. Someone had even spiked a punch bowl in the kitchen. I smiled to myself. Winston would hand everyone their ass. What were they thinking?

You could easily spot those who'd made more than one trip to the punch bowl, because they were already singing carols.

No one was getting any work done except for the accounting department. I felt zero guilt for heading downstairs.

The shop was so full, it neared breaking point. The energy in it was just surreal. "Jingle Bells" was blasting through the sound system, and the elves on every floor were milling around, visible in their green suits even in the thick crowd.

I headed straight to the books section of the shop on the first floor and picked a business book for Winston. There. That was a sound Christmas present. Professional and useful. Predictably, the line to the cash register was humongous, but I batted my eyelashes at the cashier, who ushered me forward, to the chagrin of everyone else. I wasn't a fan of shortcuts… usually. But with one hour to the party, it was time to pull out all the stops. I felt like the boss deserved more presents though. Something more… personal. Even though his grouchy, stabby personality was scaring the wits out of everyone, he was breaking his back for the company. What else would Winston like? I absentmindedly touched my hairpin and decided that I wanted to give him a gift. Something personal, something that would make him think about me.

I blamed the Christmas spirit all around for even entertaining that thought. And still, I went on with buying him a gift anyway. What harm could it do? I had fun imagining Winston's reaction to several gifts before settling on an elegant white shirt.

I spent so much time bumbling around the store that the party was about to start when I returned upstairs. I slipped the book in Jane's bag under the tree... but what to do with my own gift? I couldn't give it to Winston in full view of everyone, because it would raise eyebrows. I'd have to be alone with him.

My mouth went dry at the thought of that.

I hung the bag with the gift in the vestibule along with my coat. I'd find a moment to give it to Winston later.

Smoothing my hand over my hair, I joined the crowd already gathered by the Christmas tree. The room had a high ceiling with low-hanging lamps throughout, casting diffused lighting.

The punch bowls were set by a table to the far end of the room, along with delicious snacks like bacon-wrapped water chestnuts, cheese and crackers, and mini quiches.

I beamed, glancing around. Yes! This was already shaping up to be a success. Even the accounting department, who had to finalize the consolidated accounts within the next two weeks, seemed more relaxed.

"What did I get the boss?" Jane asked.

"A collection of biographies of successful businessmen."

"Excellent. That sounds like something he'd actually enjoy."

"I think so too."

We each took a cup of spiked punch and a cinnamon bun. I munched on it happily, already feeling myself relax. My limbs felt lighter; my smile was so bright. This evening was just how I'd envisioned it. Everyone was getting the break they needed after Black Friday and the boost of energy to keep up with the tight schedule for the next few weeks.

It was a pity that the pressure increased so much just around Christmas time—to drive sales, to organize the Christmas program. But it was all worth it, in my opinion. We made an experience out of Christmas for shoppers. Created an adventure out of buying gifts, made little kids happy by bringing Santa to them.

"Girl, I cannot believe you actually convinced the big boss to join us. How did you do it?" Mara said.

I laughed nervously. "Laid out the pros and cons. Not sure how long he'll stay, though," I added quickly, not wanting anyone to get their hopes up.

"Still a step forward. Tell me your tricks."

I winked, even though I was nervous as hell. "No can do. Have to keep my tricks for myself."

"Boss just arrived," Mara murmured, looking over my shoulder.

A jolt of energy coursed through me. I stood ramrod straight, turning around slowly in the direction of the door.

Chapter Fourteen

Sienna

I'd seen him today. How on earth could I have this reaction to him? When he locked eyes with me, I drew in a sharp breath.

The room was unnaturally silent. Half the company was intimidated by him. The other half was afraid.

Since I was the unofficial moderator tonight, I set my cup down and headed to him with large, determined strides. Winston trained that molten gaze of his on me, looking me up slowly. So damn slowly. It set me ablaze. The man had been in the same room with me for all of two minutes and I was already on edge.

How was I going to get through the evening?

"You're wearing the hairpin," he murmured when I reached him.

"Of course. I love wearing my gifts."

"Noted." His solemn expression gave way to a smile.

"So the party has started, obviously. Everyone's been waiting for you to get to the gift-exchanging part. Afterward, the catering company will serve more substantial snacks."

"And then there will be dancing?"

"Yes," I confirmed.

"Ready to keep your promise? I want to dance with you tonight, Sienna."

"Oh…" I didn't know what else to say. I hadn't expected this. I hadn't even thought Winston would want to dance (or that he knew how). "I need to get the gift exchange started."

"Go ahead."

I turned on my heels and headed to the Christmas tree. I'd volunteered to do the intro, explain how Secret Santa worked, and generally just lift everyone's spirits. Winston watched me the entire time.

The gift exchange was a cute, slightly awkward affair, mostly because of Winston's presence. No one knew how to act around him. Jane was all stressed out when he opened his gift. Winston looked perplexed, holding the socks, but he saved it with a curt thank-you and a real interest in the book I'd bought.

I'd gotten a vial of perfume and a pair of gloves from the operations manager, Eleanor. I immediately sprayed the delicious floral scent on myself and tried on the gloves. They fit me perfectly. I loved them.

After all presents were exchanged, the caterers brought in food and more drinks.

I made the rounds, happy that this party seemed to have exactly the effect I'd hoped for.

Everyone was relaxing, enjoying themselves. I'd almost forgotten about my promise to Winston... until the DJ changed the music from slow Christmas songs to rhythmic pop interpretations that were perfect to dance to.

I was at the buffet, refilling my cup with punch. Out of the corner of my eye, I saw Winston approach me with quick strides. My entire body strummed to life, pulsing with anticipation. When I felt him right behind me, I gripped my cup tighter.

"Sienna."

"Winston."

"I want my dance."

I hadn't realized how close he was until I felt his breath on the shell of my ear with every word.

"Just one, yes?"

When he didn't answer, I cocked my head in his direction. He was flashing one of his devious smiles.

"We didn't agree on a specific number."

I laughed, pressing my palm against my stomach, hoping to appease those pesky butterflies roaming around. I should have seen this coming.

"Fine, but I have one rule."

"I'm all ears."

"Suddenly allowing me to set rules?"

"Didn't say I'll agree."

"If you step on my toes, you forfeit any chance at another dance."

I expected him to fight me on it, to at least try and negotiate

But Winston merely smiled. "Deal."

He'd agreed too fast. That could only mean one thing: he was an excellent dancer.

He took the cup from me, placing it on the table. I felt everyone's eyes on us as we headed to the dance floor next to the Christmas tree.

When Winston placed his hand at my lower back, I felt as if I wasn't wearing anything at all, as if he was touching my bare skin.

I sucked in a breath, keeping my gaze level with his chin, almost afraid to look higher. His lips curled into a smile, and he pulled me even closer.

Our bodies moved in sync. He guided me with his hands, the movement of his hips. I was so on edge I could barely think, barely breathe.

"Thank you for organizing this," Winston said. "You were right. It's great for everyone's morale."

"Glad you think so."

"You have a knack for guessing what others need," he went on.

"Well, I grew up with three siblings, and then when we joined the Bennetts, there were so many of us that anticipating needs was a survival skill."

"But you like doing that, and I love this about you."

"What?"

"That you take time to do things that make others happy."

The room around us faded. I was barely even listening to the music, simply trusting Winston's body to lead me.

"I've always loved taking care of others. But it's gotten me in trouble sometimes."

"What do you mean?"

"That people either take advantage, or they consider me… intrusive."

"The world is full of idiots. Surround yourself with those who do appreciate you. Like me."

His smile was so heartfelt and his eyes so happy that I nearly melted in his arms.

"You're building a very convincing case for yourself," I teased. Only then did I realize that everyone was slowing down. The song was ending.

"I believe I didn't step on your feet once."

"You didn't," I confirmed.

"You know what that means?" He brought his mouth closer to my ear. "That you're mine for the rest of the evening."

My heart thundered in my chest. That sounded so damn appealing. I pulled back a little. *Do not look him straight in the eyes.* That was a surefire way to lose myself and give in to whatever he demanded.

"But you're the boss. You have to dance with others too."

He cocked a brow. "No, I don't."

"I think others will expect you to dance with them."

"I don't give a damn about that. I only want you, Sienna."

I took in a deep breath, steadily making eye contact—and hoping I wouldn't just cave in. There was a real risk of that. The man was simply hypnotizing.

"You said you'd like the team to warm up to you? This is what the party is about."

Winston was silent for a few seconds. "Fine. On one condition."

Damn. Nothing was ever easy or straightforward with this delicious man, but what could I say? I liked a challenge. I licked my lips as a sense of foreboding gripped me.

"What?"

"You promise me we'll catch up after the dances. Just you and me. And just a warning, if you say no, I'm not above using dirty tricks to change your mind." His voice was so impossibly rich and sinful that I couldn't do anything more than nod.

People started milling around the dance floor as the song ended.

Freddie from the sales team tapped my shoulder.

"Sienna, can I have this dance?" he asked.

"Sure."

Winston looked as if he was closer to punching Freddie than releasing me, but I gracefully extracted my hand from his iron grip.

I'd thought dancing with Freddie would give me a chance to cool down. I'd been wrong.

Every time my gaze crossed Winston's across the room, I fidgeted. Even from a distance, his presence was all-consuming.

I didn't get a chance to dance with Winston

again. I hadn't anticipated that as the official organizer, I had to dance with everyone. I spied Winston making the rounds. He also danced a few times. Progress.

The DJ switched back to ambient music once catering brought a second round of canapes. I immediately located Winston; he was leaving.

I excused myself, surreptitiously exiting the room, and caught up to him at the coat closet.

"Hey. Leaving already?"

"Yes. It's late, and I have an early call tomorrow before we leave for Burlington."

"Okay. Before I forget... I got you something." I turned to my coat. I'd hung the bag under it. I was hyperaware of every movement I made, the very dim light around us, the close space.

"You got me a present?"

Even in the dim lighting, I could see Winston looked utterly surprised. My heart squeezed. Was he not used to it?

"Yes. A shirt." I touched my hairpin absentmindedly.

"I wasn't expecting anything in return. You didn't have to get me anything."

He was definitely not used to it.

"I couldn't resist," I said in a teasing tone. "Besides, I'm surprised you're leaving. How about catching up after the party?"

A smile inched on his face. In a fraction of a second, he closed the distance between us, nearly pushing me into the wall behind. "I just realized there's no need to hurry. I'll have you all to myself in Burlington."

I was surrounded by the smell of his cologne, the heat of his body. It was all blowing my defenses to smithereens. When he tilted his head forward, I closed my eyes.

Winston kissed me ferociously. His mouth claimed mine possessively. His hands were gripping my waist. I tugged at his hair, pressing my pelvis into him. I wanted him closer, but nothing felt close enough.

Ever since he'd kissed me at my house, instinct told me that his passion would take over completely if I allowed it. The mere thought overwhelmed me, but right now, that was exactly what I wanted to do.

When we paused to breathe, I was tugging at his shirt.

"Stop that, or I'll kiss you again, and this time, I'll kiss you until you beg me to take you home."

I looked up at him, and he smiled wholeheartedly. Awww... I was melting again. Lust *and* fuzzy feelings. Now that was a lethal combo.

"I'll pick you up from home tomorrow to go to the airport," he said.

"You don't have to go out of your way. I can just Uber."

"I'm picking you up."

I smiled but didn't say anything else. I decided to let Winston just... be Winston.

I knew without a doubt that things had just

shifted between us. We were teetering on the brink of *something*, and this trip would push us right over the edge.

Chapter Fifteen

Sienna

Next morning, I was running around in every direction, packing, reviewing the presentation, wondering if I was forgetting something. I was on pins and needles, fussing about my appearance more than necessary.

At nine o'clock on the dot, Winston messaged to tell me he'd arrived. I had no time to gather my wits, because he knocked at the door the next second. He was all smiles when I opened up.

"Hey."

"Sienna. Ready to go?"

I nodded eagerly, pointing to my bag.

Winston looked at me incredulously. "You do know we're only there for a short time, right?"

"Yes, but it's much colder. Had to pack sweaters, a coat, a suit."

"So did I, but my luggage is half the size of yours. How did you manage to fill *that*?"

"Hey. Don't get between me and my packing habits."

Winston held up his hands in defense, laughing. "Forget I asked anything."

"That's more like it."

He rolled the luggage out of my house. While he loaded it into the car, I remained one step behind, unabashedly drinking him in. He was wearing a turtleneck sweater that molded over his muscles. What a sight he was. My favorite view of Winston was that of him in a T-shirt like the one he'd worn when helping me with the walls, but hey… I'd take whatever I could get.

"I'm so excited we're going to a place with snow," I exclaimed once we were in the car.

Winston laughed. I loved that I could make him laugh so easily.

"Why do you like snow so much?"

"I don't know. It's so pretty. Makes me think of the skiing vacations we went on when I was a kid."

"Where did you go?"

"Montana, mostly. I haven't been to Vermont, though."

"You mentioned that. I've made an itinerary. We have time to see a few things tomorrow after the meeting. Our flight is in the evening."

"But this is a business trip."

He leaned in closer, whispering, "We can sneak something for our own pleasure in between."

"But I've got some spreadsheets to work on."

He watched me with an amused expression. "You're already working this weekend by attending the meeting."

"Yes, but it's just a few hours."

"Sienna, you're traveling with the boss. And

I'm declaring this a work-free weekend."

"You should have told me."

"Why?"

"I would have packed even more clothes." I squirmed in my seat, realizing that no matter how much I thought that I had everything under control, Winston was actually the one in charge.

And I was supposed to spend the next day joined at the hip with this man? I had a feeling that was more than I could handle. But I smiled wider nonetheless.

***

Winston

We landed on time. The second we were out of the airport, Sienna put on a red cap that covered her ears and half her forehead. She looked around with a big, bright smile.

"Look, snow," she exclaimed. I bit back my laughter as the driver and I loaded our luggage in the trunk of the cab. Sienna kept her nose pressed to the window during the entire drive.

"Wow, this hotel looks straight out of a fairy tale. It's gorgeous," she commented as the driver pulled in front of the hotel. It had the appearance of a hut, a wooden structure with an A-frame roof, but on a larger scale. Snow was falling so thick that you couldn't see much around. The driver climbed out, announcing he'd carry our bags inside and ask for an umbrella.

"Why are you smiling like that?" she asked when it was just the two of us.

"Just… proud I booked this hotel. I thought you might like it."

I felt this incessant need to please her, to surprise her, to watch her light up.

I couldn't help but slide closer to her on that back seat. Sienna's eyes widened. She let out a shaky breath, casting her gaze down. It was all I could do not to wrap my hand in her hair and tilt her head for a kiss. I gripped the headrest instead before sliding my arm past her, reaching for the handle, opening the door. A hotel employee stood there with two umbrellas.

She climbed out of the car the next second, as if she couldn't trust herself to be alone with me any longer. After check-in, the same hotel employee led us to our rooms—adjacent suites. Knowing she'd be just one wall away was torture.

She went on to check her room and then came into mine all smiles, clapping her hands.

"This room is amazing, and I might never leave it again," she declared.

I waggled my eyebrows. "No problem. I'll lock us both inside and toss the key away."

She shrugged one shoulder. "I didn't say I want you to keep me company."

"I think you do. Why else tell me this?" I was in her personal space again. I just couldn't stay away—not that I was trying too hard.

"I'll go back to inspecting my room," she said

quickly, blushing. "Dinner in two hours?"

"Sounds good."

After Sienna left, I couldn't avoid thinking about tomorrow. It was a big day. It was just an interim presentation, but if the board ultimately didn't like where this was going, I'd have to close the store or I risked exposing the entire chain to financial risk.

I barely had time to take out the printed version of the presentation before I heard a knock at the door. It was Sienna.

She'd changed her clothes. Her boots almost swallowed her whole. She'd put on her red cap again. She looked like a dork. An adorable, sexy-as-hell dork.

"What are you doing?" she asked.

"I was just about to go over the presentation for tomorrow."

"I thought you might. But you said that this is a work-free trip, remember? You can't expect me to follow the rules if you don't. Besides, you know that presentation inside out."

"Fine. What do you want to do?"

"Build a snowman. Want to join me?"

I looked over my shoulder at the window. The snow was falling even thicker than before.

"You want to go outside now? That's a blizzard right there."

"Coward," she muttered. I laughed.

"You didn't just call me that."

"I did. And unless you prove me different, I'm going to keep thinking that."

She flashed me a sassy, challenging smile. Gripping the door tighter, I stepped closer.

"Okay. I'll go. But only if you promise to come to the sauna with me afterward."

"Oh?"

"Sauna. That place you go to sweat, wearing just a towel."

She narrowed her eyes. "I know what a sauna is. Why do you want to go?"

"Good to relax muscles after the long flight. And to warm up after we freeze our ass off outside."

"Fine, Mr. Statham. We'll do it your way."

I couldn't help myself then. I moved my hand from the door to her waist, looking her straight in the eyes.

"If I had it my way, I'd lock us together in this room and we wouldn't leave it unless we absolutely had to."

She was so close that I would just have to tip my head and claim her lips. I would have too, if a hotel employee hadn't arrived to bring wood.

"Just in case you want to light up the fire tonight."

"Thank you."

"Do you need something else?"

"We're good," I said, still looking at Sienna intently.

"I'm going to wait outside while you change into thicker clothes," Sienna whispered, eyeing the employee, who was arranging the wood as if it was a freaking piece of art. I wanted to be alone with her, damn it.

I smiled, waggling my eyebrows, dropping my voice to a whisper. "Or you can wait inside. Take a peek."

She shook her head, pointing a finger at me. "Ten minutes. Outside. Don't be late."

"Yes, ma'am."

When I stepped out of the hotel ten minutes later, I couldn't believe my eyes. Sienna had already made a huge ball all by herself. I also noticed carrots and olives in the snow.

"Where did you get those?" I asked, setting to work with her on the second ball.

"Worked my charms on the kitchen staff."

"In ten minutes?"

She laughed. "I'm very efficient. How else do you think I could have put up with you for so long?"

"I'm going to pretend you didn't say that."

I threw a small snowball at her.

She gasped, grabbing a fistful of snow herself. "It's the truth."

Just as she made to throw it at me, I grabbed both her wrists.

"So why do you put up with me?" I teased.

"Because you're smart and I like working with you. And since you've returned, you've been far more... okay."

"I'm okay. I see."

"Hey. That's a huge improvement from boss from hell." She grinned as she spoke.

"I see. And yet you dragged your boss from hell out here. Something tells me you're looking for any excuse to spend more time with me."

I let go of her wrists.

"I wanted to keep you busy. If you stayed inside, you'd just worry about tomorrow, get lost in your own headspace."

She cared about me enough to worry. I'd never been closer to just taking her in my arms and carrying her upstairs. I didn't want to share her with the world. I just wanted to have this lovely creature all to myself.

She returned her focus to the snowman.

"If I didn't love San Francisco so much, I'd move somewhere with snow during winter," she said wistfully. "It doesn't really feel like Christmas until it snows, you know?"

I laughed. "I'll take your word for it."

It took us almost an hour to finish the dwarf-sized snowman, but I had to admit, it looked damn good. Especially once Sienna placed the carrot as the nose and the black olives as eyes. Then she took off her own cap and scarf, placing them on the snowman.

Her eyes were a little misty.

"What's wrong?" I asked.

She shrugged, smiling sadly. "Last time I made such an elaborate snowman, I was a kid. It just brings back a lot of memories with my parents. Good memories."

She sighed, fumbling with the ends of the scarf.

"You should put those back on. You'll get a cold," I said gently. "And if you leave them out here, they'll get covered in snow."

She nodded, snapping a quick picture of the snowman before taking her belongings back.

"Let's head inside," I said. "The snow is getting thicker."

She nodded, but her smile was still wistful when we reached the elevator. She was the one in danger of getting lost in her own head now.

I wasn't going to allow that. Luckily, I already had an excellent plan.

Chapter Sixteen

Sienna

I sent the picture to my siblings. Chloe and Lucas didn't remember that trip, of course, but Victoria had replied with an "Awwwwww," which about summed up how I felt about the whole thing.

I took a hot shower, because my feet were so cold that I almost couldn't feel my toes. If I could have snow without the cold… But it had been worth it, spending the time out there to make that snowman. I'd intended to do it all on my own but leaving Winston alone the evening before the presentation was dangerous. I risked walking with the grinch into that meeting tomorrow.

I didn't really have to go to the sauna though, did I?

I knew I'd promised, but it felt too much like playing with fire. I should stay here. In fact, I should order room service and spend the rest of the evening by myself.

But a deal was a deal. I couldn't back out. Besides, there was still enough time for him to get lost in his own head. Yeah, that was why I was going, I told myself. For a good cause. *Not* because I wanted to see Winston seminaked and sweaty.

Wow... was I good at lying to myself or what? I'd spent so much time doubting the decision that I was nowhere near ready when Winston knocked at the door.

"One minute," I called out in a panicky voice. I put on one of those fancy sauna towels that had a clasp to keep it fastened above my boobs, grabbed the spa bag the hotel had laid out, and opened the door.

My knees instantly softened. Winston had wrapped an identical towel around his lower half, which meant his torso was completely naked. Pure muscle, everywhere I looked.

Six-pack? Check.

Biceps? Check.

Muscle-laced upper arms? Double check.

I had to force myself to look him straight in the eyes after my quick perusal.

"Ready?" he asked, his smile growing more pronounced. The honest answer was no, but I nodded anyway.

The sauna was on the top floor of the hotel. There was also a relaxation room with dim lighting, and a reading area with comfy armchairs and small lamps.

We each grabbed an additional towel, which we placed on the wood inside the sauna.

Being this close to Winston while wearing practically no clothes was more than I'd signed up for and certainly more than I could handle.

The room would have been claustrophobic if

not for the large window overlooking Lake Champlain and the Adirondack mountains in the background. The view was simply breathtaking.

"This glass… can people see inside?" I asked.

Winston smiled. "Technically yes, but we're too high up for anyone to see anything from the street. So if you have any sexy plans in mind, feel free to act on them."

Shaking my head, I nudged his arm with my shoulder. Big mistake, because that one touch made me eager for more.

Despite the grand view and the eucalyptus smell in the air, I decided after two minutes that I wasn't a fan of the sauna.

"This isn't very relaxing," I murmured, fanning myself.

"Is it the heat that makes you uncomfortable, or is it me?" His grin made my stomach flip. I was determined to last for at least five minutes, but I felt as if I was suffocating. When I couldn't take the heat anymore, I excused myself, leaving the sauna, heading straight to the counter with drinks. After downing a glass of water and one of orange juice, I finally felt as if I could breathe again.

Then I headed to the shower. Even though I'd read that icy-cold water was recommended after a sauna, to close the pores, I wasn't brave enough to do it. I spent an inordinate amount of time under lukewarm water, washing my hair too… biding my time.

I wasn't sure what to expect when I stepped

out.

When I was finally done, I wrapped a fresh towel around me and dried my hair with a second one.

I found Winston in the reading lounge. He'd showered too and was wearing a fresh towel. He'd laid another one on the armchair.

Do not look under chin level. Do not look under chin level.

"Ready for dinner?" he asked.

"Yes."

"We can also order room service, if you want."

I placed both hands on my hips. Belatedly I realized that the motion had dislodged my towel. I caught it just in time.

"Almost dropped it," I said.

"Couldn't have that, could we?"

I cleared my throat, holding the towel tightly to my chest with one hand.

"There's a fireplace in the dining room. I'm not missing out on that."

"We have fireplaces in the living room too."

"Yes, but the one on the main floor already has Christmas stockings hanging on it."

"Got it, ma'am."

"What happened to *I'm the boss*?"

He gave me a look that told me I did *not* want to know the answer to that.

"Let's go change," he added.

I nodded, walking in front of him, feeling his

gaze on me, the heat of his body and his mere presence like a physical force.

When I was finally in my room, I took a moment for myself, leaning against the door, closing my eyes. There was no such thing as a reprieve when it came to Winston.

I changed into a sweater dress. It seemed appropriate for the hotel. The atmosphere on the ground floor was cozy and just... happy. Every server wore a Christmas-themed shirt.

Winston was waiting for me by the entrance. He was wearing jeans and a black sweater. He looked like a model in a Calvin Klein ad.

To my surprise, we were shown to the table nearest to the fireplace. I couldn't believe our luck. The dining room was packed. A few seconds later, I had the slight suspicion that Winston had everything to do with said luck.

"How did you get the table?" I asked after we ordered two glasses of wine and roast beef.

"Used my irresistible charm. I knew you'd like it."

"I do. It's amazing. You look relaxed."

"I am. A certain sassy woman took care of it."

I grinned. "And how did she manage that? By talking you into building a snowman?"

"That, and also by just being herself. Fun, warm."

He placed his hand on top of mine over the table. I all but melted. Looking around the room, I noticed pictures of the family that owned the hotel hanging everywhere.

I'd been so taken with the Christmas decorations that I hadn't paid attention to the photos.

"Look, they have family pics all around."

"That's right. Hadn't seen them."

"I read the welcome letter in the room. The couple running it have been married for forty years."

"My parents celebrated their forty-second anniversary last year."

I grinned. "I know. Everyone's still talking about the party they threw for the team." Wistfully, I added, "My parents also had a happy marriage. I've been spoiled by it, and then by watching all the Bennetts fall in love. I know it sounds crazy, but I kind of thought I'd be married by now."

"Why crazy?"

"Well, you probably know all the statistics about the number of marriages going down, divorce up."

"I think statistics are just a numbers game and a matter of luck. If the right person comes along, every statistic is meaningless."

"Winston! Is it possible that you're a closet romantic?"

He glowered. I laughed. He shook his head, smiling.

"Why didn't you mention that a couple of weeks ago? I would have upgraded you much faster."

"Does that mean I'm finally in your good

graces?"

"Yes, but careful. Don't rest on your laurels."

"Wouldn't dream of it."

I shimmied in my seat, smiling. I was just so full of energy that I didn't know what to do with my hands. Put them on the table? Hold them next to me?

And why was I overthinking every tiny action?

After the waiter brought our wine, Winston and I clinked glasses. He held my gaze the entire time. I didn't know why, but I seemed even more susceptible to him this evening. The roast beef arrived quickly, and it was delicious. Usually, I'd pay more attention to the food and the ambiance, but now I was too consumed by him—feeling his skin on mine every time he touched my hand, agonizing over his nearness whenever he shifted his legs closer to mine under the table, but not *quite* touching me.

"You're happy," he stated. That dreamy smile on my face was a dead giveaway.

"This is a fabulous evening. Of course, I'm in a great mood."

I felt so in sync with him tonight, as if the mere fact that we were out of San Francisco had allowed us each to shed some of our walls, to be ourselves.

We stayed at our table long after we finished our roast beef, ordering another glass of wine and speaking about our families. We only went up when they announced they were closing the restaurant.

When had the evening flown by? I didn't want

it to end.

Winston walked side by side with me. I was so aware of his nearness. Our arms were almost touching.

I stopped in front of my door.

"Well, goodnight," I said.

Winston merely smiled.

"What?"

"This is my room."

"Really?"

To demonstrate, he held his keycard in front of the handle. It unlocked. He pushed the door open, brushing my shoulder. My breath caught. He stepped closer. He'd never looked at me with so much intensity—his gaze was almost feral.

Chapter Seventeen

Sienna

When he touched his lips to mine, I forgot what I was about to say. I couldn't even think anything beyond how much I wanted him, how much I needed him. Winston cupped the back of my head as if he didn't intend to let me go. He kissed me as if he was determined to possess me, claim me. And I wanted nothing more than to relent.

He guided us both into the room. The door closed with a bang. I shook in his arms, already overwhelmed by the sheer intensity of his body.

He kissed me so determinedly that I couldn't do anything else but give in.

Was I afraid that this would end badly? Yes. But I was more afraid of not getting to know this man who stirred so many things inside me. I'd never felt so appreciated, as if he embraced every side of me.

He feathered his fingers down my back, resting them atop of the zipper. My entire body pulsed with anticipation. He stopped the kiss, pulling back a few inches, locking his eyes with mine. The heat in them overpowered me. I was drunk on the anticipation hanging thick in the air.

He lowered my zipper, touching his fingers to my bare back. I shuddered, hungry for more of his touch. I licked my lips when my dress slid down my body, pooling at my feet. He raked his gaze downward slowly, as if determined to memorize every curve, every inch. When he snapped his gaze back up, my breath caught.

"You're so beautiful," he murmured. "Just perfect."

I bit my lower lip. He caught the gesture. His eyes flashed, and then he leaned in, licking my lower lip slowly. I shuddered, unable to hold back a moan. My entire body reacted, and when he turned his attention to my upper lip, teasing it with the tip of his tongue, my nipples turned rock-hard. An ache settled between my legs, pulsing madly. I reached for his belt buckle, undoing it. He groaned against my mouth and then kissed me so hard that I nearly stumbled backward. And then his mouth was everywhere, kissing my mouth and neck, demanding my surrender, claiming everything I had to give. I wasn't any less demanding either. Taking off his shirt, I drew my hands down his torso, determined not to leave one inch untouched. Lifting myself on my tiptoes, I kissed his Adam's apple. A low hum in his throat told me just how much he liked it.

He gripped the back of my head with one hand, pulling me into a deliciously dirty kiss. He gripped my hip with the other hand, pulling me against him. My knees buckled when I felt his erection against my lower belly. Feeling feisty, undoing his pants and pushing them down, I dipped my hand into his boxers. When I wrapped my palm around his erection, he rocked his hips back and forth, deepening the kiss, claiming more of me with every stroke of his tongue. When I drew my thumb over his tip, he let out a deep, guttural groan. And then he walked me backward until the back of my legs touched the bed.

I climbed on the mattress, lying down, admiring the view.

"Like what you see?" he taunted with a smile.

I smiled back, tilting my head to one side. "I think I do."

I drank in that gorgeous body. Every muscle was perfectly defined. I couldn't wait to run my fingers over every single one of them… and then map his body with my mouth. The feral glint in his eyes told me he had other plans for us, though.

He climbed in bed with me, resting on his side next to me. I was on my back, my breath labored from anticipation.

"I'm on the pill," I said. "And I'm healthy."

"I'm clean too."

He skimmed his fingers down my chest, and when he leaned over me, I thought he'd kiss that same spot between my breasts. Instead, he lowered one cup of my bra and sealed his mouth over one nipple, teasing it with his tongue. Pleasure curled through me. My hips bucked off the bed. Holy shit!

I gripped the sheets with both hands. I felt him smile against my breast before he reached behind my back, undoing the clasp. I pushed my own panties down my legs awkwardly, desperate to get any piece of fabric out of the way. He got rid of his boxers.

His kissing alternated between gentle and ferocious. And his touch… it was out of this world good. It didn't matter if he touched my belly or my breasts or my inner thighs… I felt every touch so intensely, as if my entire body was a sweet spot, as if every cell was wired to my center. And every time our gazes locked, I felt more exposed than I ever had.

"You're so amazing, Sienna. Everything about you just draws me in. Your laughter, the way you touch me. The way you challenge me."

I smiled, feeling our bond like a physical cord, tying us together. When he looked straight at me, I was sure my emotions were written all over my face, but far from shutting down or running in the opposite direction, he embraced it. He kissed down my chest, feathering his thumbs over my nipples before licking the spot he'd touched.

When he settled between my legs, I dug my fingers into the mattress. Anticipation coursed through me. He drew the tip of his nose along my inner thigh, then followed the same trail with his mouth, going higher and higher until he nearly reached my center. When his lips touched the sensitive skin, I gasped. He moved his mouth on my lower belly, kissing up, pausing to look at me from time to time. Every time our gazes locked, I was overwhelmed by emotions. He looked at me as if he was the luckiest man to be here with me, as if I was precious.

Gripping his erection at the base, he drew the tip downward. When he circled my clit, I gasped, lifting my hips. He pressed them back down to the mattress, smiling devilishly at me.

"I'm in charge, Sienna. Your pleasure belongs to me."

He slid inside me slowly. I felt every exquisite inch filling me while he kissed my neck before skimming his lips up to my temple, murmuring my name.

***

Winston

I just couldn't get enough of her soft skin, her feminine perfume, the way she reacted to me. I wanted to claim her pleasure, make her world tilt on its axis.

I rocked back and forth gently, wanting to give her time to adjust to me. I drank in every reaction. The way her eyelids fluttered closed, her mouth opened in a moan. I increased my pace, slammed into her without restraint. When I touched her clit, she clenched around me.

"Oh, Winston. Wins-ton." Her voice faltered, becoming shaky. I wanted to prolong this, but at the same time, I wanted to feel her come around me before I succumbed to my own climax.

I stilled, smiling at her groans of protest. Clasping my hands around her ankles, I lifted them up, placing them on my shoulders as I sat back on my haunches. Her eyes widened.

"Winston, what…. ohhhhh."

Her words completely faded when I pressed my thumb on her clit, moving inside her with quick, hard thrusts.

I had better access to her like this, could bring her pleasure in every way there was. And I could watch her succumb to it… to me. She fisted the sheets, growing so tight around me that I could barely breathe through the tension. I lasted long enough to watch her ride out her climax, thrashing and crying out. She was so damn beautiful, all flushed and spent. Her soft skin had a thin sheet of perspiration.

I came hard, buckling over, propping my palms on the mattress just in time so I wouldn't crush her. I'd never felt pleasure so intense and all-consuming. I lowered myself on top of her gently, needing more skin-on-skin contact, needing to feel her closer. I didn't want to break our connection, even though we both needed to clean up.

Just one more minute, I kept telling myself, drawing the tip of my nose up and down her neck before claiming her mouth. I kissed her lazily, wanting nothing more than to explore her. She tasted amazing. She felt amazing, and I just didn't want to let go.

I kissed her until she moaned. I was semihard

again. I felt the corners of her mouth lift in a small smile even as I kissed her.

When I pulled back, there was nothing small about it. She had a full-on megawatt smile on her face.

"What's with the smile?" I asked, drawing my thumb over the contour of her mouth.

She flexed her inner muscles, and I groaned. I'd just turned rock-hard.

Her smile turned into a grin. "No reason."

"Then I'd better give you one."

Chapter Eighteen

Sienna

After showering, I found one of those sauna towels in the bathroom and wrapped it around myself. It was so comfy that I couldn't stop touching it.

Winston was watching me with warm eyes. A smile tugged at the corner of his lips.

"What?" I asked.

"You're cute."

"It's just so soft. If I had one, I'd wear it around the house all the time. But I haven't found any that are so comfy."

He pulled me flush against him. "I'll be happy to buy you one."

"Not to look a gift horse in the mouth, but why the sudden generosity?"

"I'm not done. I have a condition."

"You and your conditions. Somehow, they're always a way for you to get what you want."

"You have to promise that you won't wear it around me."

I laughed, throwing my head back. "And what would you have me wear?"

"Nothing at all."

I couldn't stop laughing. I was seeing Winston in a whole new light. Who knew he was so wicked? I certainly hadn't guessed it, what with his perfectly ironed shirts and broody forehead.

"The great thing about towels is that you can easily get rid of them." I took a small step back, demonstrating my point with slow, deliberate moves. When I undid the clasp, he sucked in a breath. I smiled to myself—or at least I thought I did. Winston immediately noticed that I was a little too pleased with myself. He cupped my cheek, tilting my head slightly back. His eyes flashed. He stepped closer, pressing himself against my front.

"You like teasing me?" he murmured, those molten eyes trained on me.

"I like prodding you, pushing at your boundaries."

"Careful, Sienna. You might get more than you're bargaining for."

That sounded delicious. I'd make him keep that promise later.

I wiggled my ass in delight. His eyes flashed even darker. That looked very, very promising.

Since we were feeling feisty, we ordered a second dessert from room service. I wasn't ready for this evening to end, and I thought Winston didn't want that either.

Room service also lit the fireplace, and after devouring the apple pie, we just lay down in front of the fire, talking about everything.

"Want something to drink?" Winston asked.

"No, I've had enough. Just don't move too much. I've found the perfect cuddle position. This is the only semisoft part of your chest."

Deep laughter rumbled out of Winston. I smiled, happy I had this effect on him. I was pretty sure I hadn't ever heard him laugh like that.

"Didn't think there could be a downside to all this muscle-fest, but I found it."

Winston played with my hair, wrapping an arm tighter around me.

I loved this so much. Just lying here with him—well, on him, talking, discovering things about each other.

"You were right. The fire is relaxing," he said.

I grinned, looking up, holding up two fingers.

"This is the second time you've agreed with me today."

"You're counting?"

I nodded sagely. "Gathering ammunition for the next time you decide to be difficult, which I bet will happen soon."

Next thing I knew, he rolled us around on the floor until he was on top. His pelvis pressed on mine. His hands kept my wrists pinned to the floor. I was his captive, and I loved every delicious second of it.

"So I'm difficult?"

I was determined to stick to my guns. "*The* most difficult man I've met."

He drew the tip of his nose down my neck, bringing my hands down as he went even lower, until his face was level with my breasts. I squirmed underneath him.

"What are you doing?" I whispered.

"Convincing you to reconsider."

My breath hitched. He drew the tip of his nose along the underside slowly. Every cell pulsed in anticipation. When he continued the strenuous torture on the upper part, I felt like crying out. What was happening? How could every inch of my skin be so responsive? My nipples were so taut, so desperate for his touch. I wanted to grab something, tug, scratch, but he wasn't letting go of my hands. There was no reprieve for the tension building inside me.

"You've gone quiet," he taunted. The mere feel of his hot breath on my sensitive skin was driving me crazy.

Still… I wouldn't go down that easy. I had no clue why I was so stubborn, but on I went.

"Just enjoying this," I murmured.

He smiled against my skin, looking up from between my breasts. Then he trailed a path of kisses up my sternum, blissfully ignoring my nipples. He brought his mouth to my ear.

"I don't want to leave this room," he murmured in my ear. "I want to stay here, with you, so I don't have to share you with anybody."

"And you think you'd be able to convince me?"

"I'm sure."

I wiggled my eyebrows. "I think you're giving yourself too much credit."

He cocked a brow, and I knew I was in deep

trouble. He let go of one of my hands, skimming his palm downward, over my nipple. He only touched it lightly, but my skin was so sensitive that I moaned, clenching my thighs, trapping him between them.

He laughed, planting a kiss squarely on my belly. I wasn't a quitter, but I knew when to throw in the towel.

"Fine, I admit it. I'm totally on board with your plan to keep me captive here."

He laughed, leaning over me and rewarding me with a kiss that made my toes curl. I took advantage of him letting his guard down and pushed my pelvis up, shoving him away with my hands. He fell sideways, and I immediately climbed on top of him.

"What are you doing?" he asked.

"I had a plan before you sidetracked me with your bossy ways."

"And what's that?"

"Want to give all this the attention it deserves." I drew my fingers over his chest to emphasize my point.

"You ignored it before."

I shook my head. "The first step was to lie on you and cuddle."

"And the second one?"

"Wait and see, Mr. Statham. Wait and see."

I mapped his upper body with my fingers, drawing small circles, touching every line and every dent. He was patient, I had to give him that. Although, judging by the feral, barely hanging-in-there look in his eyes, I wasn't sure how long this would last.

When I placed my lips on his skin just above his navel, he let out a low grunt. Yeah… he was getting closer to that breaking point by the second. I tried not to smile against his skin… and failed. I just couldn't help myself.

When I parted my lips, dipping the tip of my tongue in the dent between his six-pack, he tugged lightly at my hair.

"Sienna," he grunted, "you're driving me crazy."

"I know."

And there I went, smiling again. I looked up, only to find him gazing at me playfully.

"And pleased about it."

"Very," I admitted.

I traced a path with my mouth upward, lying on top of him again. He drew his fingers through my hair, and for a few minutes we were silent, just enjoying each other, until he asked, "What's your favorite movie?"

"Tough call. Probably the second *Hunger Games*. Why?"

"I just want to know more about you."

I propped my chin on his chest, smiling. "Okay."

"Favorite book?"

"Anything John Grisham has written."

"A thriller lover, nice."

I narrowed my eyes. "You don't sound as if

you think that's nice."

"Anything with a murder in it gives me the creeps."

I grinned. "Winston Statham, you're afraid."

"Absolutely."

"So what kind of movies do you watch?"

"I'm not much of a movie guy, never have been."

"Well, when you have younger siblings, you quickly learn that finding them movies they like is the best way to keep them entertained. I used to play Disney movies for them and watch scary stuff myself."

"You said Lucas is in London. Why?"

"His high school has an exchange program. I'm keeping my fingers crossed for him to want to stay in the US for college. I'm lobbying for nearby schools. I miss him like crazy."

"You're an adorable creature." He pushed my hair behind my ear, then he gave me a long, deep kiss that had me all tingly and fuzzy.

Not just because the kiss was twenty on a one-to-ten scale of hotness, but because he sounded genuine. He didn't think I was a meddling mother hen.

Later, when the fire was about to die out, Winston put a fresh log on top of the burned ones.

I sighed, watching him. He looked at me questioningly.

"Just enjoying the view. I don't know why,

but watching you putting wood on the fire does something to me. I think it's possibly my favorite image of you."

"Favorite? There's a rank?"

"Obviously. This has the first spot."

"And the second?"

"I'm still debating between you wearing a suit or that hot outfit you had on when you came to help with the walls."

He laughed. "You're very feisty."

"Not always."

"So it's just for me?"

"Oh, yeah."

He sat next to me on the floor, pulling me in his lap, kissing my shoulders.

"I like how smooth your skin is," he murmured.

"Thanks."

"And this delicious little ass. It's tempting me on a daily basis at the office, ever since I saw you dance." He lowered me on my back, kissing down my neck, kneading my ass. "I like the whole package," he finished.

I laced my arms around his neck, keeping him close, kissing one corner of his mouth. I loved every word he was saying.

"I can say the same about you," I murmured.

He trailed his fingers down my back, turning my skin into goose bumps.

"What was it that convinced you? My putting logs on the fire?"

"Well, that too, but the balance started tipping in your favor a while ago. I realized you can't be too bad when you said that you want to protect your parents, so they don't worry."

He swallowed, looking up at me in surprise.

"You're something else," he murmured.

"I don't want to spoil our mood, but if we don't go to sleep, we won't be any good tomorrow."

"I agree."

I wasn't feeling sleepy at all, though. And when he lifted me in his arms as if I weighed nothing, carrying me to bed, energy bubbled up in my veins.

I had too many thoughts running around in my mind. I couldn't sleep because I was too excited by life. I was in this beautiful hotel, lying next to this amazing man. The longer I thought about it, the giddier I became.

Holy shit, if I kept going at this rate, I wasn't going to sleep a wink. How could I even be so excited? Well, the better question was how could I *not* be excited?

Just sensing Winston next to me filled me with energy. And when he wrapped an arm possessively around me, whispering, "You're sleeping here. I'm not letting you out of my bed tonight," I grinned from ear to ear, looking out the window at the snow falling.

I didn't mind at all that this delicious man was keeping me captive here. Feeling him wrapped around me like this just gave me all the feels. I was so full of energy that I could have kept talking all night, but he fell asleep almost instantly.

I just lay there, listening to his even breathing, barely able to stay still when all I wanted to do was turn around and just kiss the living daylights out of him.

I managed to stay put, looking out the window for a long time. Still grinning from ear to ear.

Chapter Nineteen

Sienna

Next morning, my head weighed a ton when the alarm clock rang. Winston's chest was pressed against my back. I'd love to be woken up like this every morning, especially when I had an important meeting ahead.

The meeting! My stomach bottomed out. I forced myself to open my eyes wide.

"What time is it?" I asked.

"Seven o'clock."

"No, no, no, no."

I jumped out of bed. Bad mistake. I was so dizzy that I nearly lost my balance. Holy shit. I couldn't have gotten more than four hours of sleep. The last time I remembered looking at the digital TV clock last night, it had been half past three, and I hadn't fallen asleep right away.

Winston walked up to me, steadying me. He looked wide awake.

"What's wrong?"

"Forgot to set my alarm clock. I wanted to wake up at five so I'd have time to wash my hair and everything."

He cupped my face with both hands. "You

look perfect."

"Don't sweet-talk me so early in the morning. I'm not awake enough to resist you."

I pointed a finger at him, attempting to sound stern. He caught my wrist, kissing the back of my hand, smiling.

"I don't have time for my routine."

"Just put on a suit, and you'll be fine."

"Spoken like a man. I need more time to get ready. But I'll have to cheat today."

"I'm gonna order breakfast to be brought here while you change. What do you want?"

"Coffee. Any form they have. IV would be much appreciated. I think I just slept three hours."

"Why? We went to bed early."

I felt my cheeks flush. "I… um, couldn't fall asleep."

"Why?"

I shrugged, but Winston's expression changed subtly. His eyes narrowed at the corners. He curled his mouth into a half smile.

"Why, were you thinking about our evening?"

"Maybe."

He continued watching me intently. I pinched his chest. "Fine. *Fine*. You want to hear me say it? I was just too excited and happy to fall asleep."

He swallowed, looking at me before cupping my face and kissing me so hard that my knees gave in. I gripped his shoulders for support, hanging on to him as I surrendered to his kiss.

I didn't want to let go. Unfortunately, duty

called. I knew that the longer I gave in, the more stressful my morning would be.

But how could I let go when all I wanted was to cling to this feeling for one more minute, or at least one more second?

When Winston intensified the kiss, walking me backward until he pinned me against a wall with his hips, I knew I had to pull myself together or I'd fall to this man's charms, hook, line, and sinker.

I pushed him away playfully, then pointed a finger at him.

"Let's set some rules for this morning. Yes to breakfast. No to kissing or any shenanigans of the sexy variety."

Winston tilted his head. "I reject all these crazy ideas."

"Winston. We'll be late!"

He pinned me with that molten gaze, and I was sure that he was going to give me a knee-weakening kiss again, but to my surprise, he took a step back, leaving me space to move, though he wasn't looking away from me.

Back in my room, I went through the motions at top speed. I usually needed at least an hour, but now I managed to be ready in twenty minutes while reciting my presentation at the same time.

I had to skip styling my hair, so I just pulled it into a low bun. It worked well with my crisp suit. I usually wore casual business attire at work, but this was different.

Suits went a long way in establishing a professional image.

I didn't want to risk anyone not taking me seriously because of my age or the way I dressed.

Winston was already in the dining room when I entered it. We ate quickly, in silence, and I knew his mind was on the presentation too. No more innuendos or flirty lines.

I debated giving him one of those kisses that pushed away every thought, because I wanted to put him at ease, but at the same time, I knew we needed our head in the game.

That didn't mean I couldn't at least mentally plan ways to spoil him afterward though.

We took a cab to the building where we were meeting the board. The drive only took five minutes.

We stepped inside together and were shown to the right room by a very helpful receptionist.

Five others joined us in no time, three men and two women. We shook hands with everyone.

"Mr. Statham, I'm happy to see you again. Ms. Hensley, great to meet you in person," one of them said. I'd emailed with him last week.

I drew in a deep breath, squaring my shoulders as I stretched out my hand.

Showtime.

I was the one who started the presentation, giving them the rundown of the rebranding purpose and targets. I'd given enough presentations by now to know that eye contact was crucial.

Even when their expressions were clearly unconvinced, I didn't back down or allow myself to be intimidated. Showing doubt was a surefire way to undermine the credibility of the presentation.

"Thank you, Sienna," Winston said after my last slide came on.

We switched places, and I crossed my legs under the table as soon as I sat on one of the chairs. I wasn't watching Winston. I knew the presentation by heart. I was watching the others, trying to read their expressions, to guess what they were writing down.

All the doubts I'd kept at bay while I'd been in the front came crashing into me.

What if they didn't like the rebrand? I couldn't imagine the store closing down. It just wasn't possible.

"Winston, I was hoping to see a more drastic plan, to be honest," one of them said.

"The charity program could be scrapped completely," another said. My hackles went up.

"Why?" I asked.

"It's occupying a prime-time slot in your Christmas program. Replace it with something you can monetize."

Winston set his jaw, narrowing his eyes. "The charity program is a staple at Statham Stores. It stays."

It endeared him to me that he was fighting for the charity program, even if he was making life harder for himself.

"Our customers expect it," I said. "They like

the fuzzy feeling of having done something good."

"The fuzzy feeling factor won't bring in revenue."

"People like to know they're contributing to a cause. I can show you the comments specifically praising the charity program in our customer surveys. It makes them happy. And when they're happy, they spend more."

"As long as you have the numbers to back it up."

"We do," Winston said confidently.

We went back and forth over several points of the rebranding campaign.

I felt as if someone had placed a ten-pound weight on my shoulders as we stepped back out on the street. Winston looked even worse.

I'd hoped this would go better. Sure, it had just been the interim presentation, but we had practically not agreed on anything. Right… there was plenty of time to worry about this later. At the moment, I had one goal: take Winston's mind off the meeting.

"So, mister. I see those frown lines have multiplied. Need to do something about them."

Winston flashed me a smile. "And what would that be?"

I tapped my chin, wiggling my eyebrows. "Still trying to decide what would be more efficient."

Winston stopped walking, training his eyes on me. The sheer heat in that look made me squirm. And then he took one step in my direction, closing the distance, wrapping me in his arms.

"Let's move our flights to tomorrow."

I blew out a breath. Wow. That was definitely not what I'd been expecting.

"You want to spend another night here?"

He nodded. "I just want you all for me this weekend, Sienna. Just you and me."

My heart was beating so wildly that I couldn't focus on my thoughts. I couldn't focus on anything other than how warm and strong he felt against me.

Emotion flickered in his eyes, and I realized this was a decisive moment. If I said yes, things would shift between us.

Last night, we'd both been driven by impulse and got caught up in the heat of things, but this was... well, different. I could fall for this man in a blink of an eye. What if I got my heart broken? The fear wasn't enough to deter me from wanting to get completely lost in him. I had to change my plans for tomorrow, but I nodded, happy that I had more time to take his mind off the meeting.

"Perfect. That means I can show you even more of the area than I'd thought."

That was music to my ears. Win-win. We could worry about everything when we were back in San Francisco.

"I'm impressed. I thought you'd just keep me captive inside the hotel."

His eyes flashed. "I plan to do that too. My suite."

I held up a finger. "Well, if you have the

fireplace lit and room service, I'm sold."

"I see. Those are the only selling points?"

"What else could be a selling point? Oh yes, a certain sexy boss making the fire, then doing me."

He kissed me right there in the street, then smiled against my lips, and my heart doubled in size because he seemed to have slipped into the same happy place he'd been in yesterday.

Then we decided to head to the hotel first and change into comfortable clothes.

"Let's check on Joey," I said when we climbed out of the car in front of the building.

"Only you can give a snowman a name."

"Hello, *Frosty the Snowman*? Haven't you seen *Jack Frost*?"

"Not a movie guy, remember?"

I glanced at him over my shoulder. "Right, I think it might be time to change that. You know what Joey needs?"

"What?"

"A friend."

Winston looked perplexed. "You want another snowman? Please tell me you're joking."

I couldn't hide my grin anymore. Winston pounced on me the next second, and we both tumbled to the ground in the fluffy snow, which somehow managed to get in everywhere: in my mouth, my nose, my hair. We were making a mess out of our suits.

I forgot all about it when he kissed me, keeping me pinned against the snowy ground.

We only headed inside after we were drenched and cold.

Winston ran his hands up and down my arms in the elevator. I was shivering.

"I'm surprised you're not trying to convince me to go to the sauna again," I joked.

"That was just an excuse for me to spend more time with you."

"And now you don't need underhanded tricks to get me alone anymore?"

"Exactly."

Chapter Twenty

Sienna

I was supposed to go to the Bennett house tomorrow. I could say that the business trip had been extended, which was only half a lie. But I didn't like lying at all. Besides, no one would believe it, so I simply decided to tell Victoria what was going on.

Sienna: Winston asked me to stay the whole weekend, and I agreed, so I'll have to miss out on the get-together.

I also sent Pippa the same message. The girls answered at the same time.

Victoria: You're doing the boss, aren't you? Good for you :-D Keep me updated.

Pippa: OMG I NEED DETAILS.

I typed and deleted about five messages to Pippa before settling on a final version.

Sienna: That would be a very long message. I'll tell you in person.

Pippa: You're mean.

Chuckling, I pocketed my phone. For sure the next time I saw them, I'd have to spill the beans on everything. I couldn't wait.

Sharing was natural to me. Victoria and I had always been close, and when we joined the Bennett family, well... Pippa took everything to the next level.

I just loved dissecting every detail with the girls. It was also helpful to uncover red flags. I wasn't kidding myself. I was naive when it came to certain things, and Pippa and Victoria had more experience. While I was with Trevor, they'd pointed out he was spending a lot of his evenings separate from me. I still remembered how small I'd felt when he'd clarified that he'd felt pressured and just couldn't deal with me anymore.

Even though I didn't want to bring up work again, I had a burning question.

"What will happen to you and your parents if the store closes down?" I asked when he came into my room after we changed out of our suits.

"They have enough savings, and I've made investments since I went to college, so I'm all set. This isn't about us. It's... the flagship store is my family's pride, and a lot of people work there. Their lives would be turned upside down. Some have been with the store since my parents ran it. They're an integral part of it. They're my responsibility, and I won't let them down."

I think I fell a little more for him right then and there. But damn, I'd had to spoil the mood by bringing this up again. Those pesky worries were weighing on him again.

"I have rules for this afternoon," I announced.

"You don't say. What did I tell you about that?"

I held up a finger. "Wait. Hear me out first. You're gonna love them. No to talking or thinking about work. Yes to having fun, and double yes to sexy shenanigans."

"I'm on board with that."

He came closer, and by the way his eyes smoldered, I knew we weren't going to go out right away.

"I still want to see Vermont," I warned.

"Whatever the lady commands."

I had to give Winston credit; he did stick to his original plan of showing me the surroundings. The city was lovely. We spent an inordinate amount of time in one of the residential neighborhoods, because I just couldn't get enough of those idyllic homes. I kept making up stories about how the lives of those inside them could potentially be.

By the time we were done, I was so drunk on Burlington and Vermont in general that I could barely believe it.

***

Winston

"I know it sounds crazy, but I could see myself living here. I mean, hypothetically, of course. I wouldn't leave San Francisco in a million years. But I could totally see myself living in one of these houses, with the white fence and the perfectly sized garden. I'd have an indoor and outdoor Christmas tree. And I'd—"

She stopped talking. "Why are you watching me like this?"

"You fascinate me, that's all."

For me, a house was a house. But with Sienna, it was a place to live, a story, a life that could unfold inside. I couldn't wait to experience more with her at my side.

"It's Saturday. That means there's a chance there is a tree lighting ceremony in the area if we're lucky," I said.

"Yes. I love those. I know we have a ton in San Francisco, but I'd love to see one in a city where we don't have palm trees next to the Christmas tree, you know?" She clapped her hands, making me laugh.

"Let me check."

I googled nearby events and stumbled upon a list.

"Here it is. Two towns over. Forty-minute drive."

"Can we go?" her eyes were brightly lit, and she was bouncing back and forth on her feet.

"Yes, we're going."

She brought her arms around my neck, kissing me. Before I realized what she was doing, she jumped in my arms. I caught her by the ass, steadying her.

"Don't do this again in the middle of the

street, Sienna."

"Why not?" she challenged.

"Might give me… interesting ideas."

"I thought we were going to see a tree-lighting ceremony."

"We are. Not much I wouldn't give you right now."

"All it takes is me kissing you?"

"Don't forget jumping me."

"I foresee lots of things going my way in the future if this is all I have to do to convince you."

The evening flew by faster than I'd hoped. I'd been in this area a few times for board meetings, but it was like rediscovering it all over again. It was very late by the time we returned to the hotel. Sienna was all smiles, chattering nonstop about the event, how we could integrate some details in the store's Christmas program.

"What would you think about adding a tree ceremony?" she asked.

"I think that you're brilliant. It works with our brand, and why not make an event out of it?"

"We're a great team."

"That we are."

When I busied myself at the fireplace, she sipped wine, just looking out the window. It was snowing again.

"What are you thinking about?"

"That I don't ever want to leave this place. It's so pretty."

"I can easily arrange that."

"Can you now? I doubt it."

"I'm the boss, remember?"

"I think I do, but if you want to remind me, I won't say no."

"I can make our own schedule, decide we need to stick around here, work remotely."

She narrowed her eyes, sliding a finger down my torso. "Somehow, I don't think we'd get much work done, would we?"

"You're right. What if we come back here another weekend?"

"Why would you do that?"

I traced the contour of her mouth with my fingers. "Look at that smile."

She tried to tone it down but only managed to turn it into a grin. Nudging closer to me, she hid her face in my chest.

"You won't hear me say no. Want to take a bath in the tub?"

"Sure."

"Awesome. That way I can get you to relax. I'm seeing some broody lines I don't like again."

I swallowed. "That obvious?"

"A little."

"I'm just thinking about the best way to secure everyone's jobs. But I don't want to ruin our mood with business talk."

She rose on her toes, lacing her hands behind the back of my head. "You're not. You can talk about it all you want."

This woman got to me in a way no one else did. The sincerity in her eyes slayed me.

"So, mister. Get in the tub. I'll give you a massage while you tell me everything that's on your mind."

She started by massaging my shoulders, but her hands kept slipping on my chest while I spoke.

"This massage is more for you than me. You're feeling me up."

"I'd deny it, but it's true."

"Maybe I should teach you a lesson. Feel *you* up. Tease you, drive you crazy for me."

"You took me to a tree-lighting ceremony. You can get away with *so* much right now. Right…probably shouldn't have given that away."

I pulled her in my lap, splashing water everywhere, wiggling my eyebrows. "Probably not."

Chapter Twenty-One

Sienna

On Monday, the celebratory vibe from the Christmas party seemed to carry on at the office. There was some leftover punch in the kitchen, though no one was starting to drink that early. Someone was listening to carols.

I smiled to myself, imagining Winston's expression when he heard it. Just at the thought of him, my palms grew sweaty. My cheeks and neck felt on fire.

It was only after I unpacked my bag at home last night that I realized we hadn't spoken about us—specifically, about how things were going to be between us from now on.

Had it been only a weekend thing? My entire body felt icy cold at the thought. It couldn't be. He'd been so sweet and loving, and the way he'd spoken had sounded as if he considered this more than a fling.

The more I thought about it, the giddier I became. When Winston arrived, the entire floor gathered for the monthly goal-setting meeting.

I worked "Mr. Statham" into my sentences as many times as possible. Perhaps a few too many, judging by Winston's amused glances, but I tried my best to be as professional as always.

It quickly became obvious we weren't on the same page. Winston wasn't even trying. He wasn't being smooth at all.

He replied with "Sienna" to my every "Mr. Statham," and the way he looked at me was downright shameless. Every time our gazes crossed, I felt as if he was physically touching me. Could anyone else feel this energy between us too?

Once the meeting was over, a few of us gathered in the kitchen for a cup of coffee.

"Anyone notice the boss smiling?" one of my colleagues asked.

"I thought I was imagining it. I didn't even know Winston knew how to smile," Mara said.

Half the team turned to me. "Sienna, what do you know?"

My ears felt on fire. "What do you mean?"

"You're closest to him. Any reason the boss is less grouchy today? We need to know what brought on the good mood so we can keep him this way."

Shit. If they could tell something was different with Winston, surely they could tell the same about me. I felt as if it was written on my forehead, as if this giddiness was just floating around me. I barely kept from grinning.

"I couldn't say."

"Well, since he's in a good mood, we should take advantage," Mara said. "Since the party was such a great success, I had an idea. Why don't we make an eggnog stand just for employees? Up here, so we don't mix up with customers. Somewhere we can stop by after the workday's over and relax? We could leave it until the New Year. The days between Christmas and the thirty-first are the most stressful for the poor schmucks like me who have to work. Would be great to have something to look forward to every day."

"I love the idea," I declared.

"Love it enough to run it by the boss?" Mara asked.

I was slowly becoming the team's messenger, but I couldn't blame them.

"I will," I assured her.

I was trying to imagine how this would play out. Even before the weekend, every interaction with Winston had left me simmering.

Now that everything had intensified by a factor of ten... Damn! My heart rate quickened simply at the prospect of talking to him alone. How was I supposed to do my job when my mind was on Winston half the time?

I was on the phone almost the entire morning, negotiating rates for the Christmas program. I'd just finished the conversation when I checked my emails. One stood out.

Subject: Urgent
Sienna, I need you in my office.

He'd sent it only a few minutes ago. Licking

my lips, I stood from my desk. Why did he need to see me? It was unlike Winston not to include any instructions in his emails.

The door to his office was open, and the second I stepped inside, my breath caught. He was leaning against his desk, arms crossed over his chest.

"Close the door," Winston said in a low, rich voice.

***

Winston

"What's this about? You didn't give any details in your email."

I'd been looking forward to this moment all morning. Having Sienna all to myself.

Was it crazy that I missed her even though I'd been with her all weekend? From the moment I dropped her off at her house yesterday, all I could think about was going back.

I tilted my head, studying her. I'd barely kept myself from pulling her out of that meeting room after every "Mr. Statham" to kiss her until she whispered "Winston" in that same shaky voice she'd used on our trip.

"I just wanted to be alone with you."

"Okay." She gave me a small, shy smile, and I lost the little composure I had. I strode across the room and kissed her right there, against the door.

Damn, this hadn't been how I'd wanted to do this. I'd planned to talk to her about our weekend first, about what would come next, but I couldn't stop kissing her long enough to talk. She tasted so sweet that I couldn't help myself, and I deepened the kiss. I pushed her against the door with my hips.

"Winston," she murmured.

"That's right. Winston. Not Mr. Statham." I looked her straight in the eyes. "What was up with that?"

"I was just... I don't know. Trying to sound professional." She blushed, lowering her gaze, shrugging. It just made me want to kiss her again, but I stopped myself. I couldn't taste her again and stop at her mouth this time.

"I've wanted to kiss you all morning." I feathered my thumb over her mouth, pressing lightly on the bow of her upper lip. Her eyes widened slightly. "You're surprised."

"I didn't know how things would be between us. We haven't talked about it."

"Yes, that's why I asked you here. To talk. And now all I want is to kiss you, touch you. The entire morning during that meeting I had to remind myself that we weren't alone. This weekend was the best thing that's happened to me in years, Sienna. Just spending time with you makes me ridiculously happy."

She grinned. "That's music to my ears, Mr. Statham."

I cupped her ass with both hands, bringing her flush against me. She exhaled sharply.

"Next time you call me that, I'll just kiss you

right where we are."

"You wouldn't."

"Yes, I would, and you know it."

She tried to wiggle out of my grasp, but I didn't relent.

"What will the others say?"

"You don't want anyone else to know?" I asked sharply.

"I don't want to keep this a secret. But I am a bit concerned that you're going to make a spectacle of us."

I grinned. "No promises."

"See? You terrible man."

She sighed, and now she did look a little troubled.

"What's wrong?"

"Nothing."

"Sienna, I want to know what you're thinking. What's bothering you. Tell me."

"Bossy through and through, aren't you?"

"You already know the answer to that. So, tell me. I'm not letting you go until you do."

"That doesn't sound so bad." She shimmied against me, and I barely held back a groan.

"Sienna, don't stall."

"Okay. Well… I'm a bit afraid that things will become weird with the rest of the team. And if we fall apart, then it'll be very strange."

I touched her chin, tilting it up, wanting eye contact. She was always so cheerful and happy that noticing that sliver of fear in her eyes felt like a punch. I wanted to erase all that completely.

"Sienna, it won't be weird. Everyone adores you."

I adored her.

"And as to this falling apart… I don't want you to waste one second thinking about that. I know it's early, and I know all we have are months of bickering and an incredible weekend, but I don't want you worrying about that. I won't let you."

"Not saying I'll worry, but just in case I do, how will you stop me?" She was smiling again, teasing me.

"I have my ways." I touched her chin before lingering on the corners of her mouth. The starry look was back in her eyes. Good. I wanted to keep it there.

"Everyone noticed that you're smiling more, by the way," she said.

I cocked a brow.

"Don't you go back to your dictatorial ways. They're just warming up to you. Oh, and everyone loved the party, and we think it would be great to have an eggnog stand until New Years for after-work refreshment."

"Why hasn't HR told me anything?"

"They think I'll have a better chance of obtaining approval."

"You're using your influence on the boss to get your way?"

"Guilty. But is it working?"

"Keep the eggnog stand. But I want

something in return."

She licked her lips. "Okay."

"Let me take you to dinner tomorrow."

"I already have plans with my family."

"The next evening?"

"We're doing the tree-lighting ceremony, remember?"

"I can't believe you organized that so quickly. After that."

"Won't it be too late? And besides, we'll eat at the event. Plus, we have dinner together every evening while we work on the rebrand campaign."

"Woman, I just want to take you somewhere. Stop giving me a hard time and say yes, or I'll kiss you until you do."

She burst out laughing, which made me realize she'd been teasing me on purpose.

"Yes, boss. Though I'll take that delicious dirty kiss too."

Chapter Twenty-Two

Sienna

I couldn't wait for the afternoon to end. Winston had a late meeting so we were skipping our evening session. Pippa, Victoria, and I were going to get drinks, which was code for having to fill them in on the weekend.

At five o'clock, just as I was gathering my things, I heard their voices in the corridor. Why were they here? We usually met in front of the store.

"Hey, girl," Victoria greeted, stepping inside my office.

"What are you doing here? I thought we were meeting downstairs."

Victoria shrugged with so much nonchalance that I immediately suspected my sister was up to something.

And when Pippa added, "I'd never seen your office. I was curious," I didn't just suspect, I *knew* they were up to something.

She and Pippa kept looking to their left and right, over their shoulders. I had a hunch I knew why the girls had come up. They wanted a glimpse of Winston.

He was still here, and I was about to reach for

my phone to send him a text, warning him that if he came out of the office, he'd walk straight into the lion's den, but I didn't get a chance. Winston's voice boomed down the corridor the next second.

"Sienna, are you still here?"

"Yes."

Pippa and Victoria exchanged triumphant looks. Yep. I'd been spot-on.

By the sinfully hot look he gave me when he entered the room, he hadn't come there with innocent intentions. Then he noticed Pippa and Victoria.

"Winston, this is my sister Victoria," I said quickly. "And this is Pippa Bennett-Callahan."

Winston shook hands with Victoria first.

"Victoria, Sienna told me you advised her about the decorations this year. Didn't get a chance to thank you."

"It was my pleasure."

"Sienna said you were booked far in advance ahead of time this year, but hopefully we'll be able to officially collaborate next year. I'm sure Sienna will love working with you in an official capacity. Of course, that is if she doesn't leave me by then."

Focusing on Pippa now, he added, "She also says you keep tempting her with offers to move to Bennett Enterprises."

"I am," Pippa said playfully.

"Fair warning, I'm going to use any and every tactic to keep her here as long as possible."

I knew the girls well enough to realize they

were both melting. Hell, *I* was melting.

Was he doing it on purpose? What was I saying? Of course he was. He was winning the girls over. He planned to keep me here, did he? He hadn't told me any of that.

This was a whole new level of charm—and I absolutely loved it.

"Right. What I have to say can wait until tomorrow, Sienna. Have fun."

Amusement flashed in his gaze.

"We'll wait for you by the elevator," Pippa said.

Victoria hurried after her. Now they were leaving, were they? After they'd ambushed Winston in his own office building.

"Did I pass the test?" he asked the second we were alone.

"What test?"

"I don't know. You tell me." He gestured with his head in the direction of the door.

I grinned. "They'll tell me later, but my money is on a resounding yes. You were quite the charmer."

"Everything I said was true."

"Including the part where you plan to keep me here by any and every means?" I paraphrased.

"Especially that one."

"And what exactly does that imply?"

He smiled ruefully, coming closer. "You'll see."

"Keeping me on my toes, huh?"

He drew a small circle on my temple with the

YOUR CHRISTMAS LOVE

tip of his nose. "I don't want to keep you on your toes. I just want to keep you."

I blushed. No man I'd ever dated had spoken to me this way. So openly and determinedly.

We were close enough that he was going to kiss me, I was sure of that. But then he just pushed a few strands of hair out of my face, smiling before stepping back.

"They're waiting for you."

"No goodbye kiss?"

Winston laughed. "If I had it my way, I'd kiss you all night. So, unless you want me to convince you to leave with me, off you go."

It was my turn to laugh. "Ha! You're awfully full of yourself if you think I'd ditch the girls for you."

"Want to test my theory?" His tone was playful, but his gaze so molten hot that I instantly lit up. He had so much power over me that it scared me. Before I could respond, he pulled me toward him, and when his mouth came down on mine, I thought I might explode from the way he claimed my lips.

I ran my fingers through his hair, tugging and pulling and just about jumping him. And when he pushed his pelvis into me, trapping me between the edge of the desk and himself, I groaned in his mouth.

I playfully pushed him away, pointing a finger at him.

"You can't kiss me like this."

"Why? Has it made you change your mind?"

I shook my head. "Of course not."

"Liar. What if I do this?" He feathered his fingers down the sides of my neck, moving them in slow, seductive circles to the straps of my dress.

"No." My voice was a little uneven.

"And this?" He slipped his thumbs under the straps. Wow. I had to pull myself together. I couldn't be *this* weak for him. When he moved one strap to the side, kissing the skin it had covered, I shuddered in his arms.

Damn.

I wasn't just weak, I was completely at his mercy. And by the way his lips curled into a smile against my skin, he knew it.

"Winston, you can't do this," I said weakly.

"Yes, I can. And you love it."

Straightening, he looked at me with mischief in his eyes before taking one step back.

"But I'll have you all to myself tomorrow. Can't be too greedy."

"Wow. I wasn't expecting you to be so generous."

"Don't get used to it. The closer I am to you, the more I want you, and I don't mean that simply in a physical way, Sienna."

The intense look in his eyes was slipping past defenses I didn't even know I had.

"I know," I whispered. "It's the same for me."

I'd never felt this burning need to spend every moment with a man, to see how deep our connection could grow if we both wanted it.

"See you tomorrow." He smiled, taking yet another step back.

"Have a great evening."

I felt him watch me every step of the way as I left the room.

***

The girls were waiting just at the elevators.

"You two. We need to talk." I sounded stern, but I wasn't deluding myself that it would have much of an effect.

"We're listening," Victoria said.

"I need a heads-up if you're going to stop by and ambush Winston. I'm not saying don't do it, because there's no stopping you if you want something."

Pippa laughed. "Thanks for giving us credit. But, Sienna sweetie, we were being on our very best behavior. If we'd ambushed him for real, we'd be interrogating him right now."

"Well, anyway, I'd still appreciate a heads-up."

"But then you'd stress out, and we just wanted to get a feel for the situation," Pippa said.

"And?" I asked.

"He is totally into you."

My heart felt lighter. I wanted to believe in Pippa's power of reading people now more than ever, but that seemed a rather hasty conclusion after such a short interaction.

"And you could tell that from the two sentences you exchanged?"

Pippa waved her hand. "Oh, no. From the way he acted when he noticed us. As if he was hoping Victoria and I could vanish into thin air so he could be alone with you."

My cheeks flushed. "Still... really. Let me know when you want to come up to the office."

"We won't come again," Victoria assured me.

"We just needed some first-hand observations so we could build a case for Christopher. We're still deciding what angle to use." Pippa waggled her eyebrows. "I wasn't sure before, but now I'm weighing his chances of surviving Christopher and the rest of my brothers at around fifty percent."

I burst out laughing, glancing at Victoria.

"You have nothing to add?"

"Nope. Pippa just about covered everything. Though I'd say fifty-five percent."

"Your confidence is inspiring," I teased.

After leaving the building, we went to a nail bar. It was the perfect combination of sipping drinks and having our nails done. We'd chosen a spot in Fisherman's Wharf, because we were having dinner later at Blue Moon, Alice and Blake's restaurant. We were overlooking the water, with a fantastic view of the fishing fleet. The boats and yachts there had been lit up since the lighted boat parade. I couldn't make out one from the other because the fog was thick tonight, but the faint colors cast everything in a fairy-tale-like glow.

In the distance, the Golden Gate Bridge was barely visible, just specks of light in the dark sky.

Pippa was a spa girl through and through. She loved getting pampered. Victoria and I had always been the do-it-yourself type. Growing up, we'd had a spa day one Saturday every month, on which we went as girly as we could: face masks, doing our nails, peelings. It was harder to keep the schedule after Victoria became a mom, though, so we snuck in an evening at the nail bar here and there. Chloe usually came with us too, but she was working on a school project tonight.

"I need to confess something," I said after taking a sip from my wine glass. "I'm glad Chloe isn't with us tonight."

Victoria nudged my shoulder, grinning. "Don't feel too guilty. So do I. Means we can get you to share every delicious detail with us."

"But maybe I should wait until we're at the Blue Moon so Alice can hear everything."

"Or… you can repeat everything once we're there," Victoria suggested with a grin. "I don't mind hearing everything twice."

"That's a great idea," I said.

Pippa did a little dance in her seat. "Start as early as possible and don't leave anything out."

"I wasn't planning to."

Chapter Twenty-Three

Sienna

Tree-lighting ceremonies were one of my favorite things ever. As a kid, I'd looked forward to any I could get to. Even as a teenager, they'd held a special place in my heart—it kicked off the magic season.

On the day of the tree-lighting event at Statham, I arrived at work even earlier than usual. I didn't go up to the office, remaining in the store instead, inspecting every detail.

Since I'd added it to the program at the last minute, we had to make a plethora of changes. I'd done my research, and other establishments closed for the few hours it took to prepare the ground floor for the ceremony, but I wanted it all out in the open. It meant extra work for us, because we had to maneuver everything around the customers—but I wanted them to be part of the experience from the very beginning.

The assembly team arrived at eight o'clock, and we got to work. I barely kept from squealing like a teenager when the giant fir tree was brought in. It would be the centerpiece of the store during the holiday season.

As I'd predicted, by nine o'clock, the store was as chock-full of customers as it was during rush hours. We'd put in place a red tape with a bow to separate the assembly team from the rest of the store until we were done. Kids cheered with every decoration we hung up. We'd only plug in the twinkling lights at six o'clock tonight, during the ceremony.

I was so happy, I had to fight against every instinct not to cheer with them too. I'd do this every day if I could. Once the tree was up, I moved on to rearranging the window display, so one could see the tree already just passing by the store. That task lasted well into the afternoon. Despite the tight deadline, everyone was relaxed and easygoing.

That was until five o'clock, when I felt a subtle change in the atmosphere. Everyone stood ramrod straight, suddenly very focused. I didn't think much of it and just went on about my task, right until I heard someone say, "Everything's running according to the schedule, Mr. Statham."

I licked my lips, feeling prickles of awareness at the back of my neck. The boss was here?

"I didn't take him for the type to oversee things like this," said one of the guys who moved around mannequins.

Honestly, neither did I. Where was he, anyway? I glanced to my right, surprised to find Winston directly in my line of vision, as if I'd instinctively *felt* where he was. He was watching me and making no secret of it.

I smiled at him before returning to my task, but my skin still felt on fire. He kept watching me, I was sure of that. When I finished the window display, I went to plug in the twinkling lights adorning it.

I'd barely made contact with the plug when I felt a burning sensation on my forearm. Yelping, I pulled my hand back. *Ouch, ouch, ouch.*

The small electric shock passed the next second, but my skin was pink where it had touched the wire. It still stung, but I tried to hide it, just requesting another set of twinkling lights, since this one was useless.

I was convinced I'd fooled everyone, right until Winston walked up to me.

"Show me your hand."

"It's nothing."

"Show me your hand," he repeated. His voice was low but commanding. I held up my arm. His eyes flashed as he inspected the pink line. It looked worse than I remembered and felt just as bad.

"Come on, let's go."

"Where?"

"The ER."

"Don't be ridiculous. I just need to put some honey on it."

He cocked a brow. "Honey?"

"It has antiseptic properties."

"Sienna, don't be difficult."

"I'm staying until we light up the tree."

"No, you're not."

"Winston—"

"You're not. We're leaving now. I'll carry you out even with everyone watching."

"I'd like to see you try."

His eyes flashed. Holy shit, challenging Winston when he was this determined was a dangerous endeavor. Still, I didn't back down. Even knowing he might make good on it, I didn't want to give in.

"I'm here to oversee the ceremony. And it doesn't hurt anymore."

"Second degree burns don't hurt right away because you can't feel the nerve endings anymore."

"Second degree… Winston," I huffed in exasperation.

I was a little disarmed because he sounded so concerned. All right, a lot disarmed. But it was a ridiculous concern. The wire had barely touched me. Still, the longer I kept his stare, the more obvious it became that if I didn't give in at least a bit, he was going to keep pushing.

"We can have a doctor look at this after we're done here."

"We're staying until the ceremony is over. Not one minute longer."

"Yes, sir."

Not wanting to give him a chance to reconsider, I strode back to my team quickly. When I glanced over my shoulder, that look in his eyes was just as intense as before, but a hint of a smile played on his lips.

I found honey in the food court, and after smearing some on the burn, it immediately felt better.

By the time six o'clock rolled around, everything was in place. I had no idea who was more excited: the customers or me. Just waiting for the lights to go up filled me with so much joy, I felt like jumping up and down.

Out of the corner of my eye, I spied Winston walking straight toward me.

"I didn't think you'd linger," I said when he was close enough. "Actually I wasn't expecting to see you here at all, Mr. Grinch."

Winston pinned me with his gaze, and that smile of his told me I was missing something.

"I had a strong incentive: seeing a certain beautiful woman."

"And who might that be? You think she knows you're here?" I asked playfully. I was swooning.

"Might have to kiss her right now, so there's no room for doubt." He dropped his gaze to my mouth. I felt warm from the tips of my fingers to my toes. He was leading this push and pull so subtly, but all it took was one touch and I became undone. Or in this case… one look.

"Winston, shhh," I muttered, biting down a smile.

The lights were lit up one by one, completely captivating me. The kids in the crowd cheered, and even some adults—I was among them. I always felt like a child on Christmas. The sixteen-foot tree was simply glorious, with huge red bows and golden ornaments. At the bottom of it were huge presents.

My heart was a little heavy, wondering if he was having a good time or if this just served as a reminder for the deadline ahead.

I looked at Winston again. He was *still* looking at me.

"You missed the lights being switched on?" I admonished him. He just shrugged, but he had a full-on smile now. It made me immensely happy that he enjoyed it, that I'd played a small part in bringing back the joy of Christmas for him.

"Ceremony's over," he said.

"My hand is f—"

I'd been about to say fine but stopped at the expression on his face.

"It's silly to go to the ER. They're busy with real emergencies. I can go to my GP tomorrow."

Winston said nothing, but his expression was mutinous.

"Fine. Let's go."

I felt his hand at the small of my back as he led me out of the store. I didn't know why, but this small gesture made me feel *so* protected. Several of my coworkers glanced at us, and I realized that everyone would put two and two together after this. And when he took it one step further, lacing his arm around my waist, pulling me closer, I just melted into his touch.

Oh, well… why pretend? I worked hard. If

anyone thought I was getting any favors, they could shove their opinion somewhere.

Once we entered the hospital, I started to feel a little ridiculous, because people lining up at the ER had serious problems, not a minor burn. We were wasting everyone's time. I tried to reason with Winston. He wouldn't hear of it.

"Sienna! We're staying here until someone checks your hand. That was the deal."

I couldn't help it. I brought my good hand up in a salute. "Sir, yes, sir."

Winston watched me for a beat before pulling me to him. He kissed me gently, as if he feared I might break.

"I know this isn't convenient but better safe than sorry, okay?" he muttered. "I'd hate for you to be in pain later just because we were too impatient."

We waited for two hours until a doctor finally looked at my arm, declaring it perfectly fine.

"There are general practitioners for this," he said sternly. "We deal with emergencies here."

"It was all his idea," I said at once, pointing at Winston, who'd come in with me. "No amount of persuasion worked."

The good doctor glanced at Winston, shaking his head. I was dangling my feet, waggling my eyebrows at Winston, who didn't even look ten percent guilty or ashamed. Then the doctor focused on me again.

"Wait until you have children. Bet he'll be one of those dads driving to the hospital for a scratch."

My cheeks heated up. Then my neck and ears. Winston was grinning from ear to ear.

"Nothing wrong with your arm. Go home and never let him bring you to the ER unless it's a real emergency."

"Will do. Thank you."

My face was still hot as I hopped off the bed, heading out the corridor with Winston.

"Where are you taking me?" I asked him.

"Hmm?"

"For our date. You bossed me into going out to dinner with you today, and instead, you brought me to the ER. I still want that dinner though. And I'm starving, so wherever you take me better serve fast."

"How about I make dinner for you?"

"Absolutely. Last time was delicious."

"We can also pick up dessert on the way."

"That sounds decadent. And I'm completely for it."

Smiling, he brought his mouth down on mine. He'd held back during the last kiss, but now?

He kissed me as if he was one step from yanking my dress away.

Chapter Twenty-Four

Sienna

Winston lived in a beautiful apartment overlooking the San Francisco bay. In the distance, I could even see the Golden Gate bridge.

I was looking around with a huge grin on my face. I *loved* being in his apartment. It was like having an inside view of who he really was, seeing this personal side to him.

"What's going on in your mind?"

"Nothing," I said a little too quickly. He immediately caught on that I wasn't exactly truthful.

"That smile doesn't look like nothing." He wrapped an arm around my waist, pulling me to him, kissing one corner of my mouth, then the other before tracing the contour of my lower lip with his mouth, giving me just the tip of his tongue. It was enough to make heat curl through me.

The way this man could light up my body was incredible. It was as if he'd discovered the secret to what my body needed—something no one had done before.

When he pulled back, he was smiling from ear to ear.

"I just like seeing your lair. Says a lot about

you," I said.

"A lot of good things, I hope?"

"Why do you think I'm smiling?"

His smile turned into a grin as I looked around. His furniture was brand-new, in shades of white and dark blue.

To my astonishment, I spotted a plastic fir tree in one corner. It was sad and lonely without any decorations whatsoever.

"What's with that?" I asked.

"The building management put one in every apartment."

"I'm not a fan of plastic trees."

"I don't like them either. We can go buy a real one if you want."

Oh my God. Was he saying what I thought he was saying?

"Mr. Grinch, let me see if I got this right. You want a Christmas tree. In your apartment."

"Yes."

I was barely keeping myself from jumping in his arms. And then I realized… why hold back at all? I pressed my palms down on his shoulders for leverage before literally jumping him.

Winston had good reflexes, only he wasn't quick enough. He realized what I was up to one second too late. He caught me, but our balance was precarious.

We barreled straight toward the couch.

He grinned, lowering me on it. "What's this for?"

"Just expressing my happiness. I promise to give you some sort of warning next time."

He touched my lips with his thumb, looking down at me with so much warmth that I just wanted to pull him closer and not let him go.

"Let me know when you want to go shopping. We also need to buy Christmas ornaments. I just moved here and didn't have time for anything. Thank God the place was furnished."

"How many ornaments exactly am I allowed?"

"Your call."

"Have you seen the office? You *cannot* give me free rein."

He touched the tip of his nose to mine.

"Yes, I can. And I am."

"Why?"

"I want you to like it here, Sienna."

Were those butterflies in my stomach? Yep, most definitely. An entire army of them.

He was still hovering above me, one knee propped on the couch between my legs.

"I want you to be happy. I want to bring you here as often as possible, keep you here."

My breath caught. His fingers touched my lips and then my neck. He looked at me as if nothing else mattered more than me.

"And what exactly do you plan to do with me?" I teased.

He pressed his thumb against my mouth. I parted my lips lightly, licking it. His eyes darkened.

"Right now, I'm going to feed you. And after that, I'll have my fill of you. All night long, Sienna."

He moved off the couch, heading to the kitchen. I shimmied in place before rising to my feet. This man had a way with words that was just more than my body could take.

"What are you feeding me?" I asked.

"Grilled cheese sandwiches work for you?"

"Sure. I eat anything."

He pointed a finger at me. "What's that semipout?"

Damn. He'd caught that?

"Well… after the delicious rice you whipped up at my house, I kind of thought you cooked gourmet food at your place. At least we bought cupcakes for dessert."

He laughed. "I don't even have food in the fridge. Don't have time to cook for myself right now. I just eat on the go."

"What do you do after you leave the office?" I asked, confused.

"Most days I head to the gym. We've got one here on the top floor. It's the only way I manage to unwind. Otherwise I'm too wired up to sleep."

I could relate, sort of. But I didn't have anywhere near Winston's responsibility on my shoulders. I couldn't even fathom how that had to feel. I could help though, couldn't I?

I tilted my head to one side, drumming my fingers on the counter.

"You have that smile again," he pointed out

playfully.

"Nothing against the gym, I just thought of a more delicious way for you to unwind."

"All part of my plan."

"Silly me. Of course, it is."

I helped him get everything ready for the sandwiches. While slicing the cheese, I accidentally dropped the knife on the floor.

"Oops. Sorry."

"You're not much of a cook?"

"Not really, but…" Tilting my head, I added playfully, "I don't know if I should tell you this next thing…"

"Tell me what?"

"I just can't seem to focus when you're around. You distract me."

He snapped his gaze up from my finger, and oh my… that look was in equal parts smoldering and affectionate.

"What exactly distracts you?"

"I could show you, but we might end up without dinner."

"I don't mind. I'm hungry for you, Sienna." His voice sounded on a lower octave than before. My body hummed, as if he was touching my bare skin.

"No, no. I'm starving, mister."

We worked side by side, and the sandwiches were ready in no time. We ate them right there at the kitchen counter. Turns out Winston was starving too.

"You know, we served appetizers at the store. If you hadn't been an ogre, insisting on going to the

ER, we could have tasted them."

Winston set his empty plate down, watching me intently, moving toward me.

"You overestimate my self-restraint if you think I would have waited any longer to have you all to myself."

Wow. What could I say to that? Somehow, he was wrapped around me again. His hands on my hips, his knee nudging my legs apart. "I've waited the whole evening to touch you. Taste you."

He trailed his lips down the side of my neck, setting on fire every inch of skin. I had no idea how my body could react so fast to a simple touch.

"I won't say no to being spoiled."

He laughed against my skin. I loved feeling the sharp exhales on every guffaw. I loved that I could make him laugh so easily. Only a few weeks ago, I wasn't even sure Winston knew how to smile, let alone laugh, and look at him now.

"So I'm an ogre when I take you to ER, but now I can spoil you?"

"Yep."

He watched me intently, touching his fingers to my cheek.

"What am I going to do with you, Sienna?"

I didn't *ever* want him to stop looking at me this way. It filled me with warmth, and so much happiness that I felt as if I was going to burst with it.

"I don't know. What are the options?"

"Still considering them."

"While you do, how about a tour of the

apartment?"

***

Winston

"Sure."

I had three bedrooms, and the master bedroom had an enormous bathroom with a tub the size of a small swimming pool.

The whole place was huge, but it had been the only one available for rent in this building when I'd arrived, and I'd wanted to be close to the store. It was a waste, because I didn't spend much time in it; though if I had Sienna here with me, I might just change that.

I'd thought that the feeling of relaxation I'd felt in Burlington had been because of the change of scenery, and because it had been the weekend.

I'd been wrong. It was all Sienna. I couldn't be around her and *not* relax. Something about her just demanded that I live in the moment and enjoy it for all it was worth.

"You don't have a home office?" she asked, after inspecting the third bedroom.

"I thought it would be better if I didn't have one officially, but I just end up working on my laptop."

Reports were lying everywhere. I picked them up as I went through the apartment, bringing them to the living room.

"I keep thinking that if I change the scenery, I'll come up with a solution I haven't seen before." I was about to launch into another conversation about the rebranding campaign but caught myself just in time. "Sorry, I don't want to talk about work again. Don't want you to think that's all there is to me."

Sienna trailed her fingers up my torso, resting her palms on my shoulders.

"Winston, I like this about you. That you feel so responsible for the team, that you're tirelessly searching for a solution. You have plenty of money. You could just close the store and be done with it. So many in your place wouldn't bother. I admire you for not choosing the easy way out."

She admired me. This was such a different reaction than what I was used to that I couldn't wrap my mind around her words, let alone answer. So, I didn't even try. I kissed her instead, long and deep, and I knew that I couldn't stop at that one kiss. I'd been starved for her ever since we returned from Burlington. Seeing her around the office all the time was a special form of torture. She was close but untouchable. Just in my reach, but not quite. I had to fight with myself constantly to keep myself from calling her into my office under any pretext and just having my way with her... because one kiss could easily escalate into more. I'd always prided myself on my discipline and self-control, but both those things went up in smoke when Sienna was around.

But now I had her here, at my mercy. I'd told her I intended to get my fill of her, but I was beginning to think it just wasn't realistic. Everything about Sienna—her laughter, the way she looked at me and seemed to understand me in a way no one else did, the way she kissed me back—just made it impossible to stop craving her.

I could just picture sharing my evenings with her like this... and the mornings.

If I told her that, she'd probably think I was crazy, and yet, I couldn't stop picturing that.

She made delicious little sounds I drank up.

I was already rock-hard, but I wanted to prolong this foreplay, explore her. Every moan I lured out of her felt like a victory.

"Winston, what are you doing to me?" she whispered.

I could ask the same thing. I felt different when I was with her.

It was the first time in months that I felt relaxed. No, it was more than that. I felt stronger, and I knew that I was drawing that strength from her.

I moved my mouth along her neck, alternating light bites with small circles with my tongue. She shuddered in my arms, and when I claimed her mouth again in a kiss so deep that I could barely think, I bunched her dress up too, needing her skin.

A light tremor went through her when I drew my fingers up her inner thigh, inching closer to the hem of her panties.

I lingered just shy of touching it, teasing her, wanting to ramp up the anticipation, even though I was already on edge.

When I finally stroked her over the fabric, I

swallowed hard at how ready she was, how much she wanted me.

"Sienna, fuck."

I pushed her panties to one side, touching a finger along her slit. She braced both hands on my shoulders, instinctively pushing herself against the wall of the living room, closing her eyes. I touched her with slow, deliberate moves, pressing my hand against her clit, drinking in the way her thighs shook, her breath stuttered.

"Winston," she gasped. When she grabbed the collar of my shirt, pulling me closer, I completely lost my composure. I let go of her dress, gripping her hips, kissing her until she pressed her pelvis against me, trapping my erection between us.

Instinctively, I rocked my hips back and forth into her.

I needed to get her to my bed, or I'd fuck her right here against this wall. I couldn't think past how much I wanted her. I needed to claim every inch of her, mark her as mine so she'd never doubt that she belonged to me.

I slid a hand to the back of her head to protect her from the hard surface of the wall before kissing her deep and fast. She whimpered, letting out a shaky breath, rocking her hips into me, seeking even more friction.

"Bed. Now" was all I managed to say. I didn't stop kissing her, touching her, on the way to the bedroom. I didn't miss her smile either. It was different than her usual one—a little smug.

"You like this, don't you? Watching me lose control."

She grinned, shrugging one shoulder. "I do. Whatcha gonna do about it?"

"You'll see."

Before I had a chance to do anything else, Sienna braced her palms on my shoulders, jumping on me again. We fell on the mattress the next second. I stopped short of crushing her, propping my palms at the sides of her shoulders.

My nose was inches away from hers. She was grinning from ear to ear.

"Thought you said you'd warn me next time."

"Yes, but not when you plan to use your sexy skills to torture me. I want you. Right now, Winston."

The way she said my name drove me completely crazy. She stirred underneath me, and it took me a second to realize she was pulling her dress up. I looked down at every inch of skin she was slowly revealing. When her panties came into view, I gave in, fisting the fabric of the dress, pulling it over her head. She was wearing a white, lacy bra that looked stunning on her. On another night, I'd take my time admiring her, but right now, I needed to run my mouth all over her, watch her succumb to pleasure.

"Take it off," I told her.

I wanted to watch her undress for me. I held her gaze stubbornly while she opened the clasp. Her cheeks became even more flushed than before. This woman was so damn adorable that I might just not let her out of my bed again… or my apartment. Or my life.

When the bra was off, I lowered myself slowly over her, hovering with my mouth just an inch away from her skin. My breath was coming out in sharp bursts.

"Winston, please."

I rubbed my palm lightly over one nipple, moving my mouth over every inch of skin I could reach.

"Sienna, I love your taste. Your skin."

She squirmed underneath me, parting her legs invitingly. I moved even lower, taking off her panties, watching her come undone from the anticipation alone. I loved seeing her like this. So ready for me, so open. I moved my mouth down her pubis until I reached her clit, and then I drove her crazy, kissing and lightly biting the exposed flesh. I teased her until she pushed her heels in the mattress, clawing at the sheets… and my hair. When her fingers pressed against my scalp, I couldn't wait any longer.

I stepped off the bed, discarding my clothes. She propped herself up on her elbows, watching me hungrily, and when I was completely naked, she reached out a hand toward my chest. I caught it midair, turning her palm up, stealing a quick kiss before lunging over her and claiming her lips. She sighed against my mouth. I rolled us over so she was on top.

"Winston," she whispered, rolling her hips

back and forth so slowly that it was driving me insane. It felt better than anything had ever felt before. I wanted to hang on to this feeling for as long as possible.

She wrung pleasure out of me so slowly that it was killing me. Every roll of her hips brought me closer to climax, every moan of hers made me want to grip her hips and take control, bring us both over the edge. I pushed myself up on my palms in a semisitting position. I needed to kiss her, just feel her closer. Then I pushed two pillows between my back and the wall, leaning against them, leaving my hands free to explore her. I trailed my fingers along her spine, feeling her skin turn to goose bumps. Lowering my hands, I kneaded her ass cheeks, running a finger between them.

"Winston..." She clenched so tight around me that I almost came. *No.* I wanted her to get there first.

We were both sweaty, desperately chasing our climax, and I just couldn't hold back any longer.

I brought one hand to her hip, guiding her moves. She relented the next second, giving in to me. I fucking loved how fast she surrendered. I wrapped her hair around my fist, first tilting her head back, so I had access to her neck, then forward, crushing my mouth to hers, suckling on her tongue in the same rhythm I was driving inside her.

Her moans grew louder as she pulsed madly around me. She was so damn close, and so was I. I didn't stop kissing her even when she came apart. I needed to own her so completely that I wanted to capture even her sounds of pleasure.

I only lasted a few seconds longer. I came so hard that my muscles clenched almost to the point of pain.

My vision blurred from the sheer intensity of the orgasm.

"Sienna, fuuuuuck. Baby. You're…"

I couldn't form a coherent sentence, so I just kept her close.

She was breathless and soft in my arms, her knees pressing against my thighs, her forehead resting on my shoulder.

I smiled when I felt her breath slow down, and she stirred a little.

I didn't know what time it was, but I was in no hurry. I just wanted to keep her like this, feel her close, enjoy her.

"What did you do to me?" she murmured, sounding exhausted.

I laughed, bringing a hand to the back of her neck, pressing my thumbs in a light massage.

"That's good."

"We should move to the shower."

"No. I just want to stay here. And I think you agree with me."

I was still inside her and in no hurry to pull out. She flexed her inner muscles around me as if to prove her point.

I groaned, gripping her hips.

"You're a temptress, you know that?"

She laughed lightly. "Wasn't my intention to tempt you, but now that you mention it…"

She flexed those muscles again, and I had no choice but to move her off me before she tempted me too much.

"What are you doing?"

"Carrying you to the shower. Who knows what you'll do if I let you go?"

She narrowed her eyes, as if preparing to say something sassy back. To my surprise, she wrapped her legs around me when I scooped her up.

"Ha! And you think this is safe?" She touched her finger to my chest. "That's temptation right there." She moved that finger lower to my abs. "So are these."

Then she shimmied against my semihard erection, and my eyes nearly rolled back into my head.

"That's temptation too," she informed me nonchalantly.

"Then I guess I'll have to do something about it."

"I like the sound of that. Details?"

I brought my lips to her ear, biting her earlobe lightly.

"You'll have to spend the night here for that."

Damn, that had come out like a command. But now it was out there, and I couldn't wait to hear her answer. My chest constricted as silence stretched for a few seconds.

I pulled back, looking her straight in the eyes.

"That sounded almost *dictatorial*."

"I meant it as a question."

"You don't really mean anything as a question." She cocked a brow, but I was relieved at the wide smile on her lips, the twinkle of mischief in her eyes.

"What's your answer? I promise I'll take excellent care of you." On a lower note, I added, "In every way there is."

She wasn't just smiling now, she was grinning. I hadn't been so happy in a long, long time.

"I'm staying, you bossy, grouchy thing. But you'd better make good on that promise."

"Yes, ma'am."

Chapter Twenty-Five

Sienna

"Well, I think we did a splendid job."

Winston chuckled. "You mean *you* did a splendid job."

I winked. "Don't downplay your role. You cheered and gave me hot looks. Very motivating."

A few days after Winston brought me to his apartment, we went to buy the Christmas tree. That was yesterday, and I'd gone completely overboard in my enthusiasm to decorate it. Winston merely watched me with amusement, then convinced me to stay overnight using dirty tricks. But guess who wasn't complaining? That's right. Me.

So even though today was a Monday morning, I was in an excellent mood.

Since we'd returned from Burlington, I'd spent quite some time with Winston. We were cooped up in the office until late in the evening and also spending a few nights at his place, since my house was still a construction site.

That meant that Winston and I arrived at the store together most days. I had a hunch that everyone knew about us anyway, judging by their not-so-subtle winks. And somehow, all requests for the boss went through me.

Oh, well. I *did* have a good track record of convincing him to approve them, so why change a running system?

Once we arrived at the store, I went into his office with him, because we needed to finalize some packaging details for the after Christmas sales.

"I've got everything I need," I said, surveying my list of bullet points.

Winston nodded. "I'm starting a conference call in ten minutes. I don't want anyone interrupting me. Except you. You can come in at any time."

I stood up from my chair, walking over to him, leaning in for a very quick peck before straightening up and nodding.

"Aye, aye, captain."

"Can't tell if that's an upgrade or a downgrade from grouchy boss."

I tilted my head playfully. "Definitely an upgrade from dictator, don't you think?"

His eyes flashed. "I'll show you an upgrade."

"No, you won't. Your conference call is starting, remember?"

I took a few steps back quickly, then left the office before this dangerous man got any more ideas.

I spent the whole morning on the phone with the packaging company. Just before lunch, a vaguely familiar woman strode in. She appeared to be in her midsixties, with gray hair flowing around her shoulders, a speck of freckles doting the bridge of her nose and her forehead. She was beautiful. I could have sworn I'd seen her before, in pictures at least.

"You must be Sienna," the woman said, striding straight to my desk.

"I am."

"I'm Everly. Winston's mom. We spoke on the phone."

"It's so great to meet you in person. I've heard so, so much about you. You're practically a legend."

"You're sweet," she said.

My stomach cartwheeled. Sweat dotted my palms. I had to impress her. Not only because she was Everly Statham, but because she was Winston's mom.

"Where is Winston?"

"He's in his office, but on a phone conference. Should I tell him you're here?"

"No need. I'm supposed to meet him for lunch, but I can wait. I arrived earlier on purpose."

"Okay," I said slowly, wondering what that purpose was. I did have a slight suspicion, though. Years of Bennett events had taught me to look for signs. I recognized when someone was on a discovery mission.

"My husband and I are expected at social events this time of the year, and since Winston is back, many of our friends want to invite him too. We just don't know if he'd bring a plus one. My husband and I were wondering if Winston is seeing someone. He doesn't tell us anything."

The corners of my mouth lifted in a smile all on their own.

"And you were hoping I might."

"Well, yes. Help out a desperate mother. Is he seeing anyone or not?"

I felt my neck become hot again. What was I supposed to say? I didn't know if Winston wanted his parents to know… actually, scratch that. He hadn't told them about us, so obviously he didn't want them to know.

Everything inside me deflated.

This is very new.

Yes, but still…

The two voices warred in my head, but I refused to be a Debbie Downer. After all, I had only told Pippa, Victoria, and Alice, not everyone in the family, even though telling the entire clan would take a small PR announcement.

"Mrs. Statham, how about I bring you a coffee while you wait for Winston?"

I hoped that my tone indicated my lips were sealed.

"Only if you drink one with me." She was *not* going to let me off the hook, but I'd had plenty of practice, and I had a good track record at resisting even under duress (read: Pippa and Jenna combining their forces in interrogation).

"Of course. I also keep chocolates at my desk. Can I tempt you with some?" I asked on a grin.

"Private chocolate stash? You're a girl after my own heart."

***

Winston

I ended the call quicker when I heard Mom's voice on the corridor. She was here early. That couldn't be good. It meant she was up to something.

I darted out of the office the next second. The voice came from Sienna's office. Further proof that Mom was up to no good. She was chronically late. If she showed up early, it wasn't happenstance. She had a plan. And when I entered the small room and saw that two of them chatting over coffee, I realized exactly what Mom's plan had been: cornering Sienna.

"Mom, you're early."

"Darling, it's so good to see you. And don't worry about me. Sienna was excellent company."

I winked at them both. "It's Sienna I'm worrying about."

Sienna smiled shrewdly.

"Don't you worry about her. She's very good at keeping your secrets."

"You can ask me whatever you want to know, Mom."

"Very well." She crossed her arms over her chest—a telltale sign that I was about to be in trouble. "Are you dating anyone? And if yes, will you please bring her tomorrow at a gallery show? Your dad and I are going, and we'd love to spend the time with you."

Mom didn't beat around the bush. I took after

her in that regard.

This was just like mom, putting me on the spot. To be fair, I had told her to ask whatever she wanted, and she'd used the opportunity to its full potential.

I moved my gaze to Sienna, who stood ramrod straight, fiddling with her thumbs. What was she thinking?

We hadn't talked about the *official* status of our relationship. I'd meant to, but every time I was with her, I got so lost in her that every detail simply fell to the background. But I wanted everyone to know she belonged to me—starting with my parents.

Suddenly, the need to know if she shared my feelings, if I was as important to her as she was to me slammed into me. I made a split-second decision, following my instinct more than anything else.

I stepped right next to Sienna, placing an arm around her shoulders. She glanced sideways at me, eyes wide, lips parted. Fuck, I barely kept myself from leaning in and capturing her mouth. Kissing Sienna would definitely clear things up. I drew in a deep breath, trying to rein in my instincts, this insatiable need for Sienna.

Words. I needed words.

"As a matter of fact, Mother, I am dating this lovely creature here."

Sienna blushed, blowing out a breath. Was it with relief or tension? Damn, I'd been too impulsive, as usual. I wasn't used to asking for permission, but I wanted to do things right with Sienna.

"I knew it," Mom said.

We both turned to her.

"You did?" I asked.

"Well… suspected it. Sienna here turned red as soon as I asked if you're seeing someone. Plus, every time you mention her, the tone of your voice is a little different. A mother can always tell."

"My mom used to say the same thing." Sienna laughed. Relief washed over me at the sound.

"Then it's settled. I'll see you both tomorrow at the gallery. Eight o'clock."

Hell, no. I loved my mother, but I put my foot down at art showings. I'd never been a fan, and I wasn't going to subject Sienna to it. We could always catch up later for dinner.

"I can't wait. I love contemporary art," Sienna said.

I glanced at her sideways, about to tell her she didn't have to put up with that out of politeness, but the expression on her face caught me off guard. She was smiling dreamily. Well, that was a game changer.

Next evening, Sienna was positively glowing. The gallery was being held in two of the conference rooms at the Westin St. Francis. When we entered the lobby, the first thing Sienna did was snap a selfie of us with the huge sugar castle in the center.

"You know, we could do this in the store after the rebrand," she said. "Some sort of holiday treat that serves as centerpiece along with the tree.

The Westin has the sugar castle, the Fairmont the gingerbread house, but there aren't many in department stores."

"I'm sure you'll come up with something brilliant in time for the next holiday season."

It was a heavy-handed hint that I wanted her to still work with me by then, but I couldn't help myself. Sienna blushed, giving me a shy smile.

While we descended the steps to the conference rooms, we could already see the crowd gathered for the event.

"Summer, the youngest Bennett, owns a gallery. She features up-and-coming artists often. I *love* it."

Mom and Dad were waiting by the entrance of the first room.

"Hi, Mom! Dad, this is Sienna."

"You look lovely," Mom said, kissing her cheek. Dad shook her hand.

"Can't believe my wife was right again," he exclaimed.

"About what?" I asked.

"She kept saying she thought you have a thing for Sienna. I was clueless as usual and told her she was imagining things."

"Don't beat yourself up too much, Mr. Statham," Sienna said. "Sometimes I think we women have a sixth sense."

Mom beamed at Sienna.

"Do you want to read the background stories of the artists featured tonight?"

"Sure," Sienna answered.

The two of them sat down, going through the leaflet. Dad and I went for drinks.

"Son, you look as if you don't want to be here."

"You know this isn't my scene."

Dad clapped a hand on my shoulder. "Let me give you a piece of advice after so many years of marriage. If something makes the woman next to you happy, do it. Even if it's not your favorite thing."

"I'll—wait a second. You've never told Mom you don't like coming to these things?"

"Why should I? She'd just feel guilty about dragging me here." Winking, he added, "Bringing joy to the person next to you is the secret to a happy marriage."

I was stunned. Dad had never shown enthusiasm, but I'd always thought it was just because he was a reserved man.

He just did it for Mom. I completely got it. A few months ago, I wouldn't have. But now I did.

Once the bartender had our drinks ready, each of us took two glasses and we returned to our ladies.

Sienna and Mom were chatting with their heads together, pointing between the leaflet and the various paintings around the room. Dad and I exchanged a glance, chuckling.

We were in for a repeat. I could feel this becoming a thing: attending an event our ladies wanted, Dad and I banding together. And hell if I didn't like the prospect of that.

I didn't resist staying away from her, though. As soon as she was alone, I went to her side, walking around with her.

"This is amazing," Sienna exclaimed.

"Glad you like it."

"Well, it's—wait a second." She stopped in her tracks, scrutinizing me. I had no idea what she was looking for, but I schooled my expression in any case.

"What's with the semi scowl? You don't like this, do you?"

Well, hell. Dad had managed to disguise his lack of enthusiasm for thirty years, and I hadn't even managed to make it through one evening without Sienna catching on.

"Not my scene, no."

She pouted. "Why did you say yes, then?"

I laced an arm around her shoulders, pulling her into me. I simply needed to feel her next to me as often as possible.

"Because you were excited about it."

Sienna lifted herself on her toes, kissing my cheek.

"I promise I'll make up for it later. In spades."

"What do you have in mind?"

"I'll show you when we're alone."

I brought my mouth to her cheek, feathering it along her skin until I reached her ear.

"How about giving me a taste right now?"

She playfully pushed me away, pointing a

finger at me.

"Winston, you're becoming more shameless by the day."

"Only because I want you so much."

"So it's my fault?"

"Absolutely."

I grinned. She returned it. We passed an empty conference room, and I saw my chance. I moved us inside it before Sienna even realized what was going on.

"What are you doing?" she admonished in a whisper.

"Giving you ideas."

"What for?"

"How to make it up to me later."

She laughed, shimmying a little. "That's cheating, don't you think?"

"Maybe. I just wanted a few minutes alone with you."

I feathered my mouth up and down the side of her neck, interlacing our fingers. I walked her backward, deeper into the dimly lit room, until we reached a wall. I pushed her against it with my hips, aligning our bodies, pressing myself against her. The contact electrified me. Big mistake. Feeling her breasts press against my chest turned me on instantly.

Now I wanted more—no, I needed more— simply craved it. I clasped her fingers tighter to keep myself from touching her anywhere else.

"We'd better return to the others. I can sense you're having dirty thoughts," Sienna teased.

"Dirty doesn't even come close."

I felt her smile against my cheek. "Well, save that for later, will you? We need to be on our best behavior right now."

"Whatever the lady wishes."

I held her close as we joined the crowd again, unwilling to yield even an inch.

***

Sienna

I absolutely loved galleries. I admired artists' courage to just put themselves out there. I did feel guilty for torturing Winston with it, though. But not too much, since I planned to thoroughly spoil him later this evening. I couldn't bring myself to cut this short either. I loved talking to Everly.

"My son has always been responsible, even as a child. I just wish he wouldn't keep everything to himself. It's not healthy, especially when you're under stress. Sharing helps unwind."

Everly was still on her mission to lure secrets out of me. I agreed with her, but it wasn't my call to make. I couldn't betray Winston's confidence.

"I promise I'm taking good care of him" was all I said.

"I can tell you are. He changes when you're around. Lights up when he sees you."

He did? I felt like doing a happy dance.

"Tell me more about Winston as a kid."

"I have so many stories."

"I'm listening."

She spoke so fast that I could barely hold back a smile.

"He's very protective," Everly finished. "He's always been like this. Perhaps too much. Usually at his own cost."

She was more spot-on than she thought. All that gruff exterior was just because he was trying to take the pressure off them. I wanted to start spoiling him right away.

I felt a rush of affection for Winston, and instinctively glanced at the corner where he and his dad had stopped. He was looking straight at me. I gave him a small smile. My heart rate was lightning quick. Was I a fool to let myself fall so quickly? Well, even if I was, nothing I could do about it.

I was powerless to stop it.

The more Everly spoke, the more I felt it growing—as if it had a power of its own and I had no control over it.

By the time the evening was over, I was a little more in love with Winston than I'd been when I'd arrived.

"Lovely lady, care to share your plan now?" Winston asked once we were in the car.

"Yes. I'm taking you home, and I'm going to take advantage of you all night long."

"I like that plan."

Chapter Twenty-Six

Sienna

The weeks before Christmas were always mad at Casa Bennett. The preparations—ranging from food planning to buying presents—were so extensive, it was like every member of the family had a second job. What with my late evenings with Winston at the office, finalizing the rebrand campaign, I felt as if I had three jobs.

Everyone was pretending they were making such a huge fuss about Christmas for the kids, but the truth was, the adults were enjoying it just as much. This year, we were having the traditional Christmas dinner two weeks earlier because we'd be on different sides of the globe on Christmas Day itself. I'd be in London with my brother. The part of the clan that wasn't coming to Aspen later on was leaving on a month-long trip to Australia next week.

I was usually on cloud nine before that dinner, but today I was fretting because Winston was joining me. I'd never had a boyfriend with me at Christmas dinner before. I squeezed Winston's hand as we walked toward the house.

"Sienna, you're quiet. What's wrong?"

"You know the saying trial by fire?"

"Yeah."

"Well, this will be trial by Bennetts."

Winston laughed, pulling me into a half hug, resting his arm on my shoulders. Being this close to him always made me feel so safe and protected. And when he looked at me with those green eyes? I felt like the luckiest woman in the world.

"What exactly am I supposed to watch out for?"

"No clue. Just make sure you don't let your guard down. The second you do, someone is bound to sniff you out and attack you."

"Duly noted."

When the door opened, I almost had a heart attack. My brother Lucas was here! Chloe was right behind him.

"Why didn't anyone tell me you'd be here?"

"No one knew. Wanted to surprise you."

I squeezed my brother so tightly in a hug that I almost suffocated him. After letting him go, I winked at Chloe. "You're safe from my hugs today."

Chloe grinned. "I'll keep my distance, just in case."

"I want to introduce you to someone. Lucas, Chloe, this is Winston, my boyfriend."

My little sister smiled at Winston, and so did Lucas as they shook hands. What was that look in my brother's eyes? I couldn't really decipher it.

"You look a bit skinny, Lucas," I said.

He groaned. "You say that every time."

"But it's true."

"Watch it, or no more hugs from me."

"Ha! As if I need your permission for that."

God, I hoped Lucas would choose to go to college here. I didn't voice that thought though. Didn't think it was fair to put that pressure on him. Everyone had their own path, and I respected that. I just hoped his path would lead him back to San Francisco sooner rather than later.

And I hoped Chloe's path wouldn't lead her somewhere else… or at least not for a very long time.

"How long are you staying?"

"Just over the weekend."

"You flew ten hours for two days?" I pouted.

"Didn't want to miss the Christmas dinner. But I have exams. I need to go back."

Chloe and I exchanged a glance. Lucas didn't miss it, of course.

"Hey! No banding against me."

Chloe opened her mouth theatrically. "Against you? We never do that."

I burst out laughing. "Never."

"Don't worry, I won't let them plot," Winston said.

Lucas whistled. "Much appreciated, man."

"Guys have to stick together."

Chloe placed both hands on her hips, tapping her foot. "Hey! Don't forget that I'm the one who lives on this side of the ocean. If you're going to have a favorite, I'm the better choice."

Winston laughed, pulling me into a half hug. "These two are even funnier than you told me."

I melted against him. There was so much warmth in his voice. I was so happy that he was here.

As we went further inside, Christopher himself came, holding his hand out to Winston.

"Christopher, this is Winston."

"Welcome," Christopher said. "Heard a lot about you. Good to finally meet you."

Whew. He looked friendly enough. I'd been expecting at least one or two frown lines. Come to think of it, I couldn't be sure he wasn't frowning, because a few rebellious strands of hair had fallen over his forehead. Wait a second! Christopher's hair was shorter.

"Max, I can't *believe* you," I exclaimed.

He grinned from ear to ear. "What gave me away? Was it the hair? Damn, I'm losing my touch."

Despite myself, I laughed. "Winston, my mistake. This is Christopher's identical twin brother, Max."

The next second, Christopher joined us on the corridor. He, too, was smiling.

"You've plotted this?" I asked them.

"Of course, we did," Christopher said.

"What's the use for having an identical twin if you don't get up to no good from time to time," Max added jovially. "We should do it more often. My skills are getting rusty."

"So are mine. We're out of practice."

Christopher and Winston shook hands. "Winston, welcome."

"It's great meeting you," Winston said with a

warm smile. I was grinning from ear to ear.

Christopher nodded. "Let's go meet the others."

The clan was spread throughout the enormous living room. There were several couches and armchairs. Victoria waved enthusiastically. We first greeted Jenna and Richard, and I introduced Winston to all the Bennetts in the room before we made our way to Victoria. Blake was with her.

"Welcome," Victoria said.

"Thanks. Heard many stories about the family gatherings. Happy to be here."

There he went with that charm of his. My ex had been completely cold with the family... probably why I didn't even invite him very often. Sometimes I still couldn't believe I'd stayed in that relationship for as long as I had.

"Make yourself at home. Christmas is always a big deal. Don't let it scare you," Christopher said. "But a word of warning: You don't treat Sienna right, you've got a problem on your hands. A Bennett-sized problem."

Totally saw that coming.

"There's a lot of Bennetts to go around," Blake added helpfully.

Well! Didn't see *that* coming.

Winston chuckled. "I'm well aware."

Blake wiggled his eyebrows just as his twin, Daniel, joined us. "Did Max and Christopher play their bit already?"

"Yup," I confirmed.

"How long did it take you to sniff them out?" Daniel asked.

"About five seconds."

He winked. "That's my Sienna."

Victoria shook her head. "So now that we have the awkward moment behind us, how about some drinks?"

"Yes. Please. Give me all the eggnog," I said. "Winston?"

"Sure."

Spending time with the Bennetts was usually my happy place, but this was pure magic, and I couldn't get enough of it.

Just looking at all the kids running around made me smile.

It was loud, it was crazy, and I loved every second of it. I just hoped that Winston loved it too. I could see us attending next year's Christmas party together, and the one after that. I was in this even deeper than I'd thought.

We never spoke about the future, and honestly, I didn't want to be the one of those nagging girlfriends. I wouldn't even know what to say, anyway.

I was head over heels in love with this man. I could tell him this, right? That was something to look forward to.

Sebastian snapped my attention back to the room. He held up his glass.

"It's not a toast, people. Just wanted to tell

everyone thank you for being here. I love that some things never change in the Bennett family. Dad will always be stubborn, we use every chance to gather as a group, and everyone meddles in everyone's business."

That just about summed it up.

"Don't forget that Blake will change alliances every week," I piped up. Everyone laughed, and we moved toward the dining room.

My favorite part of the evening was always after dinner, though. We had a tradition of hanging the star on the Christmas tree together. It was a little bittersweet for me, because Mom had hand-painted the star. Chloe, Victoria, and Lucas lit up.

It brought *me* joy too, but my heart always grew so heavy that I had a knot in my throat for the rest of the evening. Luckily, I'd always been able to disguise it pretty well.

My heart squeezed as we opened the box, taking out the star. Mom always did that. She'd take it out and polish it, then she and Dad would bicker over who would climb the ladder to put it on the tree. Eventually, they let us kids vote. They made a whole show of it.

***

Winston

I realized something was amiss the second they brought out the box. Sienna's demeanor changed. Not by much, but enough for me to notice. She seemed smaller, somehow. Her arms were crossed over her chest but not in a defensive pose, more like she was bracing herself, and when Chloe took the star out of the box, Sienna turned her head sideways, closing her eyes briefly. She was trying to rein in tears, I realized. In a matter of seconds, I placed my hand on her waist. She startled for a brief second before leaning into me. I had no idea what had brought on this wave of emotion, but I wanted to be there for her, comforting her in any way I could.

I waited until I could have a moment alone with her. When everyone returned to the couches and armchairs, I pulled her into the hallway.

"You okay?" I whispered.

"Yes. Just... Mom and I made that star. Always makes me emotional to see it. But Chloe, Victoria, and Lucas love it so much." She smiled, but it was a bit wobbly.

She felt raw every time they took that star out of the box. It wasn't easy for her, and still she did it because it made her siblings happy. I'd never met someone with Sienna's quiet and deep strength. It made me want to hold on to her and not let go.

Ever.

I drew my thumb over her lips before leaning in to capture her mouth. I needed to kiss her more than anything else, feel close to her, one with her. This woman. Did she even know everything she made me feel? I wanted to love her. Protect her.

"Let's join the others," she whispered afterward.

"If you insist."

She grinned. "I do. Come on, the best conversations are after dinner, when everyone has their bellies full."

Sienna was right. It was as if everyone had ten times more energy than before dinner. They talked about everything, and it was fascinating to watch the siblings ask each other's opinion and help in matters of business or just their personal life. Alice and Blake were asking Christopher about how to best go about implementing a new software in their restaurant and bar business. I almost did a double take when I realized Summer Bennett's husband was none other than Hollywood A-lister Alexander Westbrook. I wasn't much of a movie guy, but I wasn't living under a rock. He was currently discussing the pros and cons of using himself in merchandising campaigns with Sebastian's wife, Ava, and with Sienna.

Sebastian and Logan, the CFO, approached me after a while to talk shop. "Statham Stores don't have a jewelry section. Any chance we can get you to reconsider that?"

"I can be talked into it. It's been on my mind for a while. You'd want to be included just in the stores in the United States, or the ones in Europe as well?"

"Everywhere," Logan answered.

We agreed to meet early in the New Year and hammer out some details.

I kept a close eye on Sienna the entire evening. I had to admit, I already felt at home, so when we ran out of water, I went to bring new bottles. I'd just entered the kitchen when Lucas and Chloe joined me too. At first I thought it was a coincidence, but something in their body language led me to suspect otherwise.

"Can we talk to you?" Chloe asked.

"Sure."

"So, we just want to ask you to be nice to Sienna," Chloe said.

Wait a second… were they giving me the talk? Yes, yes, they were.

"Yes, very nice," Lucas emphasized. "Not like the last asshole she dated."

"He made her cry a few times." Chloe looked so sad that it just broke my heart. It also made me angry as hell. I should've punched that moron.

"I promise I won't make her cry. Sienna deserves the best, and that's exactly what I plan to give her."

Chloe sighed. "That's romantic. Just like in the movies. I told you he was a good guy, Lucas. He looks like a good guy."

Lucas was still watching me intently, scrutinizing me. "Time will tell."

"I promise to report if Sienna cries," Chloe said solemnly. I laughed.

"You guys have a strategy for this?"

Lucas nodded.

"Love how thorough you are."

That earned me a full-on smile from Lucas.

"We spoke with Christopher too when he first started dating Victoria," he informed me.

I grinned. Of course they did.

"Let's go back before Sienna gets suspicious," Lucas said.

"Yeah. This lasted one and a half minutes more than we planned," Chloe added.

They'd planned this down to the minute? Smiling, I followed them into the living room. I already loved these kids.

As the evening wound down, it was obvious Sienna was hoping to spend the entire weekend with Lucas. It was adorable watching her fight with herself over not wanting to encroach in his personal space too much, but at the same time wanting to spend as much time with him as possible.

"Do you have time for lunch tomorrow? And then maybe a movie?" she suggested.

"I can do lunch, but then I'm seeing some friends."

"And Sunday?"

"Sunday I have plans, but dinner is free."

Sienna pouted. "And I thought you'd come especially for us."

"You too. But since I'm here, I'm also going to catch up with my friends."

She was adorable, all frazzled and doting on him. "Okay. See you at lunch, then."

Chapter Twenty-Seven

Winston

Sienna was still a little out of it when we returned to the apartment.

"What did you think about tonight?" she asked.

"Best Christmas dinner I've ever been too. Don't tell Mom that. We just don't have an extended family, so she always invites friends, but it's not the same. Love the clan. Chloe and Lucas are great kids."

"I know, right?"

"They love you very much."

"I—wait a second, how do you know?"

"It's obvious."

"You're hiding something."

I rolled my eyes. "They might have given me the talk."

"Holy shit. They did? When?"

"When I went to the kitchen."

"They learned that from me. We grilled Christopher too."

"They told me that. It was fun."

"I can't believe he didn't tell anyone he was coming. And that he's only here for two days. I already miss him."

"We're seeing him on both days," I reminded her.

She pressed her lips together in a cute, mutinous expression. "That doesn't mean I can't miss him already. What do you want to do? It's not so late."

"I have an idea. Why don't we watch one of those Christmas movies you like so much?"

She blinked, holding her hand to my forehead. "Mr. Grinch, do you have a fever?"

"No, but I did have a few eggnogs. And I know the movie will lift your mood."

She pressed her lips together before stepping back and wiggling her hips.

"What are you doing?"

"Small victory dance. Can't believe I'm slowly luring you over to the dark side."

"I have one request."

"Nothing's ever straightforward with you."

"We have to watch naked."

She wiggled her hips some more. "Sounds like a fair deal to me."

I caught her by the waist, kissing her shoulder. "Come on. Choose something to watch."

"You're trusting me blindly?"

"Yeah."

"You might come to regret it."

"Can't be that bad."

She ended up choosing a movie called *The Holiday*. I just held her in my arms, waiting for her to share with me what was weighing on her… or not. I understood if all she needed was quiet, just knowing that I was here for her.

"This feels so good," she muttered when I closed my arms even tighter around her.

"I'm beginning to think my arms are your favorite pillow."

"Don't be ridiculous. Your chest is my favorite pillow."

"My bad. Of course, it is."

She returned her focus on the TV.

"Do you know every scene?"

"Probably every line." She was lying on top of me on the couch, squirming and shifting.

"You're a full-body, comfy pillow."

"Ouch."

"Hey, it's a compliment."

"Comfy pillow? Really."

"Muscly pillow any better?"

I cupped her head, attempting to pull her in to a kiss. She playfully shoved me away.

"Don't make me miss Jude Law stumbling drunk into the cottage."

"You know the movie by heart anyway."

"What's that got to do with anything?"

I laughed when she put her head back on my chest. Okay, so maybe the movie wasn't that bad. And Sienna was smiling ear-to-ear again.

It was past midnight by the time the movie ended, but I felt wide awake. Propping her chin on my chest, Sienna watched me intently. Her megawatt grin was back. Even her eyes were brighter.

"There's something on your mind. Work-related," she said.

"How can you tell?"

She traced her finger on my forehead. "This particular broody line only appears when you're thinking about work."

I caught her hand, biting her finger teasingly. "Need to look over a spreadsheet, double-check some values."

"Did Jo already look at it?"

Jo was our CFO.

"Haven't shown it to her yet."

She sat up on the couch, rubbing her hands. "Let's look at it. An extra set of eyes won't hurt."

"You're sure?"

"Aye, captain."

"What's the thing with the captain?"

She shrugged. "No clue. Just thought it fits you. They're all bossy in all the movies I've seen."

"Very reliable source," I teased.

I retrieved my laptop from the bedroom. When I returned to the living room, Sienna was wearing her dress.

"What's up with that?"

"I can't work naked. Feels wrong."

I waggled my eyebrows. "Do you mind if I work naked, or is it too distracting?"

She blushed, skimming her hands down the side of her thighs, but didn't answer.

We perused the spreadsheet together.

"Doesn't look like there's a mistake," Sienna said, finally.

"Thanks."

"If you close the store, is there a way to get work placements for the team right away? Especially for those over fifty? They'll have the toughest time in the job market."

"I'm working on that. It's on my list of priorities."

I fell for her even more when I realized she cared for the employees as much as I did. She had no risk. A billion-dollar company was waiting to employ her, and yet she cared.

"I think you should tell your parents. I would tell mine. Hell, I'm telling Victoria everything. Well... everyone kind of tells everyone everything in the Bennett clan."

I laughed. "I saw that."

"I'm sure they'll have an input. They have a lot of experience, after all."

"I'll think about it."

I meant it. She'd changed my perspective on several things. After seeing them through her eyes, I thought about them differently. I was paying attention to things I hadn't seen before. I'd been happy with the life I'd envisioned before, but now that this lovely, adorable woman had come along, I couldn't imagine my life without Sienna in it.

"What's with that look?" she asked.

"Nothing." My tone was teasing. She narrowed her eyes.

"I think there's more to it, and I want to know."

"Demanding today."

"Learned from a certain bossy… boss."

She straddled me, resting both hands on my chest.

"Warning you, if you don't tell me, I'm going to use my extraordinary persuasion skills."

"If that's supposed to scare me, it's not working."

"That's because I haven't started yet."

"You make me happy, Sienna. It's as simple as that."

I could see the emotion etched on her face. I wasn't the only one who felt how deep this ran, how connected we were. She shimmied in my lap.

"See, the benefits of doing me. We can go straight from work to fun."

I cupped her cheek, bringing her closer. "I'm not just doing you. I'm in love with you, Sienna. I love you. So much."

She grinned, leaning into my touch, before shifting closer in my lap. "I'm head over heels for you. I didn't know if I should say it, or if it was too soon."

"What convinced you?"

"You completely won me over with the Christmas movie."

"Love your priorities."

I kissed her the next second, getting us both off the couch. I walked her backward through the room, gripping her hips tightly, skimming my mouth over her neck, so hungry for her that I barely held back from tearing that light fabric from her body. I couldn't get enough of her to stop for a breather. I wanted to keep kissing, to keep touching. We came to a halt in the narrow, dark hallway. I pinned her against the wall, tracing the contour of her V-neckline with my mouth.

"Winston," she whispered. Hearing her say my name in that low, uneven voice was doing unspeakable things to me. I did away with her dress the next second.

I traced my fingers between her breasts and further down in a straight line to her navel. I couldn't see her but exploring her in the dark had its perks. My other senses were on alert. I felt the light tremor in her body, the way her breath hitched in anticipation of what I was going to do to her.

I dragged my thumb along the hem of her panties, feeling her contract the muscles in her belly. I slid my knee between her legs, nudging them apart. She opened the next second. I groaned when I felt her mouth on my neck. I hadn't seen her lean forward, hadn't anticipated this. I felt the touch of her tongue right along my cock. Damn, if she kept at this, I was going to take her right here in this hallway.

"Babe," I whispered, but the rest of the sentence faded when she touched my erection. I kissed her, needing her mouth, her warmth, her love. I craved all of it.

"Winston, I know I've been a bit out of it

tonight, but I promise I'll be okay tomorrow."

This entire evening, I'd seen a different side to Sienna. She'd been vulnerable and strong at the same time. I had no idea how that was possible, but I knew one thing for sure, and I wanted her to know it too.

"You were a little emotional, babe. That just shows how much you care. Never apologize for that. Never think you have to hide from me. I want the privilege of being next to you during these moments for the rest of our lives."

"I love you so much, Winston."

I felt her skin turn to goose bumps under my fingers, but it wasn't enough anymore. I wanted to see her, watch every expression, and I needed more leverage than the wall to explore her. Tonight, we weren't going to sleep. I was too hungry for her.

Lacing our fingers, I pulled her toward the bedroom, only slowing down when I heard Sienna chuckle.

"What?" I asked.

"Someone's desperate."

"And you're not?"

"Clearly not as much as you."

"Really? Then I have to do something about that."

When we entered the bedroom, I noticed her grin in the moonlight.

"Just what I was hoping you'd say."

I loved how feisty she could be, how sassy. I loved everything about her, pure and simple. She knew just what to say to rile me up. I wanted her to be as desperate as I was, as hungry for our connection as I was.

I reached for her at the same time she brought her hands down my chest.

"You were saying?" I teased.

"Oh, shut up. I just want to feast my eyes on you."

"Aha."

"And hands."

She lowered herself on her haunches, taking me deep in her mouth. Pleasure shot through me. I tilted forward, wrapping my hand in her hair, bringing her up until our lips were level. I kissed her so hard that a light tremor took hold of her body. I couldn't stop smiling while I kissed her. Pulling back, she lightly smacked my shoulder.

"What was that for?" I asked.

"You're a little too pleased with yourself."

"You're giving me all the reasons I need."

She attempted to smack my shoulder again, but I caught her arm, pressing my thumb on the pulse point on her wrist. I kissed that same spot before lowering both hands under her butt, cupping her ass cheeks, pulling her up against me. I moved her until my cock nudged at her entrance.

She whimpered against my mouth as I carried her to the center of the bed, splaying her legs wide, sitting back for a few seconds, just drinking in the sight of her waiting and wanting me. I kissed a trail up her right thigh, rubbing two fingers along her opening. I heard more than saw her claw at the sheets.

"Winston…"

Her pleading tone gutted me. I moved my mouth up her torso, lingering on her breasts, while bringing a hand between her legs. I ran one finger along her opening, teasing her before sliding it inside, moving it in a slow, torturing rhythm. When she gripped my hair, barely whispering my name, I slid in another one. Her inner muscles clenched tight. Feeling her writhe underneath me, pushing her hips into me, desperate for any contact, made me lose my mind.

"I'll make you come hard, baby. Your pleasure is mine. You're mine."

I felt close to her, but I wanted in deeper. I wanted to be part of her, to own and be owned. Not just tonight. Every night.

***

Sienna

Every inch of me belonged to this sexy, sinful man. Tonight had been… I couldn't even begin to understand how he'd made me feel. How he *still* made me feel. I only knew that I wanted to hang on to this feeling: claimed, loved, worshiped.

When he withdrew his hand, parting my legs even wider, settling his hips between them, I lifted my feet up, resting my heels just under his ass cheeks, urging him on. I exhaled sharply when he slid inside.

This felt different tonight. Every sensation

was intensified. I couldn't get enough of everything he made me feel. His kisses were as deep and frantic as his thrusts. Tension coiled through me, lighting up my entire body. I was barreling so fast toward a climax that I could barely breathe. I was chasing it desperately.

Every kiss made me whimper, every thrust made my inner muscles clench and tighten.

Winston groaned in my ear when I started to pulse around him. But then he pulled out, hovering with his mouth over my lips.

His cock was just a few inches above my belly. I rolled my hips up, but he pulled even further back. He flashed me a deliciously devious smile. That could only mean he was planning something.

He looked down at me for a few seconds before leaning in to kiss my jaw. I was sure he was going to claim my mouth next, but then he slid out, pushing me on one side until he was right behind me.

"What are you doing?" I whispered.

"I told you that your pleasure is mine, Sienna." He spoke against my shoulder while circling a nipple with his fingers. My skin turned to goose bumps, needing him, aching for him.

"Winston… please… I want you inside me again."

"And you'll have me. Soon."

The unmistakable dominance in his voice only intensified my need for him.

He moved his fingers downward in a slow, deliberate spiral. His touch was too light to satisfy, only enough to make me crave more.

When he reached my clit, I moaned, reaching behind me, needing to touch him—any part of him.

If he didn't enter me soon, I'd combust. My entire body was so on edge that I couldn't even lie still. Every cell in my body clamored for him.

"You're so beautiful," he murmured, feathering his lips between my shoulder and neck, his fingers over my sensitive spot.

"Please…" I fidgeted on the mattress, unable to take the pressure anymore, but Winston held me in place… and then he intensified the touch on my sensitive spot. He moved his hand faster, pressed harder, and I came the next second.

"I want to hear you cry out, baby. I want to hear you."

I tried to bite the pillow but gave up the fight. The pleasure took over, barreling through me, lighting up my insides. I didn't even have time to catch my breath when I felt him shift and then he slid inside me to the hilt.

"Oh, Winston."

He stilled, holding me while I was still pulsing around him, barely coming down from the wave of pleasure.

"I love this feeling," he grunted out. "You're everything, Sienna, you hear me?"

I shuddered, nodding, feeling so blissfully happy that I barely noticed the tension coiling inside me. Until Winston pinched my clit on a thrust, and my entire body vibrated with pleasure. My breath caught. My legs shook. My toes curled, and so did my fingers as I reached behind again, touching any part of him I could.

Winston's hands were everywhere. He took me closer to an orgasm with every thrust, every kiss, every touch. I lost all sense of my surroundings.

That pressure rose and rose until I couldn't think anything beyond how good this was. How close I felt to him. I'd never, ever felt so happy. I'd also never felt so much pleasure, and I wasn't sure I could take any more. My muscles clenched violently right before I exploded. My right leg straightened with a spasm. Seconds later, Winston pushed even deeper inside me, calling my name as he gave in to his own climax. He held me tight around the waist, rocking in and out of me gently.

He still held me after we both calmed down. God, I loved being held. We were both sweaty, but I loved this intimacy, feeling his breath on my shoulder, and his lips too, as if he was still not done kissing me, owning me, wanting to bring me pleasure.

"What are you doing to me? Not sure I can walk tonight. Or tomorrow morning. My legs feel like Jell-O," I said, turning around when I heard him chuckle.

He skimmed his hand up and down my waist. He still couldn't stop touching me! Man, I didn't think I could get any happier. I'd just had an amazing evening with the people I loved most, including this dreamy man who just couldn't keep his hands to himself.

He traced the corners of my mouth, raising a brow. I was an open book to him, as usual.

"I need to chastise you, bossy man."

"For what?"

"I almost couldn't touch you." I pouted, pinching his arm, and then his abs.

"I see. So, you didn't enjoy everything I did to you?"

"I'm not answering that."

He gave me one of those heart-stopping smiles. "Let's see. Legs feel like Jell-O."

He drew his hand up my outer thigh, slid it over my belly, stopping just under my breasts.

"Your skin is still sensitive."

I sucked in a breath when he skimmed his palm over one nipple and then the other. They instantly turned hard, of course. There went my cover.

"And the way you look at me… it tells me everything I need to know. I'll do whatever it takes so you keep looking at me like this."

"Fair warning. You're going to be in a world of trouble if you give me that ammunition." I shrugged one shoulder, giving him a coy, playful smile.

"I'm up for it."

I didn't doubt it. Winston was a man of many talents. My heartbeat accelerated the longer he looked at me. I was important to him!

I just couldn't contain my smile. I was so

happy I felt as if I was about to burst with it.

"So, we're back to me chastising you. I'll have my revenge, you know." I attempted to sound serious. He threw his head back, laughing. Ahh, I really needed to work on my acting skills.

"You can touch me all you want now, Sienna. Take revenge. But I don't think you have any energy left."

I pushed him on his back and climbed on top of him, shimmying in his lap to give him a taste of exactly how much energy I still had. I was brimming with it.

I leaned forward, bringing my lips level to his, unable to hold back my loony grin. "It'll be my pleasure to prove you wrong."

Chapter Twenty-Eight

Winston

I woke up early next day, but instead of heading to the living room, I lingered in bed. I kissed her exposed shoulder and arm, smiling against her skin. Waking her up was among my favorite things. Or so I thought… until she kicked me in the stomach in an attempt to push me away. Her eyes widened.

"I'm so sorry. Did I hurt you?"

"If I say yes, how will you make it up to me?"

She narrowed her eyes before turning around. "Here I was, feeling guilty."

"You should feel guilty."

"Aha."

I skimmed the tip of my nose up and down the side of her neck until I felt her shake with the effort of holding back laughter. Then I brought an arm around her waist, keeping her in place. She realized what I was about to do the second I skimmed my thumb along her underarm. She screeched with laughter, trying to wiggle out of my grasp.

I held her even tighter but stopped the tickling. I'd just wanted to make her laugh, not torture her.

"You're so bad," she said between guffaws.

I buried my nose in her hair, not wanting to let her go. If there was a happier place than this bed, with Sienna curled in my arms, I didn't know what it was, nor did I care to find out. Having her here, in my home, was exactly what I needed, what had been missing from my life.

"Are you going to tickle me again?" she asked.

"No."

"But you're still not letting me go. Do you have sexy times on your mind?"

"Not right now."

She shuddered in my arms. I loved that I affected her so much. She pushed her ass back, smacking right into me, pressing her ass cheek against my erection.

I groaned, taking in a deep breath, trying to rein in my instincts. I wanted to devour her.

"You liar. You do have sexy time on your mind."

"Always. But I have other plans for us right now."

"What?"

"Come on, lovely girl. Let's get you some breakfast."

"I like the sound of that. What are you going to feed me?"

"Let's go look."

I laced our hands as I got out of bed, leading her through the apartment. I took a good look at her while we busied ourselves around the kitchen. My woman was her usual bubbly self again, chatting my ear off, smiling for no reason.

Who knew that this spirited woman who always spoke her mind would change my life so much?

Our breakfast consisted of eggs and bacon and a lot of coffee.

"Hey, so do you want to watch a movie before we go to lunch with my siblings?"

"If it means you keep looking at me like this, hell yes!"

She grinned at me. "You're in a great mood this morning."

"Yes, I am."

"Can I take some credit for that?"

I waggled my eyebrows. "Debatable."

She pointed her coffee cup at me. "Don't try to fool me, mister."

"Or what?"

Her eyes widened as I stepped closer. Whisking the cup from her hand, I placed it on the table before drawing Sienna flush against me. I kept her exactly where I wanted her, capturing her mouth, kissing her until she moaned.

"Did I say watch a movie?" she murmured. "Because what I meant was doing you."

I laughed against her lips. "I was planning to seduce you while we watched anyway."

"Of course, you did." She sighed, patting my

shoulder. I nudged her thighs open with my knee, aligning our hips. She gasped when I pressed lightly into her, when she felt how much I wanted her already.

"How about going to a movie after lunch?"

"Wow. Really?"

She was always so surprised when I did something for her. I just wanted to keep doing it, keep surprising her, putting that happy smile on her face.

"And that's not all I have in store for you this weekend."

"It's not? What else? No, wait. I don't want to know."

"I wasn't planning on telling you anyway."

"Hey, I have a question. Do you want to come to London and Aspen with me? We'd spend a week in London, celebrate Christmas Day," Sienna said.

"I'd love to, but you know I need to finalize things with the board."

"What if I work with you while we're gone? A certain someone once told me we could work remotely."

I loved it when she used my own arguments against me.

"You could meet the board before we go to Aspen," she suggested.

"We can do that."

"So it's a yes?"

"It's a yes."

Her smile was so big that I just couldn't resist kissing her—again.

We were so lost in each other that we were almost late for lunch.

Christopher, Victoria, Lucas, and Chloe were already in front of the restaurant when we arrived.

"Chloe, Sienna and I are going to a movie afterward. Want to come with us?"

Her eyes lit up. I knew she already liked me, but I wasn't above bribery to make sure I was in her good graces.

"Ooooh, yeah. I'm a movie junkie."

Lucas grinned, patting my shoulder as we all went inside the restaurant. "You just earned some extra points for making two of my sisters happy."

"Good to know."

I wanted Sienna deeper in my life, and permanently. But this was also the worst time in my life to think about anything being permanent, when so many things were up in the air. So much depended on the next few weeks, my meeting with the board. So much was out of my control that I didn't know if it was even fair to promise Sienna anything permanent. I couldn't help myself, though. I wanted a future with her. I saw it so clearly that I could almost taste it, and I'd fight for it.

Chapter Twenty-Nine

Winston

I took Sienna's advice and spoke to my parents the following week.

"Son, I'm sure that whatever course you take will be the best one," Dad said.

Mom wasn't as calm. "Goodness, we never knew Gerald made such a mess of things. Why didn't you tell us?"

"I didn't want you to worry. This is my responsibility now."

"But it was our decision to employ Gerald. What is going to happen to everyone working here?"

"I'm going to make sure they're taken care of. Any piece of advice?"

"Just make sure you consider all options, weighing the pros and cons before deciding," Dad said.

I smiled. "You're not going to tell me your opinion?"

"No. You're in charge now. Whatever decision you make, you must be happy with it. Doesn't have to be the one we would take."

That didn't clarify anything for me, but knowing my parents trusted me one hundred percent did take a weight off my shoulders.

The next two weeks were brutal. I managed to push everything to the back of my mind while Sienna and I were lost in each other. We both even turned off our phones when we weren't in the office. But there was no ignoring my responsibilities once my phone started ringing every morning, and my inbox had over fifty unread messages, twenty with *urgent* in the title.

Sienna and I were finalizing the rebrand in the evening. I was proud of the result, but that didn't mean the board and the bank would agree to extend the credit line.

I felt so much pressure that sometimes I could barely breathe through it. There was so much at stake keeping the store afloat, not letting down my employees, my parents, and even Sienna. I wasn't sure she'd still look at me the same way if this went south.

How many times had she told me that she loved how brilliant I was? I felt anything but as I read the cashflow reports.

Every new report just brought worse news. I'd thought I could wait until after Christmas for the board meeting, but it was becoming increasingly more obvious that it wasn't feasible. They'd have to make a decision much sooner than I'd hoped.

"Earth to Mr. Statham," Sienna called. We were in my office one afternoon. She'd been giving me the rundown of a few ideas she'd just added to the rebranding campaign. I'd been listening in the beginning, but then had been too captivated by those gorgeous lips, the way she moved around the room, to pay attention.

As usual, I couldn't help but smile when Sienna was around.

"What did I tell you about calling me that?"

"Well, you've got all that broodiness going on again, so I've downgraded you all the way to grouchy boss again."

I cocked a brow. Sienna met my challenging stare with one of her own.

"What? You're scaring everyone again."

"I'm under a lot of pressure."

"I know." Her voice was softer. "Talk to me."

"I'm going to have to meet with the board sooner than I hoped. I'm flying to Burlington this Thursday."

"Shit."

"Yeah… Can you come?"

She shook her head. "I have an important meeting in the morning. No way can I cancel it. Anything I can do to help right now?"

I tilted my head. "Help? Close the door and come closer."

She licked her lips. "Not such a good idea—"

"Close the door, Sienna."

She did as I said, and when she turned around, I noticed her cheeks were pink. She was still across the room, though.

"Come closer," I repeated.

She shook her head. "No, I know what you

want to do."

"And what's that?"

She played with the ends of her hair.

"Sienna. Come. Here."

Sighing, she started walking toward me. I pushed my chair back from the desk, pointing to my lap.

"Winston!"

"Now I'm Winston again?"

She looked over her shoulder. "What if someone comes in?"

"No one dares come in without knocking. I want to hold you, Sienna."

She looked at me suspiciously. I deserved that. I didn't want to *just* hold her, but… baby steps. She closed the distance, pulling her skirt up a bit before climbing in my lap, placing her knees at the sides of my thighs. Just the smell of her perfume, breathing her in, feeling her touch instantly relaxed me. She was my beacon of light.

But I needed more than that. I needed to kiss, touch. I ran my fingers on her bare arms, watching her chest move up and down rapidly as her breath quickened. And then I leaned her back slightly so I had all the access I wanted. I kissed from her jaw, down the column of her neck, skimming my lips over her clavicle before moving my mouth even lower on her chest, where fabric met skin.

"Winston…," she whispered in a shaky voice. I opened my mouth, dipping my tongue a little, tasting her skin. She made a small sound, somewhere between a moan and a gasp that went straight to my cock. I'd never get enough of her, and I wanted her right here, on my desk.

Grabbing her ass with both hands, I lifted her from my lap to the edge of the desk.

"What do you think you're doing?" she asked. I laughed in her ear, drawing my mouth all the way to her jaw.

"What does it look like?"

Straightening up, she scooted further away. "We're not having sex on your desk."

I made to step closer, but she placed a hand firmly on my chest.

"No, not even one of your smoking hot kisses will change my mind."

Sienna had me wrapped around her little finger, which would be completely fine with me, except the troubling realization that I couldn't talk her into surrendering to me.

"Clearly, I need to refine my technique."

She laughed, lowering her hand. "I agree. I'd give you pointers, but that would totally undermine my endgame."

"Which is?"

"Grow immune to your charm at the office."

"I'd say you're succeeding."

She sighed, throwing her thumb over her shoulder. "If I was, I wouldn't have closed that door."

I caught her hand, nudging her legs further apart.

"I see." I was so close now that I felt her breath on my skin. I watched her intently and could almost tell the second I got through her defenses. She inched even closer to me. I moved my hand from her ankle to her knee, then further up under her skirt.

"Fine, one kiss. But only one. And not scorching hot, or I'm downgrading you to Mr. Statham for the entire week."

I chuckled, cupping her jaw. I'd smiled more in the ten minutes Sienna had been here with me than the rest of the day.

"I'm not giving you carte blanche," she warned, but her playful smile told me otherwise.

"I'm claiming it anyway, Sienna."

Chapter Thirty

Sienna

The day Winston flew to Burlington, I had a meeting in the morning. Afterward, my productivity suffered, because I was checking my emails and messages compulsively. He should have finished with the board by now. So far, I hadn't heard from him. I wished I'd gone with him. I couldn't change the outcome of the meeting, but at least I could be there for him, pampering him when he came out.

In the afternoon, Angela from HR came into my office.

"Sienna, can I talk to you for a second?"

"Sure."

Angela came in, closing the door behind her. Oh, shit. Something serious had gone down.

"What's wrong?" I asked at once.

"I've just received an email from the board, and I haven't been able to reach Winston. Since you're closest to him, I thought maybe you could give me some insight as to how to deal with the news."

"Okay. What did the board's email say?"

My heart and stomach constricted almost to the point of pain.

"The store will be shut down. Everyone still has a workplace for the next three months, and everyone will get a severance package. Size will depend on how long they've worked here."

I clasped my hands together, drawing in a deep breath.

"I'm not sure if Winston will be back. The board mentions that one of them will oversee the closing process and that they'll try to find work placements for as many employees as possible within the chain, if they're willing to relocate. And at the end of the email it also says that Winston will be in charge of the European stores from now on… and that he'll do that out of Paris. It doesn't say when he's leaving, and I can't reach him. What did Winston tell you?"

Nothing. I was too stunned to reply. In fact, I could barely focus on my thoughts.

"Let's wait for Winston to call," I said, finally.

"Okay. Will do." She sighed, looking around the room. "I'll be so sorry to leave this place."

Shaking her head, she left the office. The initial shock started to wear off the second I was alone. A low pressure built in my chest. I swallowed hard, attempting to focus on the spreadsheet I'd been working on. I *refused* to jump to conclusions. I'd just wait for Winston to call and explain what had happened.

I managed to hang on to that thought for all of ten minutes, after which I asked Angela to forward me the email from the board. Midway through it, I realized it had been a mistake to read it. Seeing the words in black and white made everything ten times worse.

My chest was so heavy that I could barely draw in deep breaths.

I minimized the window with the email, staring at my desk and trying to rein in my thoughts, to not let my fears get the better of me.

It wasn't working.

My body was heavy, as if I was tied to the chair. I couldn't even get up to walk off the tension building inside me.

Why hadn't Winston told me any of this? He'd always said he had a backup plan, but never mentioned that it required him moving away. And yet, the board had included it in the newsletter as if it was agreed upon and set in stone. He'd never mentioned any details. Was it because he hadn't seen a future together for us? That couldn't be.

The way he held me, loved me… the way he spoke to me was always so heartfelt. Just thinking about us, our conversations, our snuggles and sexy shenanigans made me smile. My whole body felt lighter, warmer, overpowering the sense of foreboding for a few seconds.

And yet, that damn email was weighing on me, rooting me to the spot. I just had to stop thinking about it and push it as far to the back of my mind as possible.

I pressed a palm to my forehead, forcing myself to think about something else.

Oh, yes! I was supposed to go pick up the bags Pippa had ordered for her daughters today. I'd ordered a similar one for Chloe. I shimmied in my seat imagining the happiness on their faces when they'd see the bags.

That's right. I would focus on my family. Reaching for my phone, I dialed Victoria's number. We were meeting today so I could give her the bag for Chloe, but we hadn't yet decided on the place.

"Hi! Done with work already?" Victoria said in greeting.

"Yes. Decided where you want to go?" I asked.

"What are you in the mood for?"

"No clue."

"Put her on loudspeaker," Pippa's voice sounded in the background.

"Where are you?" I asked.

"Pippa and I went to pick up some furniture. Wait, I'm switching you to loudspeaker."

Several seconds later, I heard my sister's voice loud and clear.

"Want to grab something to eat?" Victoria asked.

"Sure, sounds good."

"Wait a second. You sound a little off." That came from Pippa.

I chuckled. Pippa's people-reading skills were forever surprising me but gauging one's mood through the phone was a new high.

"I've had better days," I admitted.

"We need to cheer you up. Say no more. I know exactly what you need," Pippa said.

"And what's that?" I was super curious since I didn't even know myself what I needed.

"Nadine is at her store today. I'm sure we can talk her into staying open a while longer for us. We'll call the rest of the girls and see who can joins us, and we can have a girly evening."

My favorite girls and our usual wine in cups? *Yes, yes, yes.*

"Pippa, you're a genius."

"I know, right?"

"I already feel better just thinking about it."

"Mission accomplished."

"I'll just wrap up things here and head to Nadine's."

I practically jumped out of my chair as soon as I hung up, gathering my things. I was so excited to leave the building that I almost forgot to pick up the bags. I was already at the entrance when I remembered and made a short detour. By the time I left the Statham building, Pippa had sent me a message.

Pippa: The party is ON. Ava and Alice will join us.

Nadine's store was ten blocks away from Statham. These days, Nadine was rarely in the shop. She was usually in her studio, designing new gowns, or supervising the sewing team. Everything was handmade.

Her dresses were sold in department stores countrywide, but she also had two shops, one in New York and this one in San Francisco. The latter had hosted many a girls' night out. We loved it there; we were out of a house, but still in an intimate atmosphere.

"I'll be right out," Nadine called the second I entered the store and the bell above the door rang.

"Take your time. It's just me."

I loved it here. All these beautiful dresses, the comfy seating area in the front. Nadine also shared my love for Christmas decorations. Her store looked like Santa's workshop. Everywhere I turned were either twinkling lights, globes, or fake tree garlands sprayed with white.

Nadine appeared right away. She was wearing a stunning red dress, and her dark hair fell in loose curls around her shoulders.

She had a little twinkle in her eye. "So, I haven't told the girls to bring any wine because I have eggnog. Is that okay?"

"Is the sky blue? I love eggnog."

I beamed, already feeling lighter than I had in hours. Away from the Statham building, it was easier to forget that damn email.

"Thanks for keeping open this long."

"A girls' evening was long overdue. We can all relax a little. The weeks up to Christmas are always so stressful for everyone. Delivering orders, hitting targets. Not to mention all the holiday preparations."

"But it's the good kind of stress, right?" I said.

"You're right. You always know how to put things in perspective."

That was usually true. But right now, I was still fighting to find a perspective that wasn't bleak. Any second now I'd come up with it. Any second now. I was sure of it. Besides, eggnog boosted creativity and positivity. It was basically Christmas in a bottle.

Pippa and Victoria arrived a few minutes later, followed by Alice, who was carrying two huge bags filled with take-out boxes.

"Do I smell roast duck?" I asked, already rubbing my stomach.

Alice winked. "I couldn't come without everyone's favorite, right?"

"Gimme, gimme." I took the bags from Alice. She'd brought paper plates and cups too, as usual. Within minutes, we'd spread everything on the little coffee table between the armchairs.

"Before I forget, here are the bags for your girls." I handed Pippa the package.

"They'll be so happy. I didn't tell them I managed to place an order before they sold out. Thanks for making that happen."

"You're welcome."

We'd just begun eating when Ava walked in too.

"Is it too early for eggnog?" she asked, her eyes lighting up when she noticed the duck.

"The answer to that will always be no," Pippa answered on a laugh, pouring Ava a glass.

"Hard day?" Nadine asked.

Ava joined her palms in a prayer. "Please, please, please talk to your husband. I've been talking budgets with Logan the entire afternoon. He's still every bit as stubborn about every expense as he was when I first came to Bennett Enterprises."

Nadine held up her hands. "I don't want to interfere in your budget war."

Ava dropped her chin to her chest, sighing dramatically. "Sebastian says the same. Why's no one on my side?"

Pippa batted her eyelashes. "We all are. You're just braver than the lot of us. Any chance you can take over the budget negotiations for my department too?"

Ava's jaw dropped open. "Traitor. You'd do that to me?"

"Better you than me," Pippa said on a grin.

Ava took a sip of her glass, closing her eyes, sighing again.

"If you give me enough eggnog, I might start to consider it."

"Atta girl." Pippa held her glass up. The rest followed, and we cheered.

"To my brothers, who all married brave women," Pippa declared. I couldn't agree more. I loved these ladies.

"I have no idea how you girls handle everything," I said. "Careers, kids, and everything."

"Well, we do have pretty amazing husbands," Ava said dreamily.

Victoria nodded vigorously. "I wholeheartedly agree. They're amazing."

"Except when they're in caveman mood," Nadine said, but she was grinning. "Nah, even then. They're cute. Anyone up to pranking them?"

I perked up. "Yes, ma'am. What do you have in mind?"

"Not sure yet. Let's see if the eggnog will help with inspiration."

Several cups later, everyone was throwing ideas around.

"If we tell them that we're surrounded by a group of guys out for a bachelor party, they'll show up at the door within the hour," Nadine said.

Victoria laughed, almost spilling eggnog on herself. "They'll be here in twenty minutes tops. Christopher, at least."

Ha! Yes, he would. There was a general murmur of agreement that the bachelor idea was the best, but we decided to wait until later to put everything in motion.

By the time I was on my third eggnog, I had thoroughly relaxed. Or was it my fourth? I couldn't tell. Nadine kept refilling my cup like it was her job.

Once the food was gone, someone suggested we put on music. I danced with Victoria, Ava, and Nadine, while Pippa and Alice watched us, heads together, whispering. I had the slight suspicion they were talking about me. I wanted to pick the girls' brains, but I just couldn't bring myself to think about everything. Then Kylie's "Santa Baby" came on, and all my worries slammed into me. The next second, Pippa patted the floor.

"Come on, girl. Sit and tell us what has you all worked up."

My shoulders felt heavy again. Sighing, I sat between Alice and Pippa.

Victoria followed, sitting across from me. Well, the more the merrier.

"The Statham store in San Francisco is closing," I began.

"But I thought Winston met today with the board?" Victoria said.

"He did. And then the board sent an email informing HR of the outcome… and that Winston is going to Paris."

"Holy shit. Since when did you know this?" Pippa asked.

"Since HR told me. Winston never mentioned it."

"Did you talk to him today?"

"No. No one's been able to reach him."

My lower lip was trembling. The eggnog was *not* helping. Instead of boosting creativity, it only seemed to magnify my fears. I was clinging to every thought that filled me with love and warmth.

The way he kissed me every time? Oh, yeah.

His insistence on taking care of me after the miniburn? Definitely.

His smile when he gave me the green light to buy Christmas decorations for his apartment? The image was playing on repeat in my mind.

LAYLA HAGEN

But was I having positive thoughts? No, sir, I was not. All I could see ahead were dark clouds.

"Why hasn't he told me about these plans? If the board sent it in an email right after the meeting, it means that they'd discussed it before."

"There can be a million reasons," Pippa said wisely. "Whatever it is, we can come up with a solution. But… first we want to know how serious you are about him. We have a plan."

"Involves more than eggnog?" I asked.

"Well, eggnog and roast duck were the first step," Victoria admitted.

I chuckled. "Of course, they were. Now I will forever think of the roast duck as a means to an end."

"So, on a scale from *he's boyfriend material* to *I want to have his babies*, how into him are you?" Pippa asked solemnly.

I couldn't hold back. Not when I'd had eggnog. And roast duck.

"I was already dreaming about asking Nadine to design my wedding dress," I confessed.

Victoria smiled, exchanging a glance with Nadine. "Well… she kind of sketched something already."

"She did? Why? When?"

"I had a bout of inspiration after meeting him at dinner," Nadine said.

"Same for me. Might have designed an engagement ring with you in mind," Pippa added. "Between us girls, we already have your entire wedding planned."

I sighed, feeling my heart just grow from being surrounded by so much love. But I still felt completely overwhelmed, still hoped my phone would ring soon.

On second thought, why wait? I rose to my feet, heading toward the counter where I'd left my tote.

I was going to take matters into my own hands and text Winston. The second I tapped the screen of my smartphone, I realized the task wouldn't be as easy as I'd hoped. I was already tipsy, but I persisted.

The drinks might not have boosted creativity, but you know what it did boost? Courage.

Oh, yeah.

I typed at an embarrassingly low speed, but once I'd pressed Send, I returned to the girls feeling relieved and overwhelmed at the same time.

"You texted Winston, didn't you?" Pippa asked.

I nodded.

"Atta girl." She patted the floor again. "Come here. I know just what you need."

As I sat down, she reached for another take-out bag I hadn't seen until now.

"More roast duck?" I asked.

"Nope. Cupcakes."

"Why didn't you take them out right away?"

Grinning, she opened the carton. "Saving the best for last."

Chapter Thirty-One

Winston

After the board meeting, I moved my flight back to San Francisco from the evening to one o'clock. In the half an hour I had between packing my bags and the Uber pickup time, I went for a walk. It was supposed to clear my mind, but it wasn't working.

I'd left my laptop and phone at the hotel. I'd wanted to walk off the tension, clear my mind. Leaving all electronic devices behind was a calculated move: I didn't want to give myself the opportunity to do anything rash, like calling the board and giving them a piece of my mind. I had more important things to think about, such as mapping out my next steps.

The longer I walked, the more worked up I became, though. Last time I'd been on these streets, the opposite had happened. I'd felt relaxed, free, happy. It hadn't been Burlington, or the snow. It had been all Sienna. She'd changed the way I looked at certain things, how I experienced them. She'd changed *me*.

On the drive to the airport and the six-hour flight, I was restless. I only turned my phone back on once I landed in San Francisco. I had a dozen missed calls from the HR department, and as many from Sienna. What was going on?

Then a message popped up, and my stomach sank.

Sienna: Why did u not tell me untl now? If you're jst going to sprng on m that you're leaving, Ill b VERY VERY mad.

My stomach sank at the same time my pulse exploded in my ears. The message was missing several letters, but I got the gist of it.

I checked my email next. The board had already sent out an email?

What the hell? We had not agreed on sending this. Even though I was getting madder with every word, I forced myself to read until the end.

They'd even mentioned Paris? Jesus Christ, what a mess. Sienna must think I was a dickhead of the highest order. Just the thought that she could be hurting right now ate at my insides. I called her immediately.

She answered after a few rings.

"Well, hello, Mr. Broody Boss."

That wasn't Sienna, but the voice was vaguely familiar, even though the woman talked in a low whisper.

"Who is this?"

"Pippa. We met in Sienna's office and then at my parents' house, remember?"

"Yes. Is Sienna with you?"

"Yup."

"Can I talk to her?"

"Nope."

I tapped my fingers on the handle of my bag, worry gripping me, wrapping around me like a vise.

"Did something happen to her?"

Please say no. Please.

"Yeah. Too much eggnog. Too much duck. Too many cupcakes."

"I'm not following."

"Look, she was a little down today, and the girls and I decided to entertain her. She could really use talking to you, though."

"I agree. Put her on the phone."

"No, see... I think you should come in person. Whatever you have to say, those green eyes and your general alpha vibes will tip the balance in your favor."

I didn't know whether to laugh or not.

"Where are you?"

"At Nadine Hawthorne's store. You can find the address online. I've had too much eggnog myself to type."

"Why are you whispering?"

"Because I'm hiding from the girls."

My gut clenched. "Sienna doesn't want to talk to me?"

"She does... at least she did a few hours ago. Not sure where she stands now, which is why I'm showing some initiative."

"I appreciate it."

"Ha! Don't appreciate it yet. You hurt Sienna,

and I'll kick your ass. And I have reinforcements."

This time, I did laugh. "I bet you do. I've just landed. I'm looking up the address as soon as I hang up, and I'm coming directly there. Can you keep Sienna at the store a while longer?"

Pippa giggled. "You still have so much to learn about the way girls' nights out work in the Bennett family. I'll give you a tip: we know when they start. You can never tell when they end."

"I'll remember that. And thanks, Pippa."

I arrived at the store almost forty minutes later, and practically jumped out of the Uber before it had even stopped.

Nadine Hawthorne's shop was the only one with lights on. My eyes bulged. When Pippa had said they were on a girls' nights out, I had imagined… I didn't know what, but not this. They were having a party inside. Some of the girls were dancing. I spotted Sienna among them, and my whole body felt lighter.

I knocked at the glass door, but no one heard me over the music, so I just went inside. The bell above the door rang, and all movement stopped. The dancing girls stilled. The conversation ceased.

"Hi! Sienna, can I speak with you? Alone?"

Alice sprang to her feet, along with Victoria, who turned to Sienna and asked, "Did you talk to him?"

"I didn't. At least, I don't remember talking to him."

She frowned, checking her phone. "Oh, I did. I just don't remember doing it."

Pippa held up a hand, flashing a guilty smile. "It was me. I told him where we are."

Sienna groaned, hiding her face in her hands. "But I'm not sober."

"Details, details," Pippa said, waving her hand. "Girls, how about we give them some space?"

Right. "Space" consisted of more or less ten feet, since the store wasn't that large. I didn't care. All I cared about was Sienna.

I stalked toward her. She took a step back and wobbled. I placed both hands on her arms, stroking her bare skin just where the sleeve ended. She licked her lips before looking down at the point of skin-on-skin contact.

"We need to talk, drunk girl."

"Hey! Don't make fun of me. It's their fault." She pointed to the group of girls huddled on the armchairs.

"It is," Pippa admitted loudly. I laughed. So much for privacy.

"I can't talk here with everyone listening," Sienna whispered.

"Outside, then. Let's go."

"Hey! You can't come here all bossy and full of swagger."

I tilted forward until my lips almost touched hers. Sliding one hand down, I pressed my fingers possessively on her waist.

She gave a small gasp, and her gaze dropped

to my mouth.

"I'm this close to throwing you over my shoulder and taking you somewhere else… Outside. Now. Come on."

"Hmpf." Sienna crossed her arms over her chest, stalking past me. I followed closely. Pippa and Victoria gave me thumbs-up when I passed them.

Once we were outside, I realized that Sienna wasn't her usual self. She was fanning her cheeks, drawing in deep breaths.

"Are you feeling sick?"

"No, just… drunk. They gave me eggnog, roast duck, and cupcakes."

"You got drunk from roast duck and cupcakes?"

"No, but it made me drink more eggnog."

"I see." I couldn't tone down my grin.

"Hey! Don't mock me."

"Or what?"

She narrowed her eyes. "Why didn't you call me after the board meeting?" In a lower voice, she added, "Why didn't you tell me about Paris?"

And just like that, the ease and playfulness were gone from her eyes and her voice. I wanted to do whatever it took to bring them back.

"I wanted to regroup after the meeting. Moved my flight earlier and turned off my phone because I knew I'd lash out at them. They weren't supposed to send out that email. They followed some stupid protocol they had in place. I didn't even know about it. I meant to talk to you, explain everything."

"Paris?" she pressed, her voice almost a whisper. "Why didn't you tell me about that?"

"It was something the board and I discussed months ago. It was a backup plan for the worst-case scenario, but then I didn't give it any thought because I met a certain sassy-mouthed, Christmas-obsessed branding VP who turned my life upside down, and I fell in love so hard that I can't even see straight."

"Mr. Statham, are you trying to soften me with flattery?"

"Yes, ma'am. Is it working?"

"I'm undecided. You can keep at it though. Might tip the balance in your favor."

"Ah. I see."

"Why did you even make that deal with the board?"

"It was the only way I could get them to commit to finding workplaces for as many employees as possible. If I agreed to oversee our European operations."

That light in her eyes dimmed instantly, slaying me.

"Winston, I don't want to keep you from doing whatever you have to do to get the best deal for the team."

"Sienna, this doesn't change anything between us."

"How can you say that?"

"Because I love you." I cupped her face with both hands, needing to feel closer, to show her that our connection was as strong as ever. She belonged to me. We belonged together.

"I know that a lot of things are up in the air, but no matter what, I want us together. Don't you want the same thing?"

"I do, but… how about the deal?"

Despite leaning into my touch, she watched me with weariness. *No*. I was going to do everything in my power to erase any doubt.

"I'm not going to take it. I happen to be in love with a very smart woman. I'm sure that if we put our heads together, we'll find an even better solution for the team."

"I see. More flattery," she whispered, giving me a small smile. "Just so you know, it's working."

"Is that a yes, then?"

Her smile grew bigger, until it almost swallowed her.

"Hell, yes!"

She rose on her tiptoes, balancing her hands on my shoulders. She was the one who made the first move, touching her lips to mine, but I took control of the kiss the next second. I needed to feel that she was mine. She loved me.

She wasn't holding all this uncertainty against me. She was ready to embrace it with me.

I hadn't thought it was possible to love Sienna more, but right in this moment, I fell deeper.

I kissed her until she whimpered, pushing her hips into me. I pressed my thumb on the top of her spine, splaying my fingers on her shoulder blades, barely holding back from slipping them under the fabric of her dress. I wouldn't be able to keep a straight head if I touched her bare skin.

I needed to be alone with her.

It was all I could do not to pin her against the storefront and deepen the kiss. Instead, I pulled back. She pouted.

She was cute in her semidrunk state, rubbing her eyes and shifting her weight from one foot to the other.

I'd take care of her tonight. I'd show her I was meant to take care of her *every night.*

Before I could say anything, the door of the store opened and Pippa poked her head out.

"Not to intrude on your privacy or anything, but just thought I'd warn you. A bunch of Bennetts are joining us soon. Sebastian, Blake, and Christopher are on their way."

Sienna turned on her heels. "Crap. You went ahead with the plan to prank them?"

"No, no," Pippa said quickly, opening the door wider. The rest of the group was right behind her. "I didn't text them."

"I did," Victoria said.

Pippa groaned. "But now they're going to grill Winston. At least these two are done talking."

"How do you know?" Sienna asked through squinted eyes. Pippa lowered her eyes to her hands.

"There was a make-up kiss."

"You spied on us."

I laughed, watching everything play out.

"I… uhh… well, we could see everything

through the window. I didn't eavesdrop, though. The door was closed."

"And you haven't mastered the art of lipreading," Sienna said with a smile.

"Yet." Pippa winked before turning her attention to the street, where a car pulled up. Sebastian, Blake, and Christopher got out of it.

"Victoria, why do they look like they're on a mission?" Pippa asked.

"I… err, might have told Christopher that Sienna was feeling down… and also why," Victoria confessed.

Sienna rubbed her palms over her face. "Okay. Okay. We need a plan. No way do I want them going into overprotective mode."

"Babe, it's all good," I said. To my astonishment, she laughed. Her lack of faith was insulting.

"Pippa, any chance you can distract them?"

Pippa's shoulders sagged. "I know my strengths. Deterring my brothers when they're on a mission is impossible."

The guys joined us the next second.

"What are you doing here?" Pippa asked them.

"I'm only here because Christopher insisted, and Blake sided with him. I didn't stand a chance," Sebastian said.

Christopher focused on me. "You have some explaining to do."

Blake nodded. "That's right."

"Sienna and I are working everything out," I explained.

"Everything Bennett-related is everyone's business," Christopher said.

I was starting to realize that and was barely biting back a laugh. "We're good," I said.

"They are! I saw them make-up kiss and all," Pippa said.

"Oh," Blake said. "I'd like to promise I won't jump the gun again, but I don't like to make promises I can't keep. I'm a hothead. But I own up to my flaws. Plus, I have to protect my favorite people."

Christopher stared at him. "You usually give me shit when I say that."

Blake didn't miss a beat. "I adapt."

Sebastian shook his head. "Maybe it's time you should let everyone do their own thing."

"Sebastian, stop being so sensible. It makes us look bad," Blake said. Everyone laughed.

"I'm going to take my girl home," I said.

Victoria looked between Blake, Christopher, and me before turning to Pippa. "What did I tell you? The caveman gene is strong in the Bennett family."

Chapter Thirty-Two

Winston

I got my woman home right after that. I couldn't wait to be alone with her. I had enough self-restraint to not kiss her in the cab, but I couldn't hold back from touching her. I needed that connection at the very least. I interlaced our hands, bringing them up, touching my mouth to the back of her hand. She shuddered lightly, crossing her legs. The movement tested my self-control like nothing else.

I lost the battle with myself halfway home, tipping her chin up and claiming her mouth. Fuck, how she opened up, relenting to me right away.

I'd thought I'd appease my need for her with one taste, but I'd been wrong. If anything, it just stoked the fire. I was desperate now. When she tugged at my shirt, I deepened the kiss even more. When she let go, slipping her hand underneath, I grabbed her wrist, stopping the descent. There was no saying what I'd do if I felt her soft fingers on my bare skin. Her lips curled upwards as she tried to wiggle her hand out of my grip. I stopped kissing her, looking her straight in the eyes. She wiggled her eyebrows, whispering, "Afraid you can't resist me?"

"You wicked woman."

She laughed softly, leaning into me.

"As punishment, you're not getting another kiss until we get home," I said. She batted her eyelashes.

I shook my head. She attempted to wiggle her hand under my shirt again. I caught it—*again*. I touched my thumb along the sensitive skin under her lower lip until she started to tremble in my arms.

Not kissing her was as much punishment for me as it was for her, but it was the only way to keep from losing my head.

I congratulated myself on keeping a (tiny) distance right up until we were inside my apartment. And then I remembered that my intention had been to take care of Sienna tonight. She'd been wobbly on her legs back at the store. Even though all I wanted was to press her against the door and sink inside her, I did the gentlemanly thing.

"How are you feeling?"

"I sobered up." Touching the tip of her nose, she added, "I'm not seeing double. No need to be gentle with me. You can do whatever you want to me, Winston."

Those few words completely did me in. I pulled her against me the next second, doing what I'd been waiting all evening to do. I captured her mouth, owned her body. I lifted her sweater, skimming my fingers along every inch of skin I bared. Sienna exhaled a sharp breath, digging her fingers in my arm. When I reached under her skirt between her thighs, stroking two fingers along her panties, she gasped, lifting up on her toes, as if that one touch was already too much. And I hadn't even begun. I wanted to make her feel loved, appreciated, a goddess, which was exactly what she was to me.

Slipping my hand inside her panties, I stroked her bare skin. I teased around her clit, moving my fingers along her entrance.I peeled away her sweater and skirt with my free hand and pressed two fingers against her clit, drinking in every sound she made. It was all for me.

I kissed down her neck, and even lower, ridding her of her clothes. When I skimmed my mouth in a trail between her navel and her clit, her breath became more labored. Time to ramp up the anticipation.

When I flattened my tongue against her sensitive spot, she buckled over. I steadied her, gripping both her hips.

I alternated nipping with my lips and pressing my tongue until she cried out, thumping her palms against the wall, curling her fingers.

"You're so hot, Sienna. And sweet." I spoke as I kissed up her body until our mouths were level.

Her breath was shaky, but her hands didn't waver as she yanked away my shirt and then the rest of my clothes.

She smiled, dragging her fingers down my chest. The lower she went, the more wicked her smile became.

She cupped my erection with her palm,

moving her hand in slow, deliberate moves.

"Sienna, fuck. Baby, stop."

She was working me up too good, and I was already on edge. I needed her. To feel her wrapped around me, all warm and soft—all mine. Nibbling at her ear, I lowered my fingers down the side of her breast, to her ribcage before cupping her ass. When I pulled her to me, she braced both hands on my arms.

My cock was trapped between us. I rocked back and forth gently, watching her come apart slowly as I drew my erection along her clit. I nibbled at her lower lip before sealing my mouth over hers.

She groaned against me, pressing her nails in my skin, desperate and demanding. I loved it.

I was touching every part of her within reach, but I wanted more. When I deepened the kiss, we stumbled backward into the room. I tried to gather my faculties long enough to think where to head. Left? Right? Straight ahead? I was too lost in her for that. She was all I could focus on.

The couch. That was near, and she'd be comfortable. We lay down, laughing. But Sienna's laughter faded into a moan when I nudged the tip of my cock along her entrance, teasing her. I propped myself on an elbow, watching her part her legs. When I pushed the tip inside her, her eyes fluttered closed. She rolled her hips, but I pushed them back against the couch.

"Why the rush?" I whispered, kissing her chin.

"Winston…"

Despite being desperate for her, I slid in inch by inch, wanting to savor our connection. When I was inside her completely, I didn't move for a few seconds, just basking in this incredible feeling. Heat and energy zipped through me. Light perspiration dotted her skin.

I buckled, reaching for her breasts, placing open-mouthed kisses on the upper swell. I loved feeling the rhythm of her breath. If I remained still long enough, I could feel her heartbeat against my lips. Only, I couldn't stand still at all. I felt a bone-deep need to touch and kiss every part of her. I slid in and out of her, claiming her body, her thoughts, her love. Feeling her unravel beneath me was incredible. Cupping one ass cheek, I hoisted her on one side, driving so deep that a blast of pleasure shot along my cock, from the base all the way to the tip.

I had access to her neck this way… and with every thrust, my pelvis pressed against her clit. I could feel it every time she pulsed around me.

My muscles tightened until my body held so much tension that I knew I wouldn't last too long.

"Come, baby. I want to feel you come all around me."

I stilled the movement of my hips, bringing my hand over her clit, drawing slow, deliberate circles with my thumb. She grew so tight around me that I thought I was going to lose my mind. I was sure of it. This was too good. Too intense. But I didn't pause, didn't even slow down. I wanted to tip her over the edge, watch her succumb to pleasure—feel it.

When she gritted out my name, her inner muscles clenched so tight that I could barely breathe through the pleasure. I pushed my hips forward the next second, unable to stay still anymore, pushing in and out of her through her orgasm. I kissed her shoulders and her neck before capturing her mouth, tangling our tongues in the same wild rhythm. I couldn't get enough of her. I wanted to claim every inch of her, feel that she belonged to me completely.

I came so hard that my entire body clenched tight. My muscles were burning, but I didn't stop, didn't relent, just kept rocking in and out of her until we were both spent.

Then I shifted us until she was on top of me, lying with her cheek on my chest.

I drew my fingers lazily up and down her back. My woman had worked up a sweat.

"Don't," she chastised.

"Don't what?" I tried to sound innocent. Failed.

"Don't laugh at me for being sweaty."

I just couldn't help myself and chuckled. "How did you know I was going to do that?"

She looked up at me, propping her chin on my chest, wiggling her eyebrows.

"You have this way of touching me when you're holding back laughter. Dead giveaway."

My woman knew me well.

"I'm so tired, I can't even get up from here," she murmured.

"Works for me. I get to touch you all I want

like this."

"Pervert. Taking advantage."

"Always."

I placed my hands on her ass, fondling it. She tightened her inner muscles around me.

I groaned. "And here I thought you were too tired."

"Not for this."

"Who's the pervert now?"

She grinned and did it again.

"Sienna, don't," I warned in a low voice.

"Stop me if you can."

"That's the thing, I don't want to stop you."

Her mouth formed an O, but before she could react, I flipped us over to one side. I was getting hard again. I slid out of her, and when I pushed back in, her eyes widened. I came closer, feathering my lips on the tip of her nose, then repeating the movement over her mouth.

All day today I'd felt as if I'd been trapped under a rock and couldn't breathe, right until I'd had Sienna with me again.

"What are you thinking about?" she murmured.

"That you're amazing, and you changed my life."

"I did? How?"

"I can't explain. The way I look at certain things, experience them."

She smiled, hiding her face in my chest. "You're making me blush."

"Looks good on you."

"I see. Flattery. I think you have an ulterior motive, mister. And your ulterior motives are usually not so innocent."

"Maybe." I grinned. She looked up when I caressed her shoulder with the back of my fingers. I couldn't stop touching her when she was this close.

"I knew it."

"Come here and kiss me, woman. Tonight, you're all mine."

Chapter Thirty-Three

Sienna

Next morning, I woke up with a remarkably clear head. No hangover, not even a headache. I had to thank this gorgeous man for insisting I drink water last night in between our sexy shenanigans. Right now, he was fast asleep, with his back to me. That was no good. I wanted to study him. As surreptitiously as possible, I moved to the other side of the bed. Much better. I could watch him to my heart's desire right now. I feasted my eyes, but then the temptation to touch him was too big. I dragged my fingers down his chest in a featherlight touch.

Wait a second! He wasn't sleeping. There was a slight movement in his eyes behind his eyelids. The corners of his lips twitched.

He'd been pretending. Well, well. I could play this game. I placed my hand back on the bed, waiting him out. One minute passed, then two. Then five. Right... clearly he was better at this than I was. Unable to hold back any longer, I poked his shoulder.

His eyes flashed open the next second, and he broke into laughter.

"I was curious how long you'd hold out," he

said between guffaws.

"And here I was, trying not to wake you up."

"Your hands were all over me. How's that trying?"

I shrugged a shoulder, smiling coyly. "I said I tried. I didn't say I was successful."

"You deserve a lesson for waking me up."

"You weren't sleeping. It doesn't count."

"*You* thought I was sleeping, and you did it anyway. It totally counts."

I licked my lips. "So, what's the lesson?"

I didn't realize what he was up to until he went directly for my armpits. I shrieked with laughter, unable to defend myself. He only stopped torturing me when I was completely out of breath.

He laughed wholeheartedly. "How is your head?"

This right here was an excellent opportunity for some blackmail.

"If I pretend I'm hungover, will you take care of me?"

"I'll take care of you anyway."

He kissed my forehead. His words warmed me all over.

"And how?" I murmured, loving the feeling of his lips on my forehead, his hand cupping the side of my face.

I had no idea how he made me feel so many things at the same time, but I couldn't do anything else except bask in it.

"First step. Breakfast."

"Now that you mention it, I'm hungry."

"Stay here. I'll be back quickly."

"In bed? You're pampering me."

"My pleasure."

He kissed my stomach before getting out of bed. I admired his holy hotness for all of two seconds before deciding I wouldn't miss the sight of him walking around naked.

But when I attempted to climb out of bed, he cocked a brow.

"So staying in bed was a demand."

"You bet it was. You should at least hydrate before getting out. I'll bring you water."

That was just too adorable. I was tempted to stay in bed just so he could dote on me. But… I was more tempted to spy on him naked around the apartment.

"I'm fine, Winston."

He glowered. I laughed. He glowered some more.

"Besides, you can hydrate me all you want while we're in the kitchen. You hydrate me. I spy on you naked. Win-win."

"Fine, but any signs of a headache, and you come back to bed."

"Aye, captain."

I'd downplayed the reason I wanted to be near him. I wanted to gauge his mood, check how he was really doing after yesterday's events.

I kept a close eye on him during breakfast. We devoured pancakes with maple syrup. I also had coffee and plenty of water under his watchful gaze.

Once we were done, I rose from my seat and walked over to him. He was sitting far enough from the table that I could comfortably climb in his lap.

I'd given Winston shit when he'd insisted we throw on some clothes, but now I could see the benefits. Less distraction, even though the fabric of his shirt stretched so thin over his chest that I could practically map out every muscle.

"Now, bossy man, I want you to tell me the truth. How are you holding up with the store's troubles?"

He rested his hands on my waist, kissing my chin once before straightening up.

"I was thinking about taking on a partner. You know we've had inquiries from several companies."

"Wow. Okay. I didn't think you'd even consider that. You were very categoric when I first brought it up."

"I told you that you've changed me." He winked, but I could tell he was serious.

I placed my palms on either side of his face, caressing the edge of his lips with my thumbs.

"You're serious?"

"Yes, I think it was a mistake to believe I could do it all myself, even though you think I'm brilliant."

"Hey, it takes a brilliant man to admit that his way didn't work and he needs to pivot. How will you decide on a partner?"

"I have this smart branding expert I'd love to help me veto them."

"Yes, sir, at your order."

I shimmied in his lap in a little dance of victory.

"Sienna. Stop, or this conversation will be very short."

"Oops. That wasn't intentional. Really. When do we start?"

"Right now."

I loved that he trusted me so much. I'd never felt so empowered and appreciated.

Climbing out of his lap, I first headed to the bedroom, returning with a thicker shirt for him.

"What's this for?" he asked, perplexed.

"For you to wear. The one you're wearing is so transparent you're practically naked. Does not help my concentration, trust me."

He barked out a laugh, nodding. Guess what I hadn't taken into consideration? To put on the new shirt, he first had to get rid of the old one, which meant I got an eyeful of his naked torso.

"God, you're sexy."

I only realized I'd said that out loud when Winston laughed.

"You could have just closed your eyes."

My cheeks heated up instantly. "I could have. But where's the fun in that?"

Winston had his laptop here. I didn't, but I worked just as well with pen and paper, especially because at this stage, I was basically just making a huge pro-con list for every company.

We judged based on several factors such as general brand appeal, capitalization, benefits other than monetary value, and so on and so forth.

Four hours later, we had fifteen pages worth of notes and a spreadsheet with three hundred values. We still had a lot of work ahead of us, but this was a solid start.

"My eyes are blurry," I said on a yawn.

"Let's call this a day. I've been overworking you."

I batted my eyelashes. "You totally have, and you can make it up to me for the rest of the day."

"The lady needs to relax?"

"Yes, she does."

"Always happy to make myself useful."

"I'm warning you, I'll be very demanding."

He scooted closer on the floor until our thighs were touching.

"I can't wait."

A smile was playing on his lips.

"Okay... I have to admit, I thought you'd be more... how do I say this... stressed out isn't the right word."

"Neurotic?" he suggested.

"Well, yes."

He leaned in, whispering conspiratorially, "Being around you has this effect on me. I'm calmer, I see things clearer."

"So basically, you just need me with you all the time so you're not grouchy?"

"Exactly."

I kissed his cheek, smiling from ear to ear. "I can totally do that."

"Damn, and I thought I'd have to work for it."

"If you insist, I can play hard to get."

"Come here." He pulled me in his lap. My thighs were pressing against his. I wiggled my lower body for good measure.

"How do you always manage to get me where you want?"

"This isn't where I want you, sweetheart." His voice was suddenly lower.

"And where do you want me?"

"In bed. Panting, calling my name. Writhing when I have my mouth on you."

And just like that, my entire body felt like a livewire. But I was determined to hold my ground. A certain someone deserved to be teased.

"Well, doesn't sound that promising."

"Really?" He drew his hands up my arms, lingering with his fingers on my shoulders. "I have other ideas too."

"Don't you dare tickle me again."

I scurried away, just out of his reach. He waggled his eyebrows. I shook my head, eying him carefully. I was still reluctant to lower my guard when my phone beeped with an incoming message.

"I'll behave. I promise."

"I don't believe your promises right now, mister."

He held up his hands in defense. I reached for my phone quickly.

"Victoria just texted me. She's asking if we want to go to their house for dinner. Apparently half the family will be there. Want to go?"

I looked up at him hopefully. There was no better way to spend an afternoon than surrounded by a bunch of Bennetts.

"Look at that smile. Think I stand a chance of saying anything except yes?"

"Good to know. I'll add it to my list of emotional blackmail tactics."

I'd thought Victoria was exaggerating when she meant half the clan was there, but she wasn't. Yesterday's group was here, plus Logan and Alice's husband, Nate, and Blake's wife, Clara. She was pregnant, and Blake was constantly doting on her. It was fascinating to watch Blake completely transform around his wife. They had a boy, Maddox—who was a mini-Blake—and they were expecting a girl.

The second I entered the living room, I glowered at Christopher.

"I'm on my best behavior today, I swear," Christopher said.

Blake nodded quickly. "Me too. In fact, I'm on extra good behavior to make up for last night."

I narrowed my eyes. "Blake, I'm having trouble believing you. You're getting more intense every time I see you. Careful, you're turning into Logan."

Blake clutched his heart theatrically. "You wound me, Sienna."

"Hey, I heard that," Logan called from further inside the room. I grinned sheepishly but didn't say anything else. I wasn't wrong.

Sebastian was the levelheaded one, Logan the hotheaded. Christopher was close on his heels. Blake was laid-back about everything. Usually. I was learning that roles were not set in stone.

"It's because we're having a girl. His protective instincts are getting sharper," Clara said.

That sounded like a solid explanation.

When Victoria asked me to help her bring some ice for the drinks, I seized the chance to question her.

"What's with the impromptu get-together?"

Victoria blushed. My spidey-senses kicked in. What was going on?

"Um… so you know that we all had a little too much eggnog last night," she began.

"Yeah…"

"And you know I'm usually not one to tell about other's secrets."

Um… that was debatable. Very debatable. But making that point now wouldn't help my goal.

"Sister, spill it."

"Well, Christopher and I spoke about Statham and the board. And he talked to the rest of the Bennetts, and they have an idea."

"Okay…"

A Bennett-wide conspiracy? I *loved, loved, loved*

those.

"Sebastian will explain everything."

I was looking at the gang with fresh eyes when I returned to the living room. Now that I thought about it, everyone was already here when we arrived. What was going on?

I wanted to wait for Sebastian to bring up the subject... and I resisted all of ten minutes, until we all sat at the dinner table.

"Sebastian, Victoria said you wanted to talk to Winston and me about the store."

Victoria laughed. Sebastian looked between the two of us with a smile. Next to me, Winston sat straighter in his chair. I should have warned him, but it completely slipped my mind.

"Yes. Winston, we have heard that the banks won't extend the grace period to solve the liquidity troubles and the board will close this store."

"That's right."

"We held a family meeting at lunch, and we have a proposition for you."

A family meeting? Wow. That was superinvolved. How had they even managed it? Summer, Daniel, Max, and their families, plus their parents were in Australia.

"We've told you before that we're interested in having our jewelry in Statham Stores."

"Yes."

"We'd only talked about you building a jewelry section before... but how about making it exclusive for Bennett Enterprises? In exchange, we'll invest the necessary amount to even your liquidity ratio. We'd be silent partners, only getting involved in decisions regarding our products."

Holy shit. They had actually gotten together today and discussed this.

I'd felt part of the Bennett family ever since my sister started dating Christopher, but never more than now. I had a sudden urge to hug everyone at the table.

"That's a very generous offer. Thank you," Winston said. He sounded stunned. I could see how that might seem perplexing to anyone who didn't know the family as well as I did.

"Take your time and think about it," Sebastian went on.

"I'll get back to you quickly. I need to talk to the board first. Just to clarify, you've already got all the involved parties to agree to a partnership?"

Sebastian smiled, exchanging a furtive look with Logan and Pippa.

"Shares are distributed between family members. We debated it in the family meeting at lunch. Summer, Max, and Daniel participated via video calls."

"You decided this… in a family meeting." Despite still sounding perplexed, he was smiling.

"That's how we do things in the Bennett clan," Christopher said.

"Once we stop giving you shit," Blake clarified. "See it as a rite of initiation. And now that we got business out of the way, let's change the subject. Wouldn't want to scare Winston into thinking that's all we do when we get together," Blake said. Everyone laughed, and there was a general hum of agreement.

The rest of the dinner was a leisurely affair. Business wasn't mentioned again, though I suspected it was on everyone's mind. It definitely was on mine.

I was really, really hoping Winston was considering it. I would have said yes in a heartbeat, but well, I was biased, of course. I was so full of energy I could barely sit still.

My euphoria kept intensifying, reaching a high point during dessert (chocolate chip ice cream with caramel and pistachio sauce).

I wanted to be alone with Winston and hear his thoughts on the proposal, but guess what's the one thing you can't get during a Bennett get-together? That's right—alone time.

During after-dinner drinks, I managed to tone down my euphoria somewhat. I needed to be levelheaded and objective when Winston and I spoke about it, make a pro-con list, like we'd done this morning for all the other prospective partners. I started mentally making one. Honestly (and objectively!), this was the best deal of all. Sure, it would be an investment to add the jewelry division in the stores and include it in Statham's branding, but the payoff was stellar.

And then there was me! Ha! I knew Bennett Enterprises, could make the whole process run much smoother than with a different company. I would definitely put myself in the pro list.

A dark thought popped in my mind. What if Winston didn't? We'd been together for a short time. What if he thought that this offer came with strings, with expectations from my side? *Oh my God.*

Sometime in between dinner and drinks, I fell into a rabbit hole. My previous euphoria was completely gone. I was now trapped in the clutches of fear. Did he feel pressured?

By the time we left Victoria's house, my heart was in my throat.

I fiddled with the hem of my sweater during the entire drive to my house.

"What's on your mind?" Winston asked once we were inside.

"Just what Sebastian said."

What was *he* thinking? I couldn't tell.

The house was semidark. My pulse was so intense that I felt almost nauseous from the rhythmic pumping in my ears.

"So… I was thinking it's a great offer. I've already made a mental pro-con list, and it's the best bet."

"Sienna… why are you nervous?"

Crap, of course he'd caught on. He stood right in front of me, and, as usual, having him so near was messing with my senses. Actually, now much more than usual. Perhaps because I was afraid I might lose him.

"Because I don't want you to think that this alliance between the companies means I'm expecting anything… that things between us have to change. Don't feel pressured. Because I'm happy with the way things are between us right now," I said quickly.

Winston was silent for so long that the thumping in my ears turned to pounding.

"I'm not, Sienna."

"What?" I whispered.

He stepped even closer, until the tip of his nose touched my cheek.

"I love our relationship, but I want even more." I felt his lips curl in a smile against my cheek. I couldn't do anything other than cling to every word. "And clearly, I'm not doing a great job showing you how much I love you if you think this is scaring me. Pressured, huh? You can pressure me every day of the week, love." He pinched my ass, dropping his head to the side of my neck, biting it playfully before planting a kiss.

"I'm your man, Sienna. Your man, you hear me? I want to share my life with you—the smooth sailing and the bumpy rides. You came into my life unexpectedly, and I fell so hard, so deep. I won't let you go. I love you unconditionally. Never forget that, you hear me?"

"Yes." My voice was semiwobbly with emotion, but what did he expect after those beautiful words that just melted my heart?

"Now we're talking." He pinched my ass again.

"Hey, stop that," I teased.

"I don't intend to. Mine to pinch, pat, kiss,

fondle. You're mine, Sienna. Every part of you. Every inch of you."

I pulled at his collar until our lips were level. I wanted a kiss. He obliged me, and then some more.

He kissed me so deep that I felt my heart was about to explode. I never wanted the kiss to stop.

His chest pressed against my upper body; his hips touched mine. Masculinity was rolling off him in the way he gripped my hips, fisted my hair, deepened the kiss.

We were both laughing as we stumbled through the house. Then he flipped me around, keeping his arms wrapped around my middle, his chin in the crook between my neck and shoulder.

"Let's watch where we're walking," he said.

"But I could touch you before."

"You can touch me all you want once we're in the bedroom. And as to the offer, I plan to say yes. I wanted to say yes at the table but wanted to talk to you before. I'm sure the board will agree."

I squealed, shimmying my hips right against his crotch. Heat curled through me when I felt how turned-on he was.

He groaned. I did it again. He lowered his hands from my waist to my hips, keeping them firmly in place.

"I do have one condition, though," he said.

"Oh?"

"I want you to be in charge of everything related to the partnership."

"That sounds promising."

"You'd be working for both Bennett Enterprises and Statham Stores. I've been looking for a loophole to keep you with me this entire time, and finally, I have it."

I laughed as we came to a halt at the entrance to the bedroom. I immediately turned around, lacing my arms around his neck, before lowering one to his arm. I wanted to touch and kiss him everywhere at once.

"So, what do you say?"

"Yes, sir."

"I see. So we're back to sir? Is that an upgrade, a downgrade? I can't even tell anymore." He was grinning against my cheek.

"Definitely an upgrade."

Chapter Thirty-Four
Winston
Four months later

"Son, if your mind isn't on the car, you'll get us both in trouble."

"Sorry. I'm focusing now. Promise."

I'd come to help Dad work on one of his newest acquisitions. We were both bent over the engine, trying to determine what exactly was broken.

Ever since signing the deal with Bennett Enterprises, things became considerably more relaxed. I'd spoken to the board right before I flew to London with Sienna to visit Lucas on Christmas. They'd been surprised that I was willing to go into a partnership and immediately agreed. Since I was staying in San Francisco for good, we had to send someone else to Paris. One of the operations managers volunteered to go, and he was the perfect fit.

Since I finally had some room to breathe, I'd made some changes to my lifestyle. One of them was regularly stopping by here.

"You know what? Today's a big day for you. Let's talk about that. The car can wait."

"No, no. It's fine. I can multitask."

Dad winked. "Doesn't look like that from where I'm standing."

We worked on the car in silence for a few minutes before Dad said, "We're happy you went into that partnership, Winston. That's exactly what your Mom and I would have done, but we thought it wouldn't be your way."

"A few months ago, it wouldn't have been."

"That pretty girl you're crazy about is a great influence on you."

"She is."

"How's that *proposal strategy* of yours coming along?"

I could tell Dad had a shit-eating grin without even looking at him. He'll be mocking me for a long time for saying that.

"So far, so good."

Every great achievement begins with a great strategy.

My goal: ask Sienna to marry me... when she least expected it.

I was heading to Bennett Enterprises this afternoon to pick a ring right from Pippa's desk. Before that, I was meeting Lucas and Chloe.

After leaving Dad's garage, I headed straight to the restaurant.

I'd already talked to Victoria and Christopher, asking for Sienna's hand, but I wanted to talk to Lucas and Chloe separately as well. Lucas was here for his spring break, so the timing was perfect.

I arrived first and waited for them at the table. Chloe waved at me enthusiastically as soon as they stepped inside, hugging me when they reached the table.

"As you know, Sienna and I have been dating for a few months," I said once we sat down.

Chloe nodded eagerly. "And you are the perfect boyfriend." Turning to her brother, she added, "You can take notes."

Lucas's eyes bulged. I laughed.

"I want to marry Sienna, and I wanted you two to know that before I propose."

They were close, more than siblings usually were, always looking after each other.

Chloe squealed. Lucas laughed, shaking his head.

"Man, you really worked hard at winning Chloe over. She's your number-one fan."

"I do what I can," I replied.

"Well, every *report* I received was that Sienna's happy, so this is a great thing." Then he groaned.

"What?" Chloe and I asked at the same time.

"Nothing. Wondering what the cut-off age is… before they start getting on my case about a steady girlfriend."

"Lucas. You're seventeen. I think you're safe for now," I said.

"You never know with the Bennetts."

Truer words were never spoken.

Chloe grinned, rubbing her hands. "I didn't know you were afraid of that. This is excellent blackmail material. If you bug me, I'll give them ideas."

Lucas groaned again, but he was smiling. "I leave for half a year, and she forsakes me as her brother."

"No… just… you know, filling my Lucas-free time with the Bennett girls."

"Yeah… I can see you've gone over to the dark side. Let's order."

We ate three courses. Chloe gave me tips about rings the entire time, with Lucas looking at her as if she'd grown an extra head.

By the time I arrived at Bennett Enterprises, I was already feeling very confident about my plan. Christopher was waiting for me in the lobby. He'd insisted on going with me and spouted off survival tips—his words, not mine—the second I joined him.

"Did Pippa already drill you about rings?" he asked.

"No, she doesn't even know why I'm coming."

I'd been in the building a few times since signing the papers for the partnership.

Christopher threw his head back, laughing. "For your sake, I hope you're right. But decades of experience tell me you're not."

The creative department was bewildering, at least compared to the floors above, where everything was orderly and everyone had a separate office. This was an open floor plan with sketches and prototypes scattered on the desks. Pippa was waiting just by the door, hands clasped together.

"Already got the rings on my desk. I have the newest collection here, as well as some of my personal favorites. Plus, Sienna's favorites."

I was… stunned.

"How did you know I'm coming for a ring?"

She flashed a cat-ate-the-canary smile. "There are two main reasons anyone ever comes here. One: to talk budgets. Two: pick a ring."

"That is scarily accurate," Christopher pointed out.

I laughed. "Well, then. Let's get started on choosing that ring. I can see it's a group activity."

Christopher grinned.

Pippa laced her arm around mine, escorting me to her desk. "Everything is in the Bennett family."

Epilogue

One day later

Sienna

"Sister, I know your matchmaking credentials are impressive, but you can't claim any credit for Winston and Sienna," Alice said to Pippa.

We were all in the Statham building, ready for the inauguration party of the revamped store. The group was huddled in a corner, away from everyone else.

"I know, I know," Pippa said.

I laced my arm with Pippa's, dropping my voice to a conspiratorial whisper. "I wouldn't say that. All those dangerous ideas you planted in my head about doing the grouchy boss... definitely helped."

Pippa's smile was so smug that I couldn't help laughing. Next to us, Blake shook his head mockingly.

"Don't encourage her, Sienna. Every time someone tells her she's right, that's one more battle I lose."

Pippa narrowed her eyes. "Brother of mine, you're being unfair."

"Did you or did you not side with Clara when we picked our girl's name? *Hermione.*"

"But I also talked Clara into giving her two names, so you could have yours as well. Does that not count for anything?"

Blake winked, shaking his head. "The women in our family will be the death of me."

Pippa patted his shoulder. "Don't be so dramatic. We girls have to stick together. Clara and I have our secrets."

Blake looked positively frightened. "What does that mean? Actually, I don't even want to know."

"Shhh... it's starting, and I want to pay attention," I said.

Bennett Enterprises became an official partner of Statham Stores four months ago. I loved, loved, loved my new duties. I was still working on all aspects of branding, but Bennett duties were making up a big chunk of my tasks. It was even better than what I'd envisioned whenever I'd planned my future at Bennett Enterprises. Lesson learned. Sometimes it's worth keeping an open mind instead of planning in too much detail.

We closed this building for renovations right after the deal was signed, to add the jewelry section and to implement the rebrand Winston and I had worked on. The result was simply beautiful. The core structure had remained the same, but with the added playground in the food court and the mini entertainment corner on every floor, the place was more alive and inviting than ever before.

I couldn't *wait* for the next Christmas season.

Winston went up on a small stage we'd set up right next to the entrance.

"Welcome, everyone. Thank you for joining us at this opening party. My mother and father have left me a legacy I'm proud to carry on." He looked at his parents, who were only a few feet away, beaming. "We're entering a new era for the Statham Stores. I couldn't have done this without my smart and beautiful girlfriend, Sienna Hensley, as well as the support of the entire Bennett family. It's my honor to welcome them as official partner in Statham Stores."

Everyone clapped, I even harder than the rest. I watched with pride as my man walked toward us, smiling from ear to ear. God, was he sexy or what? All that swagger, that muscle-laced body moving with all the confidence in the world.

"I need to steal Sienna for a bit," he told the group, placing an arm around my shoulders. What was going on?

"What is it?" I asked, as Winston led me upstairs.

"Just wanted to do one last check on the party room."

"Okay."

We'd gone over every detail quite a few times, but I guessed one last check wouldn't hurt.

We were hosting a party for the team in the same room where we'd held the Christmas party all those months ago.

I perused the details again: the small stage, the long table where servers would bring food. Wait a second. There was a box on it that hadn't been there before. And it had my name on it!

I looked sideways at Winston, who grinned. I hadn't gotten him anything!

"That's for me?" I double-checked.

His grin widened. "Has your name on it."

"And I can open it now?"

"That's why I brought you here."

"Gimme, gimme."

I felt like a kid on Christmas morning as I opened it quickly. There was yet another box inside. I looked at Winston speculatively, hoping for a hint. He gave nothing away.

I opened—what? Yet *another* box, only this one was tiny. What could fit into a box this small? I wasn't materialistic, but well… when it came to presents, the bigger, the better.

Winston watched me closely as I opened it, and all that heat and intensity rolling off him wasn't helping matters. It made me jittery.

He reached inside the box before I could see what it was, and then I gasped, placing a palm over my chest. I felt as if my heart might spring out any second now.

I was looking at a gorgeous princess-cut diamond in a platinum band that was set with tiny rose quartz stones.

Winston was holding it between his thumb and forefinger, and I felt my eyes turn misty at the corners. I'd always thought that knowing you've found *the one* was going to take time... until I was sure. But this felt so perfect that I was close to bursting with happiness. I didn't even know it was possible to feel so much joy. It was like a physical force, like a pressure from the inside out.

"Yes! Yes!" The words burst out of me loudly. I grinned sheepishly.

Winston chuckled. "I haven't even asked yet."

"It's a yes anyway."

I held my hand out for him to slide the ring on. I was jittery. I didn't care, didn't even try to hide it. This was Winston. My Winston.

His hand held mine strong and steady, but I thought that his breathing pattern was a little uneven.

"Sienna, here, in this place where we fell in love, I'm promising you that I will cherish you every day of our life. You're smart, beautiful, kind, sweet. Sassy when the situation requires it."

"Which is almost always."

He laughed. "I agree."

He touched my cheek with his fingers, dragging them down my chin, resting them on my neck.

"I promise to love you and make you happy, always, even if it means letting you turn these offices into Santa Land every Christmas. I'll even help you."

"Now I'm suspicious."

He waggled his eyebrows. Now I was even *more* suspicious.

"In fact, let's make this a rule. You can only

hang the decorations outside of business hours, and only if I'm watching. Every time I hang something where you can't reach, you take off an item of clothing."

I doubled with laughter. "Now I get it. You're just hoping to get me naked."

"Well, I just like being around you. Naked time is a bonus."

"I can't believe you went from being a broody boss from hell to being a seductive—if opportunistic—fiancé."

"All your doing."

"Well, here is my vow to you: I promise to love you and shake up your grouchy ass whenever you need it."

He was grinning now. "I'm counting on it. I wasn't in a good place when we met, but you came into my life and… you gave me no choice but to fall in love with you."

His fingers went even lower, touching the necklace hanging around my neck slowly, seductively. My breath caught. He brought my hand to his mouth, placing a small kiss on my engagement ring before placing an open-mouthed one on the exposed skin under my necklace. I felt the touch of his lips and tongue reverberate through my entire body. Every cell was clamoring for his touch, his kisses. That pressure in my chest magnified.

When he straightened up, his gaze was even more intense than before, full of fire. Gripping my hips, he aligned our bodies. I was trying not to think about how close we were… almost touching, but not quite. Thank God, because I didn't think I could feel him against me and not jump in his arms. Then he pressed me to him, and I was certain I was about to combust.

The second his mouth came down on mine that pressure in my chest spread like wildfire through every limb, every cell. I nipped at his lower lip. Winston groaned against my mouth. The sound fueled me on. He touched one thigh in a possessive and delicious grip, lifting it, pressing his hips between my thighs.

"Winston," I whispered when he kissed down my neck. "We should go down. Everyone will know we're missing."

He groaned, lowering my leg. "I know. Worst idea I've ever had, thinking I could keep this short. I can never get enough of you. You think I would've learned my lesson by now." Straightening up, he kissed the tip of my nose. "Let's stay here for a few more minutes, just the two of us. I want to memorize everything about this moment. The way you're shaking in my arms, the way you look at me."

I wasn't shaking only because he'd just touched and kissed me wickedly. It was just that… I hadn't ever imagined that I could be loved this way.

I cleared my throat, attempting to push him away, because if we were this close, he was bound to get dangerous ideas again. And if he didn't, I would for sure.

"Nah, I'm not letting you go."

"Winston, you're being bossy again."

"Always." He traced his thumb over my lips, pressing it lightly at one corner. "I might not be a grouch anymore, but I'll always be bossy."

That he was... and I loved it.

By the time we returned to the celebration, everyone was holding a glass of champagne. Catering had also brought out plates with canapes. We went straight to the corner where all the Bennetts and Winston's parents stood, talking.

I'd already thought about a few sentences to announce the news, but my lips curled in a smile so big that my cheeks were hurting.

"Look, the ring." Victoria pointed out, before everyone started congratulating us at the same time.

"We were wondering where you'd disappeared to," Pippa said.

Blake winked. "Of course, half of us guessed what was going on since we heard you went to the creative department yesterday."

Winston chuckled. "I was expecting that. Why do you think I only waited one day between buying the ring and proposing? Didn't want to risk the other half finding out too."

Blake whistled loudly. We all laughed as Winston and I also picked up champagne glasses.

"Here's to fast learners," Christopher said.

"And romantic proposals." Victoria's smile was as dreamy as I imagined mine was. Everyone huddled closer for a toast.

Over the sound of clinking glasses, Blake said, "Winston, welcome to the Bennett family."

Other Books by Layla Hagen

The Bennett Family Series
Book 1: Your Irresistible Love
Book 2: Your Captivating Love
Book 3: Your Forever Love
Book 4: Your Inescapable Love
Book 5: Your Tempting Love
Book 6: Your Alluring Love
Book 7: Your Fierce Love
Book 8: Your One True Love
Book 9: Your Endless Love

The Connor Family Series
Book 1: Anything For You
Book 2: Wild With You
Book 3: Meant For You
Book 4: Only With You
Book 5: Fighting For You
Book 6: Always With You

The Lost Series
Book 1: Lost in Us
Book 2: Found in Us
Book 3: Caught in Us

Standalone
Withering Hope

***

CPSIA information can be obtained
at www.ICGtesting.com
Printed in the USA
LVHW111306291119
638940LV00001B/22/P

9 781699 176207